JOSH & ANNA

and

GABE & CLAIRE

Eliza Freed

Also by Eliza Freed

The Lost Souls Series
Forgive Me
Redeem Me
Save Me

The Faraway Novels
The Devil's Playground
The Lion's Den

The Shore House Novels
Full Share

Short Stories
The Best Man
Finding Faith
The Dark Horse (an erotic short)

JOSH & ANNA

and

GABE & CLAIRE

Brunswick House
New York

Josh & Anna and Gabe & Claire
Copyright © 2016 by Eliza Freed
Excerpt from *The Devil's Playground* © 2015 by Eliza Freed

Edited by:
Rhonda Helms

Copyediting by:
Ashley Williams, AW Editing

Proofreading by:
Nichole Strauss, Perfectly Publishable

Interior Design and Formatting by:
Christine Borgford, Perfectly Publishable

Cover Design by:
Design by James, GoOnWrite.com

Brunswick House Publishing
244 Madison Avenue
New York, NY 10016
First Brunswick House ebook and print on demand edition: November 2016
The Brunswick House name and logo are trademarks of Brunswick House Publishing, LLC.
The publisher is not responsible for websites (or their content) that are not owned by the publisher.
Manufactured in the United States of America

ISBN 978-1-943622-06-1 (ebook edition)
ISBN 978-1-943622-07-8 (print on demand edition)

To Tricia, for when I was paralyzed with doubt telling you every detail of Josh and Anna and Gabe and Claire's story, you told me to, "Write it exactly like that. Don't change a thing."

You're a gift.

"You need to be careful with perfect. It's brilliant at hiding its flaws."

~Jason Leer in REDEEM ME by Eliza Freed

STAGE I

INTOXICATION

1

Anna

HE THRUST INTO ME ONE last time before relaxing his muscles and resting his weight on my chest. He was breathless, panting softly against the crook of my neck as I ran my fingers through his hair and kissed the side of his face. I didn't have an orgasm, but neither of us cared. That wasn't what our sex life was about anymore. We were trying to have a baby. Desperately trying. We no longer wanted each other in the same way we once had. Before the irregular periods and the journals, logs, and temperatures. Before I asked my husband to jerk off in a cup so we could analyze his sperm.

Back when I didn't hate myself.

Now, our sex life was a new job that wasn't working out.

"I love you, Anna," he said. He always said it.

Josh had wanted a baby more than I did. He'd brought it up first, but once we'd started trying, I'd become consumed with the idea of a little one joining us. "Fixated"—that was Josh's word for my focus on conception. When he drank too much, he used the word "obsessed."

He rolled off me and walked to the bathroom. The dim light highlighted his ass, which hadn't changed since the day I'd met him in a dingy room of an off-campus house party. His eyes were a soft blue, and while he was a few inches taller than I was, his body was soft as well. He wasn't rock hard like the gym crew, but gentle in his stance. Something about his exterior had told me he was kind. When he'd made me laugh that first night, I'd told him I thought we were going to be married, and two years later, we were.

This morning I felt as if I'd been tricked all those years ago, and Josh seemed to feel nothing. Like a soccer star playing with tremendous skill but only half a heart because he thought he might not survive the big game loss, Josh had launched the idea of our family and then disconnected when we didn't score on our first try.

"I think we should have a baby," he'd said. I'd always assumed someday I'd get married and then have children, but I'd been happily not planning past the next few months of my life, and those plans had *not* included a baby.

At the time, I'd been a bridesmaid in my college roommate's wedding, and I'd already bought my plane ticket for the upcoming bachelorette party in Las Vegas. Babies weren't welcomed on girls' weekends. Josh had been quiet and irritable the entire week leading up to my departure. My new shoes and fresh highlights had done nothing to quell his abrasiveness.

"I guess you're not getting pregnant this month," he'd said, as if we were already trying. I hadn't even gone off the pill.

"Why does it have to be right now?"

Josh had never answered. Somehow over time, when there'd been a lull in the weddings, the birth control had been thrown away, and my focus had shifted from my own life to creating another. The first few weeks of trying had been the happiest of our marriage. It was inconceivable how we'd gone from him wanting me pregnant two years ago to me crying alone every month when my period came. The concept of a child wasn't as appealing to Josh if we had to work for it. With each month I didn't get pregnant, a baby became the only idea I'd let in my head.

Josh turned off the light and returned to our bed. He picked up his phone and read the screen while his sperm made itself at home inside me. I laid still. His carefree movements beside me annoyed me. He'd done the very least he had to for me to get pregnant and turned his attention to an article about the Eagles preseason. Everything he did, besides coming inside me, told me he didn't care if we had a baby or not. His face reacted to something in an article, making his lips pull up at the edges. I resented that look. Why did a piece of technology get it when I didn't?

I already knew I wasn't pregnant. I could sense the emptiness. The same feeling of being alone I had every day.

"Did Claire ever tell you what time we're supposed to meet them tomorrow?" Josh asked without looking up from his phone.

I stared at the popcorn ceiling above us and sifted through the endless things Claire had told me about tomorrow. What she was wearing. Why she absolutely had to get out of her house for the night. Gabe's dimmed enthusiasm. Her lack of care regarding Gabe's opinion. "Seven, I think."

"Why so late? It's Friday."

Partying with Gabe and Claire always started early and ended late, or rather, whenever we all passed out somewhere. Josh preferred couples to girls' trips. He'd be happy if we spent every weekend with them, even if Claire drove him mad.

"Gabe said he has a late meeting tomorrow."

Josh stayed perfectly still, clueing me in to the lie that had passed between a different husband and wife. If Gabe had a meeting, Josh would know about it. They ran a group of three hundred people together.

I rolled over and rested my head on my husband's shoulder. "But there is no meeting, is there?" I remained nonchalant.

"There must be something if Gabe said there is." It was the

perfect answer. Non-collusive, non-committal, yet seemingly in agreement.

"I'm sure he'll tell us all about it." At this, my husband stiffened. I wrapped my arm across his stomach and closed my eyes. Josh was the least fun person to torture. Josh was a rule follower, but he struggled with his dual role of my husband and Gabe's friend whenever the four of us were together. I'd save my torture for Gabe. He didn't struggle with anything.

"Why don't I come home early and we'll go somewhere first. Just the two of us."

"Just like it will always be." The words escaped before I could catch them. The wave of regret they rode upon was always flowing below the surface. No matter how hard I tried, I couldn't stop the thoughts.

"Would that be so bad?"

I was sick of the question. I'd considered the reality a thousand times. When I was driving in my paid-off car, when I arrived each night at our lovely home, when we were laughing with Claire and Gabe over possibly nothing but the fact that we were all hilarious to each other, a little voice would always lament, *it is that bad*.

"I love you, Josh." He didn't want to hear the rest. Even if I spoke the words, they wouldn't penetrate through his own disgust at our situation. Josh acted as if it didn't matter, but a baby was the one thing he'd failed to plan. He couldn't provide a son or a daughter. One came when God decided.

He kissed the top of my head, and I fell asleep next to my husband.

2

Gabe

MY WIFE WAS DRUNK. NOT completely wasted, but drunk. I watched as she poured herself a glass of water, trying to detect whether this was the pull-my-dick-out-and-suck-it drunk, or the hateful-crazy-bitch drunk. I was a fan of the former. Terrified of the latter.

Claire sipped her water. Her large almond-shaped eyes softened the harsh edges of her latest haircut. The style accentuated the sharp collar bones that protruded like a shelf her head rested upon. She watched me over the rim of her glass and said, "I talked to Anna today."

Fuck.

I wasn't getting a blow job.

"Oh yeah?"

Anna was Claire's best friend. Closest friend was probably a better definition. They were together at least two weekends every month. Sometimes it was every weekend. They drank. They gossiped, and they left Josh and me alone to quietly enjoy our beverages. Anna balanced Claire. She stabilized her, but Claire couldn't get past some minute piece of jealousy when it came to Anna. When she drank, it came out in these ridiculous conversations.

"It's so funny . . ." Nothing would be humorous about this. "I still can't get over how different she is than I expected." Claire had met Anna four years ago. Anna was funny and gracious and always kind to Claire. Even when my wife's over-the-top ideas of what we should do or where we should go would have exhausted any other acquaintance. Under the umbrella of Anna's acceptance, Claire and her ideas didn't seem so ridiculous.

"Really?" I walked up the stairs to our bedroom, leaving my crazy wife to her insane thoughts.

She followed me. "Really."

Claire wasn't going to leave me alone. I'd neglect her to avoid the subject of Anna Montgomery, but to ignore the topic altogether would only enrage her. "What did you expect?" I asked.

"Well, having met Josh, I thought she'd be ultra-respectable."

I brushed my teeth. My reflection in the mirror was as confused as I was. I shook my head a little. "Anna's not respectable?" I needed to get my wife to sleep. Especially if there was no hope of a blow job.

"Of course she is. I guess I just expected her to be prim. Not so much fun." This was her bait, and I wouldn't let her catch me.

I'd spent hours with Anna. Every single one of them with my wife, too, and I'd never felt a thing from her but warmth. She wasn't as loud as Claire. Not as obvious. Her humor was dry and almost obscured by her petite figure and tailored politeness, but she could be as hilarious as the rest of us. "I haven't really thought about it. I had no expectations before I met her, and now I have no opinion."

Claire huffed past me, hiked up her dress, and sat on the toilet. She'd taken to the ugly intimacies of a relationship the same way I'd embraced her naked body the first time—without a thought. Within the first week of knowing her, Claire had flossed, peed, and snored in front of me. Ours was like a five-year-old marriage within days of its conception.

The toilet paper roll wobbled on the holder, and I continued to brush my teeth without looking at her. There was a time when I couldn't keep my eyes off her. Claire's openness had been intoxicating. Strangers, coworkers, and friends all fell under the spell of Claire's connection to this life. She shared pieces of herself without a thought. The longer we were together, the more I understood how small those pieces were.

Claire's loud laughs and monologues on the meaning of life were only to distract her audience so she could examine each person further. Her hair and attire were mere props to trick the eye. The people who fell under her spell never knew the real Claire. They only ever knew the parts she'd arranged. Most people we met were mesmerized by her, but I was unnerved. It was getting worse. A chill ran down my neck.

I replaced my toothbrush in its holder and walked out of the bathroom. If I could be asleep in the next three seconds, that'd be great.

"What are we doing tomorrow night?" she yelled from her perch.

I waited for her to finish in the bathroom and climb into bed with me. "Where were you tonight?" I asked, hoping to find a new topic. One which pleased my wife.

"My team went to happy hour. We finally finished the acquisition and deserved a good night out." It worked. She was satisfied with my attention.

"Congratulations." I kissed her cheek and rolled over in bed.

"What are we doing tomorrow?" she asked as if I'd answered and she'd already forgotten what I'd said.

"Meeting up with Josh and Anna. You made the plans." Claire's mind was a scary place.

"Oh, yes. That's right." She intertwined her legs with mine, and her cold toes rubbed against my shin. It was almost painful. Within minutes, her breathing deepened and fell into an ominous rhythm. When I knew she was asleep, I finally allowed myself to relax as well.

3

Anna

CLAIRE'S SHIRT KEPT FALLING OFF her left shoulder, exposing her burnt-orange bra strap and the top of the lace cup. It was like the sunrise you waited for with anticipation or, in Claire's case, aggravation. I pulled the fabric up again to her shoulder.

"You know where we should go?" she asked and waved her hands in the air causing her shirt to fall again when she dropped them.

"Where?"

I couldn't fake intrigue. I had barely been able to breathe since Josh called that afternoon to say the fertility tests were back and that he was fine. He had rambled on about a few other things, which had no bearing on my becoming a mother, and had to get off the phone to work more.

I was left staring at the floor. Josh was "fine." I was the problem. I couldn't have a baby because there was something wrong with *me*. I went for a run—I hated running. I showered and dressed. After every tiny decision I made—left, right, blue shirt, green—my mind returned to my body denying me a child.

Claire leaned in as if the rest of the bar around us might steal her fantastic idea and beat us there. "Greece," she whispered conspiratorially, withdrawing me from the horror inside my mind.

"I'll go." There wasn't a second of hesitation. I needed to get out of here. To focus on something other than what was wrong. Greece, Italy, France, Ireland, Germany. The list went on and on of countries I was determined to visit before I died. I'd begged Josh to take me to Italy for our honeymoon, but his idea of exploration was crossing a time zone within the United States. We'd finally settled on Puerto Rico, which was beautiful and I was happy to go. It just wasn't Italy.

"What's so great about Greece?" Josh asked. He wanted to ignore Claire, but to do so would only wind her up, and she'd already taken the stage two vodka and sodas ago.

"We'll eat and drink all day until we take a nap, and then we'll eat and drink some more," she answered, and I could picture myself there. Claire could steal me from the barren Northeast and deliver me to the rich Mediterranean. I'd be sipping my ouzo on the rocks and staring out at the Aegean Sea. Warm breezes. Moon rises.

"And then we'll make love," I said and inhaled as if I could smell the sea air.

As I exhaled and returned to Pennsylvania, Gabe laughed at me.

"What's so funny?" Claire demanded to know.

I braced myself for his gentle dig.

"Nothing." He tipped his head toward me. "For a minute there I thought Anna was actually in Greece." Josh examined me closer and sipped his drink. "That's all."

Claire pushed her hair behind her ears. She was taking a minute. Regrouping. "Well, what do you say?" She was only asking Josh. Gabe would do whatever Claire asked, and I already admitted I wanted to go.

"I say, what about Vegas?" Josh offered, and Claire's eyes rolled back in her head.

She fell backward against the seat of the booth we were

sitting in and unknowingly pushed my purse onto the floor. The contents spilled everywhere. I bent down and corralled my belongings as Claire went on. "Vegas. Please. We've done Vegas. We can't go back." I peeked my head above the table to watch her. "Why would we even go?" She held her drink in the air just above her head. "It can't compare the islands of Greece." She finished her speech with, *"Ne."*

"What are you, a horse?" Gabe asked her as I found my wallet.

"Ne is how you say yes in Greek."

"Of course," Josh said.

This was why I loved Claire. She was unstoppable and always prepared to support her position. She'd probably searched Greek words on the way over tonight in preparation for this conversation.

"Where do you want to go?" she asked my husband. I rejoined the group and put my bag on the opposite side of me from Claire.

"I want to stay right here. I don't need to go anywhere." I glanced at Josh and I tried to remember if I'd known about his dislike of traveling *before* we were married and whether I was accepting of it.

He leaned into the table and touched my leg as if he knew what I was thinking and wanted me to stop. He may have known. Josh often did. His hand caressed the back of my knee, which was the most ticklish spot on my body, and I squirmed and squealed.

"What the fuck is wrong with you?" Claire asked.

"He's tickling me."

She was shocked. Something was going on Claire wasn't aware of. She looked under the table for evidence. "What else is he doing under there? Why, Josh, you naughty boy."

Josh stood. He smoothed out the wrinkles in his Phillies

tee and grabbed his pack of cigarettes off the table. Without a word, he walked out of the bar.

"I'm going to go keep him company," Gabe slid from the booth and followed Josh outside, where he'd stand by while Josh inhaled carcinogens and exhaled them into the air.

I shook my head a little as I watched them leave. A man so structured and uptight smoking on the curb . . . the alcohol and cigarettes hid his rigid personality in college. He couldn't break the habit. Or was it the rules and expectations that hid an addiction? Even after being with Josh for eight years, I wasn't sure, but he drank too much and smoked too much and had too many rules that he followed.

I wanted to tell Josh and Gabe and every other man of child-bearing age around us to not smoke and not drink and not wear tight underwear and get plenty of rest and exercise. Everything I've read to increase sperm count, but to do so would ruin Josh's night. He only smoked when he drank, but every sip of a drink . . . every drag of a cigarette . . . moved me further away from getting pregnant. At least it did until this afternoon when he'd told me it was all my body—not his.

Left alone, Claire scanned the bar. She was always conscious of who was around her. Of who was aware of her. She'd recently cut her hair into a blunt bob that hit just above her shoulders. She'd said she could pull it off because of her almost platinum color. She also mentioned that I should keep mine long because a honey blond needed a softer silhouette. I didn't disagree.

"Have you and Gabe talked about children?" I sipped my drink to hide the urgency of the question. I'd never brought it up before. Claire and Gabe hadn't ever spoken of children, and I feared they'd somehow agree with Josh's silent retreat from the idea. I didn't want there to be any support in his abandoning my quest to get pregnant, but it had become too large a part of my life to not talk to her about it.

"Gabe doesn't want kids." She was unaffected by her words. They fell to the pit of my stomach. Without really thinking about it, I'd always assumed Gabe would be a dad someday.

I searched for him by the front door. I'd have to see him to believe it. "What?"

She smiled at a group of guys across the bar. "Yeah. He doesn't want babies."

"Why?" Gabe would be an amazing father. He was the kind of guy who'd hoist them up on his shoulders to walk the board-walk and then tuck them in at the end of the night. He was a big teddy bear.

"He's a dick." Claire took out her lip gloss and swiped the wand over her lips as if she didn't care if she ever had children either.

I'd never heard Claire speak so harshly about him. She usu-ally reserved the word "dick" for my husband and only used it on occasions when Josh kept her from getting her way. Gabe had been demoted. Unfairly, in my opinion. "Well, you have plenty of time to change his mind. You're twenty-eight. You've got at least twelve more years to get pregnant. Do you want children?"

"Not necessarily." She tossed her lip gloss in her bag and spun the ice in her glass. "But I like options. Life's not about what happens, it's about what *could* happen." Claire was intoxi-cated by her own words, and she was drowning me in the haze. "You can't plan life, Anna. You can only live it. Don't waste your time worrying. We're only here until we're not." Claire lifted her glass to me. "It's only life. You know?"

I didn't know, though. To me, life was everything. For Claire, it was her current activity. I believed we were here to live. To fight for the next breath. Death row inmates would choose a life in prison over a shot and a chance at the next thing. Claire was as ready for the afterlife as she was for the shore house the four of us had rented for vacation.

"What's with all the baby talk? You're not pregnant, are you?"

I lifted my glass between us and downed the last of my drink. "Not preggo."

"Thank God. I'm not taking you to Greece if you can't drink. The shore would be tragic enough. Greece," she raised her eyebrows in warning, "is out of the question."

Josh and Gabe sat down across from us.

I inhaled the stale cigarette smoke trapped in Josh's clothes and his hair. I exhaled the hope I'd ever get pregnant. On my way to the bathroom, I stopped at the back bar and did a shot all by myself, and then I did another one on the way back. One to forget I wanted to get pregnant, and one to forget that I couldn't.

When the night was finally over and we said our goodbyes near our cars, I climbed into the passenger's seat and gave my husband a blow job in the parking lot. I had plenty of time to get pregnant. I didn't want to be a failure. Somehow, a parking lot blow job felt like a triumph. From the look on Josh's face, he felt the same as I did.

I needed to be more like Claire. More interested in planning a vacation than the rest of my life. Greece, Italy, Spain—those were the things I'd been *obsessed* with before Josh had pushed for a baby. I was a loser in my mind, but the only thing I was losing was myself.

4

Gabe

I CRACKED OPEN A BEER and set it on the coffee table in front of me. It was two in the morning, which was hardly the best time to drink another, but I didn't care.

When we got home, Claire breezed by me and up to our bedroom. I sat in the middle of the couch and stared at the television above the mantel. I'd told Claire it was too high, especially since the couch was so close, but she insisted it was perfect. On Sundays during football season, my neck ached by the eight o'clock game.

I think she did it on purpose.

I flipped through the channels. ESPN, History, DIY, Cinemax. Two blondes were going at it. The toilet flushed upstairs, and I turned to the Discovery Channel. I stopped paying attention and rewound the night's events in my head. Claire, as usual, suggested an extravagant escapade that Josh said no to. Anna had drunk a shot by herself at the back bar. Before I saw Anna pay the bartender, I'd thought the guy next to her had bought it for her. I was about to get up and walk back there because I knew Josh wouldn't. Not that he ever had to with Anna. She never put him, or herself, in a situation that required that kind of protective gesture.

I downed half my beer, still thinking about the shot. Why drink alone? We would have bought her ten shots if she'd wanted them.

The lights in the kitchen turned off behind me, and I cringed. There were no sounds of footsteps or words of greeting. The lamp next to me clicked off. Even after five years of marriage, Claire only had sex with the lights off. It was one of her many contradictions.

She practically fell onto my lap. Her bony ass dug into my thighs, and I shifted her weight on top of me, seeking a soft spot. "Why aren't you in bed?" Her words were raspy from the alcohol, which had swollen and deepened her voice. "Don't you want to make love to me?"

I set my beer on the table next to us. "Of course I do." I took off her shirt she couldn't seem to keep on all night. The orange lace of her bra covered thick padding that I never felt was necessary. Her tiny tits were great. She'd already started talking about a boob job, so that would happen by the end of the year. Five grand to still touch my wife's boobs in the dark.

Claire slid off me, and I could hear the swish of fabric as she removed her bra and pants. Then, she was back, sitting just to the side of me so she could rub my dick through my shorts. She reached low, below my balls, and I forgot about the boob job. I arched my back a little and inhaled the thick citrus scent of my wife's shampoo.

Claire unzipped my pants and released my dick. "We should make a baby."

In all our years together, children had been an abstract concept. Something other people had and were part of the fairy tale we'd begun, but we had never talked about them as an actual part of our lives. That would require long-term planning, and that wasn't Claire's style.

I almost lost my hard-on at the suggestion, but I was a professional when it came to wood. I flipped Claire onto her back. If I didn't get my dick in her soon, she'd ruin this.

One ankle on the back of the couch. One on the coffee table, and then I slid into her as if we were a perfect fit. She pulled my hair and moaned. It felt perfunctory and boring. I could do more. I *should* do more, but Claire liked to be covered, even if it was with my body.

I closed my eyes and thought of the two blondes going at it. The one with the black roots at the base of her fake hair color was between the other's legs. I thrust into Claire. She could control everything but what was in my mind. That she couldn't have.

Claire was warm and wet. My dick had no complaints about my wife.

"Oh, Gabe," she whispered into my ear. I wanted her to stop talking.

I leaned back and took her nipple in my mouth. It was selfish. Claire wouldn't want to be that exposed, but . . .

"'Til death do us part, baby," she said and drug me back up and into her.

There was no way to touch her and stay on top of her. I could have jerked off with more creativity than this. I pictured Anna's neck as she threw back the shot, pulled out of Claire, and came on her stomach.

I didn't want to be the father of her baby. It might be as scary as Claire was. That seemed impossible, but I couldn't take the chance. I climbed off and got her a paper towel from the stainless steel contraption that was more a piece of art than a paper towel roll holder. I was going to turn on the light so she could see better, but that would be cruel, and I loved my wife.

Gone were the days where she'd fucked me anywhere. In an alley, in the car, in the laundry room at my parents' house while everyone was having Thanksgiving dessert. I was too busy coming to realize all of those times had been in the dark.

"You ready for bed?" I asked her when she didn't get up.

"In a little while." She rolled over and faced the television. She didn't look up at it though. Her gaze rested on the fireplace across from her. It wasn't lit. Just a dark shadow beneath the blaring light of The Discovery Channel.

As Claire laid there quiet and alone, I remembered how much I loved her and that I promised to take care of her. In my family, we didn't abandon our problems. We didn't really fix them either. For better or worse . . . I lifted Claire into my arms and held her close to my chest.

She tightened her arms around my neck. "What are you doing?" She laughed a little as I walked up the stairs.

"I'm taking my wife to bed."

Claire kissed me on the cheek and rested her head against my shoulder. There was nothing that made my wife happier than something unpredictable. She was easy to please once you understood her. "You're crazy," she whispered in my ear.

That made two of us.

5

Anna

MY EYES FLUTTERED BUT REFUSED to open and face the day. I shut them tight again and rolled over toward the wall.

"Are you ever going to wake up?" Josh said as he walked into our room with a light step that told me he felt fine.

"Shh. Not so loud." I covered my exposed ear with my arm. Glimpses of shots touched the edges of my mind, leaving me with a bad taste in my mouth.

"I brought you green tea." He put the cup on my nightstand and sat on the bed next to me.

"You're too good to me." I'd never get over the power of a blow job.

"I know," he said, and just the sound of his voice made me feel better. "You seemed different last night."

With my head still on my pillow, I thought of Claire. She'd never let herself fail. She always moved forward and dragged the rest of us with her. I was going to be more like her even if it killed me. "Why?" I sat up and took a sip of my tea. It was the ideal not-too-hot temperature. The man was perfect. "Because I gave you a blow job in the car?"

Josh blushed. He always treated me like a lady, even if he loved me acting like a whore once in a while. I could only do it when it was just the two of us so our reputations would stay solidly intact. "That's part of it." He kissed the end of my nose, returning innocence to our union. "But you drank more than usual. It's a good thing I was okay to drive."

"It's a miracle if you ask me."

"I'm not that bad," he said, but it was always me driving or Gabe if we were with him and Claire. "There was nothing looming over us," he added with a soft voice as if he could erase the way I just snapped at him.

I stared down into the yellow-green potion in my cup. I'd been killing us slowly with the concept of a baby. I'd lost perspective of what was important . . . on what I already had to be thankful for. "By nothing, you mean a baby?"

Josh pushed my hair away from my face and hooked the unruly strands behind my ear. "A few weeks ago, you would have never *attacked* me in my car." Only Josh could exaggerate "attacked" and still sound sweet. A few weeks ago, I would have never wasted his biological materials on a blow job. The realization of that truth hit me right before the guilt of what I'd been putting him through did.

"We're the lucky ones," I said, and I meant it. "If someday we have a baby, I'll be thrilled." I teared up and hated myself for it. It was robbing my words of their sincerity, because although I could force myself to say them, I couldn't bring myself to believe them. "But every single day until then, I'm going to be thankful for you."

Josh took my tea and found a safe spot for it on my nightstand. He leaned down and kissed me as if it were the first time our lips had met. Every touch, every breath on my skin sent his love coursing through me. When he was secure with the details, there was nothing quite like being loved by Josh Montgomery.

I rolled him over and ran my lips down his bare chest until I took his balls in my hand. "Does this remind you of last night?"

Josh blushed again. It was the morning after the safety of the drinks and the darkness. I stroked him and kissed the inside of his thigh until he lifted my head by my hair. "What are you doing?" he asked.

I wasn't sure. The only thing I knew was that I wanted to be different.

I climbed on top of him. I rode Josh in the light of the morning as I basked in the love in his eyes. We were back to the beginning, and we were going to be fine. I laid my hands flat on his chest and watched as he reached down and touched me.

"Come for me, Anna."

My head fell back as the heat rose up inside me. It'd been weeks since either of us had cared if I came. I focused on his dick inside me and the taste of it in my mouth the night before. A wet heat surrounded him between my legs. I kept going, pushing myself against him. Then, with one smooth movement, Josh rolled me under him and pressed deeper inside me. I lost myself to him, and I came right before he did.

He flung himself down beside me. "Old habits," he said. "Just in case."

Just in case today was the day I was supposed to get pregnant. One of the eight thousand articles I'd read to him about conception suggested the female should be on the bottom at the time of orgasm.

"Just in case." I stared at the ceiling.

He caressed my arm until I almost fell back asleep. "Did you have fun last night?" His question pulled me back to the morning light.

"I always have fun with Claire . . . and Gabe. What do you think about Greece?"

"No way."

"Why? And why do you have to answer so quickly?"

"Because if Claire plans it, the trip will be twenty grand."

"But it'll be amazing."

"Nothing's that amazing. Gabe's going to need to get a

second job."

"Maybe that's what his meeting was about."

Josh ignored the question and slid out of bed to put his clothes back on.

"Did you ask him about it?" I wasn't letting him off the hook that easily.

"Nope."

"Why not?"

He leaned down and kissed me again. "Because it's none of my business."

"You know. Don't you?"

He smiled and stood up straight. "You sound as crazy as Claire."

"Maybe she's the sane one and the rest of us are crazy."

"I love you." Josh wouldn't waste our time evaluating Claire. "Let's go to Brandywine and hike."

My head still pounded. "I might be dehydrated."

"Bike ride?"

"Better. Let me take a shower and we'll see where we are."

"I'm exactly where I should be," he said.

A tiny voice inside my head said, *I'm not.*

6

Gabe

"I KNOW WHAT WE SHOULD do." The urgency in Claire's voice was a warning siren. There were many pressing issues to Claire that only cost me money and time.

I hadn't even opened my eyes, and Claire was already making plans. I wondered again if she ever truly slept or just stayed awake plotting. "What?" I asked since resisting was futile.

"We should rent a boat and party on it all day."

"You want to rent a boat."

She leaned across my chest smiling at me, but her mind was mulling over ideas that I couldn't begin to guess about. "Not just a boat. Maybe a yacht."

"Claire—"

"Don't 'Claire' me. We're only young once. The weather is beautiful. We live near the water. We should be on a boat." She spoke in the same tone the Surgeon General used to advise everyone they should eat healthier. Claire reached across me and grabbed her phone off the nightstand. Her elbow dug into my chest as she typed and swiped through different pages on the screen. "BaySail. Havre de Grace. Half day rentals."

"Claire—"

"I'm going to text Anna."

She used her elbow as leverage to sit up, and my chest threatened to cave in around it. I rubbed the area as I looked at the time. "Are they even up yet?"

"Who cares?" Claire left me alone in bed. In peace. I closed my eyes again, knowing I'd soon be packing a cooler or searching for sunscreen. Just like that. Plans had been made. A few minutes later she returned, triumphantly holding her phone in my face. "See?"

The text back from Anna read: "Yes Yes Yes"

We were spending the afternoon on a boat.

It was five hundred dollars when we factored in tax and tip. Maybe a few dollars more, but only two-fifty a couple, and for a Claire-led plan, that wasn't too bad. Josh shook his head a little and laughed as he peeled the twenties off his wad of cash.

"She's never been known as a cheap date," I whispered so Claire and Anna couldn't hear us.

"No," Josh said and handed me the money. "Better you than me, man."

Anna and Claire were already on the boat. Their backs were to us as they gazed out at the water and laughed. Their bodies intertwined in the intricate dance moves of a tribe with their own language. I could hear Claire's laughter. Sometimes they were like two little girls rather than our wives. I thought that was why Claire loved Anna. In spite of her jealousy, she never giggled with anyone else the way she did when they were together.

Anna's bathing suit was a one-piece and conservative compared to Claire's bikini, which was nothing more than thin straps holding together minute pieces of fabric. When she looked up and smiled, she reminded me of a sprite or a pixie. As if she might float away with a glitter trail behind her. Anna was more like a woman. Her suit was black and simple in the front with a respectable V-neck. When she turned around, the straps formed a pinwheel of color across her back. It was interesting, but it didn't scream for attention. She looked like someone's wife. My gaze followed the contours of her hips in the suit, and I remembered she *was* someone's wife.

Claire began mixing everyone a drink. I waited for Josh to insist on a beer, but he took the red cup containing whatever concoction she'd created without argument. She raised her glass, and we all reciprocated, holding ours high in a circle above us as Claire proclaimed, "To us . . . and to today."

We tapped cups and dispersed into seats as the boat departed the dock. The only open spot left was next to Anna, so I stood and tried to keep my balance. Claire was smiling at me, but the sentiment didn't touch her eyes. It was a cold expression. She was examining me and my choice to stand. Constantly having to consider my own actions made drinking with her tedious and exhausting. I took a small sip from my cup and sat next to Anna. This seemed to please Claire.

"Do you think when we're sixty, we'll still be spending our weekends together drinking on boats?" Anna asked.

I assumed we'd be with our families. Children and grandchildren, but I didn't dare answer. It was an odd version of my life since I wasn't getting Claire pregnant.

Josh said, "Of course," without much assurance in his voice.

"Nothing lasts forever." Claire stared at Josh as she spoke, and he only rolled his eyes.

There were nights when Josh drank too much and I braced myself for him to tell my wife what he really thought of her. He never did, though. He teased her, and they drove each other crazy, but he was always kind to her.

Anna stood and walked toward the back of the boat. The captain asked her if she wanted to help raise the sail. She hesitated, and I knew she was considering how her agreeing would look to Josh. If he'd consider the interaction flirting or if she shouldn't draw attention to herself.

Josh was watching her as he drank. The liquor in his glass seemed to interest him more than his wife this afternoon. My judgments were unfair. Anna might not care what Josh thought. Maybe she was always careful and respectful because that was how she was. I just wasn't used to reserved behavior. I assumed it had to be required of someone.

As if in denial of my thoughts, Anna looked back at Josh, seeking approval.

He didn't move. Just stared at her until I almost said something. I turned back to Anna, who was entranced by her husband sipping his drink. She didn't seem angry or sad, as if she'd detached from him when the boat had taken off from the dock.

Anna nodded at the captain. He moved her to the side of the sail without touching her—the guy still had a tip to worry about—and instructed her on what rope to pull. I watched them work until Claire wrapped her arms around my waist and buried her head in my chest. I hadn't seen her coming. I was lost inside my head.

7

Anna

"YOU SURE YOU WANT ANOTHER?" I asked my sloppy husband. I could tell where the night was going—where most nights went—but it was still early, and Josh just kept downing drinks as if he were trying to drown out a stressful week.

He ignored me and waved his hand toward Claire to order another. I'd switched to beer after the first round. I couldn't figure out exactly what Claire was mixing in the drinks, and that was never a good sign.

She handed him a cup and came to lay next to me on the warm fiberglass of the boat. I moved over and shared my towel with her. "I'm going to have to take care of him," I said.

"Isn't that what wives do?" We peeked back at Josh and Gabe. "Some days I swear that's the only reason they married us. To take care of them."

"Gabe seems pretty self-sufficient." He was leaning against the side of the boat facing away from us. Through the fabric of his shirt I could see the muscles in his back, strong and defined.

"Oh, he is when it comes to drinking. He said he left his bender days in the Army."

All the drunken nights together ran through my mind and caused me to smile. "I've still seen him drink a lot," I said to regain my composure.

"I know. Imagine what it used to be like back then. He never talks about it."

"Never?" I leaned down and whispered. If Gabe didn't talk about it, neither should we.

Claire laughed, knowing exactly what I was doing. "Well, just enough to not make it weird. He was out of the service and had gotten his MBA before I'd met him, so that time felt distant to me."

"I think Josh would have liked the military," I said.

"He definitely loves rules." Claire leaned into me and laughed.

I joined her at Josh's expense. "And expectations."

"And consequences."

"And predictability." We were practically rolling over laughing so hard. "Stop, or I'll divorce him tonight."

"Shh. He'll hear you and hide all the money."

"He can have it all," I said and stopped laughing.

"I'll run away with you." Claire put her arm around my shoulders. I believed her. She'd come away with me if I wanted her to. "You remind me of my brother."

I rolled onto my side and faced her. She was solid in her expression and her posture. Just waiting for the words I'd say. I didn't want to disappoint Claire. Ever. "I didn't know you had a brother."

"He's gone now. It's just me." Claire turned gray. Her eyebrows pulled together until her eyes almost closed completely.

I wanted to ask Claire his name and if he'd been younger or older than her. I couldn't imagine her with a sibling. I'd found Claire in this world alone, and my trying to match her with someone else was throwing me a little. Claire's eyes shut. She didn't want to talk about him. She *couldn't* talk about him.

"I'm sorry, Claire."

Josh always said that Claire acted the way she did because she was an only child. I told him that was a good reason to have lots of kids.

"Do you guys want a drink?" Josh yelled too loud in our direction.

Claire brightened and turned toward our husbands. "We're good. Thanks, though." She faced me again as light and airy as she'd been a few moments ago. I wanted to ask more about her brother and how he'd died, but her switch to despair and back again was so swift it left me speechless.

Josh tripped on the way to the car. He didn't fall, but since he was resting his heavy arm across my shoulders, we both dipped toward our knees. I caught us before we hit the wooden planks of the pier and stood us up straight again.

"Whoops," he said like an elderly woman, and I knew he was drunk.

I'd predicted it when he let Claire mix his drinks. She firmly believed every drink should be a stiff one. "What is the point of a weak drink?" she'd say and pour another shot over the ice.

"You okay, big guy?" I wasn't in the mood to take care of him. Claire should have to. She'd put him in this condition, she should have to manage it.

Claire was still on the boat, having Gabe take pictures of her on every corner of it now that it was safely docked. She wasn't exactly the caretaker type. The breeze blew her white gauze dress tight between her legs. It grazed her waist and showed the perfect silhouette of her taut body. She was as pretty as the boat floating by the dock.

"I'm glad I didn't marry Claire," Josh said and steadied himself against Gabe's car.

"I am, too." I laughed at the improbable idea. I was sure Claire felt the same way.

"She'll bankrupt him."

Gabe helped Claire off the boat and laced his fingers through hers as they walked toward us.

"They have plenty of money," I said and stared at our friends. Josh never held my hand. Not unless it was completely necessary, like when we'd walked down the aisle after our wedding and the entire church had been watching us. Otherwise, he cited gait issues when I tried to grab his hand. I'd joked with him about how many men would love to hold my hand, but he still didn't budge on the subject.

"Not just money. She's going to suck the life out of him." He was slurring worse than he was ten minutes ago, and my chest tightened at the thought of Claire overhearing him. "What are you talking about? You sound crazy."

"Nothing. Mark my word, though. They're not going to make it."

"What do you know?" My expression was stern. I wanted Josh to sober up and tell me what he was talking about, but if he sobered up, he'd shut up, too.

"Nothing. Come here and kiss me."

I crossed my arms at my chest and watched Gabe and Claire. Claire was happy, and Gabe looked . . . satisfied. He was happy, I was sure of it. Holding his wife's hand during the rare moments she was quiet and content.

"Come here."

"No," I snapped, but then I smiled at him to soften the blow. I didn't feel like kissing him.

"Where to?" Gabe asked when they reached us.

"Iron Hill," came the voice of the drunk behind me. He thought a brewery was a good idea.

I raised my eyebrows since Josh couldn't see me. "I think it might be time to go home."

"What's one more?" Claire said and opened the passenger door of the car. She placed Josh into the front seat, as if he were completely pliable, and climbed into the back seat behind him.

"He'll sober up on the way," Gabe said and opened my door

for me.

"Promise?"

"We'll stop and pick him up a roll somewhere."

Josh leaned over the front console and beeped the horn.

"Or six . . . rolls," I said.

We rode up I-95, going well over the speed limit. The windows were down, and my and Claire's hair blew across our faces. We had to hold it close to our heads to even see. Our sunglasses were on. The sunroof was open, and the waning sunlight poured into Gabe's black Lexus. When he turned up the volume on the radio, I was transported to my teens. I couldn't sing. I couldn't speak. All I could do was enjoy the ride.

In the reflection of the rearview mirror, I could see the top of Gabe's head. His sunglasses hid his dark eyes, but his black hair was blowing in the wind. Josh's hair was always cut tight to his head. Gabe let his grow out a little. It was thick. Wavy. I assumed Claire dictated his haircut. He was smart to succumb to her suggestions. I smiled at the term. Nothing was really a suggestion with Claire.

She reached over and held my hand on the seat between us. I hadn't held another girl's hand since before kindergarten. "I love you, Anna," she yelled over the radio. The wind and the speed were intoxicating to her, too.

I winked at her, and she laughed. I could always make her happy. The same way I knew to wear a one-piece bathing suit and not to laugh too hard at her husband's jokes. Claire was loud, but sensitive. Based on her short list of close friends, I assumed she was difficult to manage, but I found her to be pretty clear about what she needed. I only slipped up occasionally.

A new song came on. One we'd heard a hundred times before, and Claire tapped Gabe on the shoulder and told him to turn it up. He obliged, and we all careened north without a care in the world. I was invincible in the back of Gabe's car. Young and beautiful. I could fly as long as Gabe was driving. Claire squeezed my hand, and I closed my eyes and let go of my hair. It blew wildly around my head and blocked out any thoughts that didn't include the music and the wind.

"Gabe, go faster," she yelled.

I settled into the ride with Claire.

8

Gabe

EVERY WEEKEND WAS ABOUT THE same as the one before. Except for wedding weekends. Claire had called it the season of weddings. I wasn't sure if she was referring to the past few months or our late twenties, but we were going to a lot. She'd been a bridesmaid in one. The last two were coworkers, and tonight's was my corporate counterpart in Manhattan's nuptials.

We had four hours until we picked the girls up from the salon, and I was in the middle of cleaning my car out when Josh pulled up.

"Is that all you brought?" I nodded to the two small overnight bags he had.

"You're funny." He set both of them on the ground by my trunk. "There are also two garment bags with our outfits for tonight."

"Did she threaten your life if you forgot them?"

"It was implied."

"Claire took up the whole trunk with her dress and told me if it doesn't make it to Manhattan, I may as well not either."

Josh pointed at me. "I believe her. She scares me."

"You and me both. Are they all crazy?"

"I tell myself they are," he said, and I mentally reviewed every item packed and its location within the vehicle. If it wasn't in there, it wasn't meant to be. "Ready?"

Josh was placing his bags on the floor of the backseat. "I think so." He set Anna's upright behind him and closed the door. "Let's make them check everything before we leave the salon. Just in case."

"Just in case." I backed out and shut the garage door. "Let's hope they like their hair."

"Oh, God." Josh shook his head and stared out the window as we drove out of my development.

They both looked beautiful. I was careful to only tell Claire, though. I at least wanted this night to have a placid beginning. She loved her hair, and that was all that mattered. If she'd hated it, we might be dropping Anna and Josh off at the train station so she could repair it.

Because of said hair, we rode up the New Jersey Turnpike with all the windows and the sunroof closed. Anna was behind me in the car. She always was, as if that was her assigned seat for our escapades.

"I got us adjoining rooms," Claire said, reminding me once again who orchestrated everything around us.

"Why?" I asked. "Aren't rooms next to each other enough?"

"Because if I want to tell Anna or Josh something quickly, I don't want to have to go out in the hallway. This way, all I have to do is knock on the center door and wait for them to answer. It's more efficient."

"You could call," I said. Josh was characteristically staying out of this, but I was sure he wanted as many doors as possible between him and Claire. "Or text."

"Or walk through the door I made sure was between the rooms," Claire said, dismissing all future comments.

The door would become a stress point for the rest of the night. I'd let her bait me. With what, though? A door? I went over the conversation again in my head. The minute anyone walked through the adjoining door, her face would light up with satisfaction, and the second I disagreed with her it would be "about the door." The way I was becoming able to predict the crazy was scarier than the actual situation.

"I can't wait to get there," Anna said. She was leaning forward, her head almost even with my and Josh's shoulders. "I haven't been to the city since we came up last Christmas to see the tree."

"You bought me my red coat that trip," Claire said and stole the conversation.

"I love that coat." Anna let her have it. She always gave in to Claire. Claire was lucky to have her.

"Thank you."

Claire and Anna sat back. I turned on the radio so I could drive the rest of the way in peace. We valeted the car at the hotel and went to our separate, but connected, rooms.

Everything—the ceremony, the cocktail hour, the reception—was taking place at the Le Parker Méridien New York. The rain fell against the giant windows in the ballroom, but it didn't matter, because no one had to go outside. Claire was disappointed we couldn't experience the terrace. She voiced her concerns a few times. I found the bar a few times.

Josh was approached by a bald guy halfway through the cocktail hour. He hugged him while I stared in shock. Josh and I had been inseparable for years now, and I couldn't think of a time he'd hugged me. Shock didn't even describe the emotions I felt when the guy lifted Anna off the ground and swung her in a circle by the pasta station.

"Gabe, Claire." Josh waved us over and pointed to his lovable friend. "This is Conrad. He was my fraternity brother at

Penn State."

I extended my hand. "Nice to meet you."

"I was also Anna's best friend before this guy met her." I raised my eyebrows at Conrad and Anna. "He stole her from me."

Josh punched him in the arm. Also something I'd never seen Josh do before.

"I can't believe you're here." Anna regarded Conrad as if he might rise up and float above us at any minute.

"Gina's cousin is the bride. I'm supposed to be here. How did you two get in?"

Claire was suddenly aware of all our attention being given to someone other than her. She introduced herself and stood between Josh and Conrad as Anna explained, "Josh and Gabe work with Gina's cousin."

"Wow. Small world."

"Can I get you guys another round?" I offered. My glass was empty. I could see Anna's and Josh's were, too.

"I'll go with you. Help you carry them," Josh offered. Really Claire should have. She didn't know Conrad.

"That's all right. I got 'em. You guys catch up." I walked away and left Anna, Josh, and Claire to reminisce with Conrad.

The bartender made our drinks, and I watched Claire from across the room. She was nodding and smiling and laughing. She was a part of a conversation that had nothing to do with her. She looked utterly uncomfortable, and eventually, she stared out the windows beyond Anna. If Conrad didn't move on, Claire would be grabbing the mic out of the singer's hand to make a toast just to get attention. Or taking off her dress. Or kissing the groom's father. Nothing was outside the realm of possibility. Not when it came to Claire's need for validation as the most interesting person present.

Josh awkwardly watched as Anna laughed at something

Conrad had said. His examination focused in on his wife as she touched the guy's arm and laughed some more. From where I was standing, he looked as much of an outsider as Claire did.

It was odd to see Anna and Josh with a stranger. Over the years, I'd forgotten they'd lived their early twenties without us. College, first apartments, St. Patty's Days, Oktoberfests, whatever they did about all of those things, they'd done it without us. They'd been with other people.

I handed Conrad his drink as the crowd began moving into the ballroom. He nodded his gratitude and left to find his wife. The band was already playing. People were congregating on or near the dance floor. It seemed too early to dance. The lights were still on, and the bride and groom hadn't been announced yet.

"What a crazy place to see him. Do you guys still keep in touch?" I asked Josh and Anna as we made our way to table number twelve.

Claire's scowl made it clear how she felt about talking of Conrad even after he'd finally left. "Dance with me," she said, but the request wasn't to me. She was asking Josh.

Josh hated to dance unless it was late at night and he'd had a few. Even for Claire, the invitation was desperate and highlighted my ever-growing surprise at how far she'd go to fill her endless needs, but Josh let her yank him away.

"So, do you guys still keep in touch?" I asked Anna.

"No." I thought it might be all she'd offer, but after she took a sip of her drink, Anna added, "Josh doesn't believe a man can be friends with a woman."

I laughed. Josh had plenty of female friends at work. Sure, they weren't the kind of friends who called each other on the weekend or really ever saw each other. I thought back over every close friend I'd ever had, searching for the women among the group. There were none.

"Would you count us as friends?" I asked.

"The best of friends, but we're different."

"How so?"

Claire lifted Josh's arm and spun under it. If she could have made him dip her, she'd be parallel to the ground. "We have them. They make our friendship easy."

I'd never heard Claire described as easy before. Anna and I watched as the song ended and Claire and Josh clapped with the rest of the small group on the dance floor. Josh leaned down and said something only Claire could hear. She lit up at his statement.

STAGE II

RECKONING

9

Gabe

"I'VE GOT A LATE MEETING," I said to Josh, expecting his acceptance of my delay without question. He had the knack of knowing when to ask more questions and when not to. Actually, he just didn't ask any.

"Another meeting, huh?"

Until today.

I gauged his interest in my whereabouts. I was thankful he hadn't brought it up in front of our wives. "You're going to have to trust me on this. It's no big deal."

He studied me for a moment, probably searching for signs of drugs or another addiction he'd be forced to address. Of course there were none. "If you say so." He nodded and walked out of my office with a light step.

Why couldn't things be as easy with my wife as they were with Josh? Claire was becoming increasingly jealous. Over nothing. I'd never even considered cheating on her. My father had cheated on my mother once. My sisters and I had listened to our mom cry late at night in the weeks that followed. If I even thought about an affair, my sisters would come to my house and beat the shit out of me, and I was better than that. Better than my dad.

I left the office a little early. Vacation had begun. We were meeting Josh and Anna for happy hour tonight, we had Rob's wedding tomorrow night, and after that the four of us were sharing a beach house for a week in Sea Isle. Just the thought of not coming into the office for a week relaxed me.

I pulled into the gym parking lot and parked two spots from the building. Not many people here on a Friday night. Everyone had something to do. So did I, but I was suddenly hiding my workouts from my wife because somehow my staying in shape equaled me hunting for someone new to have sex with.

Since the day Claire and I'd met, incidentally at a gym, I'd worked out. She always loved it. Especially in the beginning, she'd comment on my body all the time, but recently, it took on a dark connotation. Nothing I said convinced her it was still me just sweating and smelling while I exorcised the demons of the work day. So, instead of fighting with her about it, I hid it from her as much as possible. It wasn't really a lie. I was working. Just not at the office.

My workout was an abbreviated one. I showered and re-dressed in work clothes. I hid the gym bag in the trunk of my car to be emptied and washed during a time when Claire wasn't home. I rolled my eyes at the absurdity of it all, but if it took me hiding my gym shorts from my wife for her to feel secure, I'd hide them.

Claire was sitting on the front porch waiting for me when I drove up. The house seemed bigger with her there. Her tiny frame swung back and forth on the swing as she waved to me. She was Main Street and apple pie gazing out at our neighbors' pristine lawns. Even with her constant need for attention, there was something quite innocent about Claire. Leaving her would be like returning a dog to the shelter because it was too much work.

She met me in the garage and said, "Another Friday meeting?"

I kissed her on the lips. She was calm, and I glanced at the glass of wine in her hand "Starting without me?"

"Well, if you don't come home on time . . ."

"Just give me a minute to change, and then I'll be ready to properly commence our vacation."

She kissed me again, this time wrapping her arms around my neck and pulling me down toward her. "Sounds good."

"Unless you want to come upstairs with me . . ." I tilted my head toward her in invitation.

Claire's posture straightened. "Josh and Anna are waiting." Her voice had a resolved tone. The lightness of our vacation discussion was lost. I wasn't sure where.

"Okay. I'll be right back."

"I'll be on the front porch drinking and yelling at little kids as they ride by," she recovered. I only watched as she laughed a little.

"Oh. Just like my grandmom."

Claire and I both said, "God rest her soul."

We ate at Half Moon and then all drove down to Victory for drinks. Kennett Square was far from both our jobs, but it had just enough bars to keep Claire and I satisfied. We kept trying to convince Josh and Anna to move up here from Delaware, but they kept waving off the idea.

The parking lot at Victory was packed. I stepped out of the car as Josh slid into a spot two rows back from us. Construction machinery and port-o-potties dotted the landscape behind us where new townhomes were being built. Anna and Josh should move there. The site was quiet since happy hour was in full swing, but it didn't stop the couple that was climbing out of the car next to Josh's from fighting. It was none of my business, but I couldn't stop listening.

"You're such an asshole," the woman said and slammed

her car door. She stormed into the restaurant with him barely following behind her. I'd been there before. He was thinking. *I should leave her. She's crazy.* I imagined him just turning around and driving away. Claire took my hand. She was staring at me, and the hurt in her eyes ripped the smile from my face. As if I'd spoken my thoughts aloud.

Claire led us to the last two open stools at the bar and ordered a round without anyone's input, and then handed a glass filled with tequila and soda to Anna.

"Tequila again?" Anna asked. "You already got me two others at Blue Moon." Anna stared at Claire forlorn with the evening's consumption. It was still early.

"You're only young once, Anna," she said and clinked her glass of Jack and Coke against Anna's drink.

The couple from the parking lot were standing off to the side, still arguing. The woman came up next to me and held out money to the bartender for a drink. The tension between them poured over the four of us. Anna was looking behind me. Josh's gaze followed hers. When Claire realized no one was listening to her story, she noticed, too, as the guy came up and yanked the woman away from the bar.

"Get the fuck off me," she said and ripped her arm from his grasp.

"You're a crazy bitch," he said, reaching for her again.

"Back off." I was standing between them before I had time to figure out what exactly was going on.

"Mind your own fucking business, dude." The guy leveled off, faced me, and sized me up. He was stocky and had the stance of a fighter. He'd probably lifted weights for years but had lost his routine because he appeared soft.

"I'd like to, but your business is right next to me, and your girl just told you to get the fuck off her."

His cheeks reddened as the blood rushed to his face. His

hands clenched into fists. He didn't like the way I was talking to him. I was about to drop him because I was done talking.

"Babe." Suddenly his girl was calling him babe and hanging on his arm. "Babe. It's okay. Let's just go."

"You sure?" I asked her, and the guy's head nearly exploded.

"Problem?" the bartender asked, scrutinizing the both of us.

I didn't take my eyes off the hothead in front of me. "I've got no problem." Even if he took a swing, I had none.

"We're leaving," the woman said and pulled him away. As they always did, he kept glancing back, ready to lunge at me at any second. I stared him down until he exited the door and the adrenalin quieted inside me.

I turned to see Anna staring at me in complete and utter admiration. Her mouth was open just a tad, and her eyes were bigger than I'd ever seen. She scanned every inch of me from my chest to my head as if in awe.

Claire stared at me, too. She looked at Anna and back at me. Her chest rose a little with the stifled breaths of a woman who was about to cry. I felt the sudden urge to apologize to my wife. She'd witnessed something and was making it into much more than the harmless look that it was. I was a dead man.

10

Anna

I COULDN'T STOP STARING AT Gabe. Suddenly, the angle of his jaw and the contour of his arms were making me hot. While Josh had just dismissed the couple as if they were trash, Gabe had stepped up. I was enthralled. It must have been some primitive natural selection taking hold, because I wanted him to kick the shit out of the guy and then put his dick in me.

I blushed and looked at the floor. He was Josh's friend . . . and my friend . . . and my best friend's husband. He was just Gabe, but he was strong and completely unafraid and standing up for someone who needed him to.

Gabe went to the bathroom, and Josh focused his attention on the bartender to order us another round.

"I don't want to be here anymore," Claire said. Her voice was soft. She was talking to herself more than to me.

I didn't want to be here either. I wanted to be underneath her husband somewhere. I lifted my hair off the back of my neck, seeking some cool air. Claire sat next to me, deflated. Something had brought her down since we'd arrived at Victory. I rolled my neck and regained my senses. *He's just Gabe.* I nodded to solidify the thought. "It isn't that big of a deal. The guy left," I said.

Claire wasn't appeased. Her expression didn't change at all, not even when I rubbed her back. When Gabe returned from the bathroom, she announced, "Let's get out of here."

"Yeah, I'm done, too." Josh was suddenly no fun either.

"Why? We just got here," Gabe said and didn't take his eyes off Claire. They stared at each other, having some private, silent conversation Josh and I would never comprehend. As close as we all were, we weren't a part of their marriage.

"Let's go back to our house," Claire finally said.

"Fine." Gabe gave in. "I have to stop for gas on the way."

We left as a cohesive group, but when Gabe held the door for us as we exited, we somehow broke apart. Gabe walked ahead of us to his car. Claire and Josh were several feet behind me, walking in silence. None of us seemed together anymore.

Josh and I followed Gabe and Claire out of the parking lot and toward their house, all the while Gabe's chest and shoulders flashed in my mind as their car's tail lights blinked on in front of us.

"You're quiet," Josh said.

I peered across the car at him and managed to smile. I'd been sad. Maybe even depressed, but over the last twenty-four hours, I struggled to fight back the resentment and anger. It was all aimed squarely at him.

"Are you still upset about not having a baby?"

Just the word wounded me a little. I stared down at my hands in my lap. The engagement ring he gave me represented less and less as the days of our marriage moved forward. Josh's call to tell me about his test results still beat at the inside of my head, even after two weeks, and I swallowed back the bitterness rising in my throat. "I'm trying not to be."

"Maybe it's not meant to be."

I took a deep breath to spare him from the horrid thoughts about him rushing through my mind. "Maybe."

"We're fine without children."

"You're fine. Do you even care what I am? Or are you

just happy we can't have kids and you're not the problem?" I spewed the words at him. My anger was on the verge of being unleashed, and I didn't want to have this argument with him. Not in this car.

Josh shifted in his seat, leaning forward a bit as if the lumbar was the source of his discomfort. "What do you mean?"

"We've had one test, and you're ready to be kid-free for the rest of our lives. There are so many other options. Why is this the end for you?"

Josh reached across the console for my hand. It was a calculated move, and I hated him for it, too. I moved it away from him. "Anna, I don't want us to get any deeper into this than we already are. Counting days, taking your temperature. Arguing about sex. If we're meant to have a baby, it'll come. That's how life works."

I stared at the lines in the center of the road. I hated him. "Is it?"

Gabe's car pulled into the Sunoco and up to a pump, and Josh turned in behind him, coming to a stop in a parking spot in front of the double doors.

"I'm going to get some soda. Do you want any mixers?" Josh asked.

With the strength of a warrior, I managed to get out, "No."

Josh left me alone in the car with a solitary thought: *I hate him.*

He seemed relieved that it was my body that was the cause. He didn't want to have a baby, but he wouldn't be the reason I didn't have one. He thought he'd just hold my hand as I mourned what my own body wouldn't give me.

"Hey," Claire said and hopped in the back seat of our car. She slid across the seat until she was in the middle and leaned into the front seat with me. "Why do you look that way?"

I squeezed my eyes shut tight to hold back the tears. Claire stayed completely silent. "There are several reasons, but the most pressing right now is that I want to have a baby, and Josh doesn't." I felt like a child throwing a tantrum. That was how Josh made me feel. Senseless about the whole thing. *Thing* being a child.

"I know," she said, and my eyes snapped open.

"How do you know?" If Josh discussed this with Gabe, I was going to kill him.

"Little comments you've made. The way you ogle every baby that comes near us." Clare leaned against the side of Josh's seat and stared at me sympathetically. "You don't look at him the same way you used to."

"I don't?" I could feel it. If Josh felt it, too, that would explain his coldness about the subject of children. It still made no sense. I wouldn't forget wanting one. It wasn't something a woman got over.

"No. He's your husband and should be the father of your children. If that's not going to happen, it's going to change the way you see him."

"Do you think I'm terrible?"

She shook her head. "I love you. Gabe and I both love you, and I'm sure Josh does, too."

"This will be the end of us." I scanned the windows of the convenience store. Josh was leaning down and reading labels of bottles in the refrigerators.

"Someday, all of this will fade. You'll only remember it as a terrible, horrifically sad few months." Claire was inside her own mind. It didn't seem as if she was still talking to me. "When it does, I want you to remember one thing."

She looked into my eyes. Hers were different. She wasn't excited about a thing. All the energy that usually poured out of Claire was silenced. "What?"

"That I always knew you were going to be a great mom."

The tears fell down my cheeks. She knew exactly what to say, and my husband could only find all the wrong words. I pulled Claire into my arms and cried on her shoulder. "What if this doesn't work out?"

"Trust me. You're stronger than you realize. Find what you need and take it." She rubbed my back.

I put myself back together and watched as Josh paid at the register. The way he stood there like the most important thing going on in his life was a bottle of Coke Zero enraged me all over again. "I'm starting to hate him."

"I understand." Claire was looking at Gabe in the rearview mirror. Her jaw was tight. Her eyes narrowed.

I leaned toward the window to distance myself from whatever she was going to say next.

She took a short breath, turned to me, and smiled. It was warm and loving. "Go ride with Gabe. I'll ride with Josh and talk to him."

I shook my head before I'd fully processed the offer. "Oh, no. We're fine."

"Not about the baby. Just about life and how it's all so fleeting. He's wasting your time, and he needs to know that it can all slip away in an instant."

He did need to know. He thought we could continue going to happy hours until we died, but there was so much more to life than what drink was on special.

"I'll make him understand. I promise."

"Go easy on him," I said and laughed. If nothing else, the ride with Claire would annoy Josh, and I wanted him to suffer.

Claire climbed between the seats and sat beside me. "I love you, Anna. I've got this."

I wanted to believe her, but Josh was stubborn. Maybe even more so than Claire. I started to make a joke, but the cold determination in Claire's eyes stole the words from my lips. Claire could do anything. I shouldn't underestimate her.

She nodded toward the store. "Josh is coming. Go get in the car with Gabe. Tell him we'll follow."

Claire got out of the car when I did. She met me behind it and hugged me, holding my body tight against hers. She released me and took one last look at me. She finally said, "We were meant to meet." She was so divinely correct when she spoke this way.

She climbed into Josh's passenger seat. I waved to Gabe before climbing in his car next to him.

"What's up?" he asked.

"Claire's going to ride with Josh. She said they'd follow us."

Gabe rolled his eyes as if Claire's plans exhausted him. I thought deep down he loved it. He must have loved her. His would be a lifetime of wondering what was next. One adventure after another. He pulled out and made a left as we drove toward their house.

11

Gabe

I DIDN'T GIVE A FUCK what the reason was, I was relieved to have Anna in the car with me instead of Claire, especially since it was Claire's idea. She must have gotten over whatever she thought she'd seen inside Victory.

A sweet, floral smell followed Anna into the car. It floated around me, and I inhaled it deeply into my lungs. It was the same smell that always shocked me when I was close to her. Next to her in an elevator. Randomly seated beside her in a booth. Reaching across her shoulder to pay for drinks. This was the smell of Anna. It was her smile, and the color of her eyes against the bay, and the way she quietly laughed at all my jokes.

Anna was in a flowy red dress that was completely innocent unless she sat just the right way, shifting the fabric high up to her mid-thigh. I kept my head pointed completely straight and snuck a second glance at her legs. I gripped the steering wheel hard and released the image from my mind. What the fuck was wrong with me? She was Josh's wife. Claire had legs, too. They just weren't as long or perfectly shaped as Anna's.

I inhaled deeply and turned off Baltimore Pike.

"You ready for vacation?" I asked. Normal topics should be discussed. I needed to fill the car with conversation so Anna never suspected how I felt about her. She'd end this friendship immediately. She'd never let any of these emotions exist behind

Josh's back. She was *that* good, and so was I.

"Oh, man. I can't wait." She scrunched up her nose. "I do have to work a little, though."

"What?" I practically yelled, dragging out the one syllable as if it was a full interrogation.

She laughed at the way I asked the question. I could always make her laugh. "I'm working on a new logo for work, and the mock-ups are supposed to come back on Thursday. They'll want the final turned around quick."

"You and Claire would kill us if Josh and I brought work to the beach."

"The same rules don't apply to us." In the space where she'd usually laugh, Anna only stared out the window and ran her hand up and down her seat belt.

I turned into the driveway and hit the garage door opener button. The silence was thick between us, but it was comfortable. Anna was easy to be around. It wasn't until I'd pulled into the garage and closed the door behind us that I realized something was wrong. Anna was still turned away, but there was a faint shimmer on her cheek. Was she crying? I leaned forward for a better look.

"Are you okay?"

She nodded. "Fine." Something was definitely off.

I listened for Josh's car to pull in behind us. In the silence the garage light clicked off, and Anna and I were completely in the dark.

She didn't say a word. Only sat next to me as if the two of us in a dark car in a closed garage was normal, when in fact, there was nothing less casual than the way I felt sitting next to her.

"We should go in," I said and yanked the door handle.

When our vacation was over, I was going to have to back off this friendship. Claire and I would have to stop doing so many things with Josh and Anna. Really just with Anna, but that'd be weird. I'd tell Claire I needed some space from Josh. That working with him and hanging out with them socially all the time was wearing on me. She'd understand. Based on the way she looked at me tonight, Claire might fully comprehend the issue. It was the right thing to do.

Anna opened her door and followed me into the mud room and through to the kitchen. I hit the on button for the radio attached under the cabinet in the kitchen. It'd been left by the previous owners, but Claire still used it all the time. I told her we could get Bluetooth speakers and upgrade the entire house with surround sound, but she said it was fine where it was. The simplicity of her needs on this subject had confused me. Rarely was Claire simple.

I tossed Anna a few limes. She took the cutting board and a knife out of the drawer in the island. If anyone knew this kitchen as well as Claire, it was Anna. She sliced the limes into tiny wedges for our beers. I found the lighter and lit the citronella candles on the back deck.

"Where the hell are they?" I asked when I came back in. "They should have been here twenty minutes ago."

"Text them." Anna didn't even look up from her task of washing the knife and cutting board.

"Leave them." I nodded toward the sink, but she was already done.

"It's not a big deal, and your house is always perfect." I inspected the room. Not an item was out of place. "My phone's been dead for hours," she said.

I took mine out of my pocket and texted Claire. The entire communication consisted of one question mark. She'd know everything I was asking. *Where are you? When are you getting here? What is taking so long?*

Anna pressed lime slices into two beers and handed one to me. "Let's go outside. They'll be here any second." I followed her back out.

She sat on the glider. If Claire and Josh were here, I'd have sat with her. Claire always sat in the chaise lounge. Josh angled the table chair toward us and rested his feet up on another. Anna and I glided. We all joked that no one else could stand to rock with her. The more she drank, the faster she went. She was in that dress, though, and every time she swung forward, the hem flipped up a bit.

I sat in Claire's chaise.

"Maybe they're doing something crazy." Anna's face lit up with the possibility, and I wanted to laugh. She didn't know her husband very well, considering not even Claire could talk Josh into "something crazy."

"Like what?" I asked. Anna rocked back and forth without a care in the world. "Sneaking across the Mexican border?"

"Cow tipping, drag racing . . ." She played along, smiling and staring at the cloudy night sky above us. "Tree climbing, peeing on the side of the road . . ." She looked back at me and took a sip of her beer before adding, "Running from the law."

"All possibilities, I suppose."

"Less probable, considering it's the two of them together, but you never know how things will turn out."

"Life would be boring if we did."

Anna laughed at some inside joke I didn't understand. She stopped and tilted her head at me when she noticed my confusion. "Claire would never let us live a boring life."

I nodded and took another sip of my beer. I didn't tell Anna how I'd appreciate a little of the expected when it came to my marriage. We were all best friends, but complaining about my wife to Anna was a line I wouldn't cross.

12

Anna

"I'M GOING TO USE THE bathroom. Text them again. You know they're screwing with us," I said and left Gabe to figure out what was going on.

In the hallway, right above the table covered in colorful little tiles, hung Gabe and Claire's wedding picture. It wasn't a posed shot like everyone else's our age. Theirs was a picture of Claire running through the crowd, holding Gabe's hand behind her as everyone around them threw confetti over their heads. Gabe was turned slightly away from the camera, waving as he exited the reception.

Claire's eyes were bright and shining. She smiled the same way she did when she thought of a new plan. She was in motion, and her tight sheath dress clung to her legs. I almost laughed at her headpiece. Not because it was anything less than spectacular, but because I could still hear Josh asking, "What the hell is on her head?" every time he saw the picture.

The movement of the photo perfectly depicted Claire in life. She was always running ahead and dragging the rest of the world behind her. She and Gabe's relationship was like a roller-coaster, and if you stood close to the base, it'd blast you with air as the cars roared past on the tracks. It was terrifying and exhilarating and illogical how it always stopped safely after the ride.

My husband couldn't understand Gabe and Claire or the

appeal of their relationship. Josh preferred a slow and controlled life. He planned for his retirement. Josh shopped for mulch with the same level of attention other people used when buying a house.

Josh watched Claire and Gabe with a healthy amount of self-assurance that we weren't them, but for me, they were inspiring.

The doorbell rang. They *were* screwing with us.

I unlocked the door and swung it open. "What are you idiots—"

A uniformed police officer stood on the other side of the door. "Is this the home of Claire Heller?" he asked. Claire's last name threw me, which it normally did when I heard someone use it. She'd chosen not to become Mrs. Gabe Hawkins.

I looked past him, hoping Claire and Josh were hiding over his shoulder. Maybe Claire had somehow convinced him to come here and scare Gabe and me. They weren't there.

"Miss?"

I took a few steps backward. When my heel hit the bottom stair, I reached out for the bannister to steady myself. The weight of his expression was pressing on top of me. He was almost stone-faced, except for sympathetic eyes that didn't make for a good practical joke at all.

"Gabe," I yelled through the house. I steadied myself and my voice. "This is Claire's house."

"What's your name, miss?"

"I'm Anna Montgomery." The words were automatic. I kept waiting for him to smile. To end whatever this was.

"Do you know a . . ." He flipped a page in the little notebook in his hand, scanned whatever was written there, and then turned his eyes back to me. "A Joshua Montgomery?"

Gabe walked up beside me, and I moved my hand from the staircase and held onto him. "He's my husband."

"What's going on?" Gabe asked.

I couldn't breathe. When I tried to swallow, there was an acidy taste in my mouth.

"There's been an accident," the officer said. "There were two people in the car, and their identifications were Claire Heller and Joshua Montgomery. We started with this address. Were they in a Honda . . ." He reviewed his notes again. "Accord?"

"Yes. Oh my God," Gabe said. "Where are they? Are they okay?"

It felt like an hour before the trooper spoke. My fingers dug into Gabe's arm. "They've been airlifted to Christiana." I heard my breath suck in, and then I stopped breathing. Airlifted. The trooper noted the beer in Gabe's hand. "I have some questions for you. I can drive you down."

"Let me get my wallet." Gabe rested his hand on mine until I let go of him. He looked back over his shoulder to me and the trooper as he crossed into the kitchen. I was left standing in the doorway, staring past the trooper to the front yard. They weren't coming. Claire wasn't joking around.

Gabe handed me my purse when he returned, and we followed the trooper to his car. I held Gabe's hand for the entire thirty miles to the hospital. I sat silent as Gabe answered the officer's questions of where we'd been, what time we'd left, and who else had been with us. I didn't really pay attention to Gabe's answers until the trooper asked, "How many drinks did your wife have?"

"What does it matter?" Gabe asked.

The trooper glanced back at both of us in his rearview mirror. "It's standard to assess how much the driver had to drink."

"Claire wasn't driving," I said. "Josh was."

"I assure you she was."

I squeezed Gabe's hand in mine to ward off logistical

thoughts. I wouldn't answer any more questions. "What happened? Were they hit by a car? Did someone run a stop sign?"

The trooper pulled up to the Emergency Room entrance, climbed out, and opened our door from the outside. "It was a single car loss. The vehicle collided with a tree."

I followed Gabe out of the car and didn't let go of his hand. I squeezed it tight and kept my other hand on his forearm to hold myself up. I didn't let go until I was face-to-face with a man who was telling me that Josh hadn't made it. My head tilted as I tried to make sense of what he was saying. I let go of Gabe as if I could hear better unattached to everything and everyone around me.

"He was just with me." The words came out of my mouth, but they were foggy and distant.

"I'm very sorry, Mrs. Montgomery."

I was taken to a seat and given some juice. I didn't taste it. My mother came. She appeared as if she'd been painting her house when she'd received the call, but it was late Friday night.

"Were you painting?" I asked.

My mother leaned back and tilted her head to see me from a different light. Her gaze flitted to every corner of my face. "Anna, I think we should get out of here." She was standing right in front of me, but still seemed very far away.

"Claire's in surgery. I don't want to leave without her."

My mother left me to my silence. She sat on a chair by the window and frantically texted whomever she was updating on my wellbeing. Gabe's parents came, too. I listened as he called Claire's parents in Minneapolis. His words didn't make sense, but I assumed that had more to do with me than him.

When hours had passed, my mother approached me again. This time, she was less careful. "Anna, he's gone. Josh is dead," my mother said. She was standing above me. Hovering as mothers often did. Her eyes were wet with tears, but mine were completely dry.

"I know," I said. Every person standing around me stared at me without saying a word. "I'm waiting for Claire." I turned to Gabe, who was still sitting at my side. "She's going to make it."

"Anna, you should go. Go home with your mom." I watched his lips as he spoke. He didn't mean it. He choked up before lowering his head. I pulled him toward me, rested his head on my shoulder, and covered him with my arms. "I'm so sorry," he said, but he had nothing to be sorry for.

"Shh."

We stayed like that, huddled together on hospital chairs while our families stared at us in dismay. Gabe and I didn't move until a man in scrubs entered the room and asked for Gabe.

His statement began with, "I'm very sorry . . ."

I don't know what it ended with.

13

Gabe

ON THURSDAY AT ELEVEN IN the morning, I was standing at the front of the church trying to hold myself together. I'd glanced up as soon as Anna walked in, as if something inside me told me she was there. I was sure we'd forever be connected and wished it weren't in this way. She wore a black sleeveless dress that had a belt cinching it at the waist. As long as she kept her sunglasses on, she was stunning, but when she took them off and put them in her purse, it was clear she was damaged in a way few people in the room would ever understand.

We made eye contact, but she skipped the receiving line and sat alone in the pew four rows back. I had to look away from her and to the next person in line who wanted to tell me how sorry they were that Claire was dead. I nodded to each person, shook their hands, hugged them, and all the while I didn't let their words touch me or their gestures move me. It couldn't have been my wife they were talking about. Not Claire.

I lost track of Anna after the church. I assumed she moved to the burial site with the rest of the mourners. I'd attended Josh's entire services the day before, and I knew she would do no less for me. Hundreds of people came from Josh's and my office. Between them and family, college housemates, childhood friends—many of the people at Claire's funeral attended because she was married to me. It was because she'd grown up in Minneapolis, but it would have pissed her off if she'd been here.

She probably would have hated most of today. Except the lilac chiffon dress Anna had picked out for her to wear. That she would have loved. Claire's mother had chosen a suit, which I'd mentioned to Anna. She'd come over the next day, walked by me to Claire's closet, and returned with the dress, shoes, and a small silver purse in her hands.

"What's the purse for?"

"Claire always completed the look."

I'd nodded. "That she did."

"This is her last one. It has to be perfect."

"She loved you, you know?"

Anna had flinched as if the words had hurt her. So few words had gotten through to either of us during the days following the accident, but these had hit her in the chest. "I know. I loved her, too."

Gravestones littered the green grass. The rows went by without notice as Claire's parents and I rode out of the cemetery. We didn't say a word to each other. The only subject we'd both shared was lowered in a wooden box into the ground.

Over the next two weeks Anna didn't answer my texts or calls. The guilt I had that it was my wife who had killed her husband was almost unbearable, and most nights I would wake up to crushing nightmares of not driving all of us home that night. Why hadn't I offered to? Why hadn't I followed them? Why did I drive off and leave them behind? Had I even checked to see if they were following? The list of things I felt shitty about went on and on. The thing that topped it was that I'd been relieved that Anna was in my car instead of Claire. That guilt threatened to crush me.

Instead of sending a text for Anna to ignore, I picked up a pizza and a twelve pack and drove to her place. The house was dark. I knocked. She opened the door and barely looked like herself. She was too thin, and her skin had lost the tan glow it'd still had at the funerals. Anna was fading away.

"Can I come in?"

She opened the door wide and moved to the side. I entered my best friend's house with dinner for his wife. There were two boxes at the base of the stairs. Josh's shoes and sweatshirts were stacked neatly in the one on the left. The other held winter coats and clothes. Skis, golf clubs, several garment bags with hanging clothes all rested against the furniture in the living room.

I swallowed hard. "You've been busy."

Her gaze followed mine around the room. "My mother told me to do all of this. That it would help me."

I hadn't done a thing. I hadn't even so much as opened Claire's closet door since the day Anna had come over. "Has it?"

"No." She shook her head. "I feel like I'm erasing him." She looked from the skis to me. "Or trying to."

"I brought dinner."

"Thanks," she said, and the knot in my chest loosened a bit.

I followed Anna into the kitchen I'd eaten in a hundred times with our spouses. She took two beers out of the box and opened the fridge to put the rest inside. I saw past her thin frame to the empty shelves. Anna's life seemed a lot like mine these days.

I forced the pizza down. I couldn't expect her to eat without me doing the same, but the words I needed to say to her were choking me—the limited answers I had about the night our lives had ended with our spouses.

"I talked to the police today." I wiped my hands and crumpled up the paper towel. I tossed it on top of my plate.

"You did?"

"Have they contacted you?" I'd spent the day hoping Officer

Reeves had already shared the details with Anna.

"About what?"

I exhaled the disappointment that the information would come from me. "The accident," I said, but that was obvious. I hoped she didn't take offense. I couldn't really speak any longer.

"I haven't heard from them since the funeral."

"They called to tell me Claire's blood alcohol concentration was zero."

Anna looked up as my words registered. I watched as she ran through her memories and waited for her to catch up to every moment of the day Josh and Claire had died that I'd already reviewed in my own mind. "But that's impossible. She drank that night."

"When I came home from work, she had a glass of wine in her hand and said she'd started without me."

"And then she ordered drinks with dinner and at Victory afterward."

"Did she? Did you see her order the drink?"

Anna thought again. I gave her time, knowing the reminiscing was probably hurting her. "I thought so."

I gauged whether she could handle my next statement. She had to at least know what I was apologizing for when I wanted to die of guilt. "He also said Josh wasn't wearing his seat belt."

"What?" Anna was appalled. Her complete disbelief hung at her open jaw. "There's no way." Her husband was always safe. Even if Josh had been completely drunk, which he wasn't that night, he'd have his seat belt on.

"I know." I'd been trying to make sense of it since I'd talked to the police the day before. It was as if the two people in the accident hadn't actually been her husband or my wife.

I took a long swig of my beer and steadied myself for the answers I needed to hear. "What do you remember about that night?"

"Gabe . . . I don't think we should."

"Please."

I leaned on the counter across from her so we were at eye level. Anna took a deep breath and exhaled. I didn't say a word. I'd wait forever if I had to.

"I remember having a great time. I remember laughing. As usual," Anna said.

"Was she supposed to be driving?"

"No. When we left, Josh was driving. Claire only said she was going to ride with him."

Why did I let them drive?

As if Anna could read my mind, she said, "You didn't do this. You're not responsible for any of it."

I peeled the label off my beer, running my thumb back and forth over the sweating glass until the corner rolled back to the middle. "I wasn't drunk. I swear."

"I know you weren't." She shook her head. "I'd never felt anything but safe in the car with you." I tried to believe her. Anna leaned in closer to me. "Or anywhere else with you."

I sipped my beer and stared down at the bottle in my hands. I'd failed all of them. This was my fault. I always got us home safely.

"How come you weren't in the car with her and Josh? Why did you ride with me?"

Anna shook her head. She was lost in her own thoughts and crumbling in front of me. There was something that she wasn't telling me.

"Anna?"

"I don't know." I'd pushed her too far. Her eyes were filling with tears. "You and Claire knew the directions. You were familiar with the area." She shook her head before adding, "It was decided before I knew what was happening. I hugged Claire, and she was getting in the passenger seat of Josh's car. You and

I left first and never looked back . . . I don't know why I wasn't with her."

"Why'd they switch?" I asked aloud, but there was only ever one explanation . . .

"Because Claire wanted to," she said and sighed.

My jaw clenched. "Claire was so fucked up."

"It was an accident. A horrible accident." She pleaded with me to believe her, but it didn't make sense. Anna, the police, the insurance companies . . . everyone was satisfied with the version of facts that had been documented regarding this car accident, but the evidence didn't take into account who Josh was and what Claire was capable of. "Claire shouldn't have been behind the wheel. The police have the blood alcohol wrong. She was drinking. She must have gotten confused about where she was, or maybe she wasn't as sure as she thought about the directions." Anna was pleading with me to agree with her.

"Claire had been down that road tons of times before. She wasn't lost. She knew it like the back of her hand." None of it made sense. "The toxicology report will take a few months, and then we'll know for sure."

Anna stood up straight in front of me. "What are you saying?"

"Nothing." I wouldn't take it any further. I couldn't hurt her anymore. I pulled her to me. "Don't listen to me. The accident's fucking with my head." She exhaled into my chest and closed her eyes. "I have no idea what I'm saying. It was an accident." I held her tight against me. "It's haunting me, though. I can't stop going over it in my mind. Every detail I can remember. You had on a red dress. It was odd."

"What was odd about my dress?"

"The dress was fine. It was unusual for you to wear the color red."

Anna stepped back and studied me. "My mother had bought

me the dress the weekend before and had insisted I looked beautiful in it. She kept going on and on until I believed her."

"You were beautiful in it." I didn't have to hold back a compliment, but I was cautious around Anna. I was careful because of me.

"I don't usually wear red," she finally said.

"And Josh was out of money, which was also weird." We both laughed. Josh had to pay for dinner with a credit card, and he always had cash on him.

"We should have gone home the minute he realized he had no money." She sat back down, still laughing. "There was obviously something wrong with the world."

"And Claire kept ordering Jack and Coke instead of her usual vodka," I said, suddenly able to picture my wife holding the dark brown drink that night.

"You're right. I'd commented on it. I'd never seen her drink anything that wasn't clear and sparkling like her." The memories were slow to return, but Anna's contribution was helping. "Claire had said, 'Change is the only way to stay forever young.' She'd ordered me two tequilas under the same vein."

"I think Claire was drinking a lot by herself."

Anna let that sink in. She played with the edge of her paper plate before looking me in the eyes. Her stare was colder than Claire's body in the lilac dress closed inside her coffin. "Were you having an affair?"

"No!" I yelled at her. "God, no. Did Claire think that?"

She shook her head. "I don't know if she thought a thing, but I knew you'd been going to a lot of meetings that Josh hadn't been going to."

I took both her hands in mine and squeezed them until she faced me again. "Anna, I swear to God I was not cheating on my wife."

She closed her mouth and swallowed before breathing

through her nose. Her features softened, and her gaze dropped to our hands. "I'm sorry. Of course you weren't. You loved her."

I held on to her hands, hoping she wouldn't notice any difference in my own features at her last statement.

"I should go." I put my empty beer bottle in the sink. "I'm sorry to be bringing all this up again."

"No. It's fine." Anna didn't seem fine. She appeared to be in worse shape than she'd been in at the funeral. "Whatever you need."

"My father tells me I need to get back to work," I said.

"Funny, because my mother swears I should take some more time off. I think she wants me to take her somewhere."

"Any thoughts on where?"

"With my mother? Nowhere. I might go somewhere, though."

"Where?"

"I'm not sure."

I'd never seen her lie before. She was terrible at it. Everything was different now.

Our goodbye was awkward. We were broken. Both individually and apart from each other. As soon as I backed my car out of her driveway, the emptiness returned. I left, unsure if I'd ever see her again.

14

Anna

THE FUNNY THING ABOUT CAR insurance—as if there were ever anything funny about that—was that since Claire had been driving our car, our insurance was her primary coverage. So, I apparently had a claim against Claire for the death of my husband, and the first company to pay on that claim was my own. They offered me the policy limits immediately. Then there was Claire and Gabe's insurance, and since they'd been as careful to protect their personal finances as Josh and I had been, they had a personal umbrella policy as well. With all the auto coverage and Josh's own life insurance, I was suddenly a wealthy woman.

A wealthy widow, I kept reminding myself.

Gabe got nothing. He'd lost the same thing I had, and he got nothing. Maybe a payout from a small life insurance policy through Claire's work, but they had no children, and she wasn't the primary caregiver of anyone. Not even herself usually, and she was at fault for the loss. I could barely face Gabe the first time I saw him after the insurance people explained all this to me.

"I'm just happy you're not going to sue me," he joked, but he didn't smile. He barely laughed.

"I would never."

"I know you wouldn't." I hugged him because I didn't know

what else to do. "I'd sue you, you know," he said. He was teasing me the same way he used to.

"I'll bet Claire had a huge policy on you," I joined in and hoped I hadn't gone too far.

"Are you kidding? She probably had ten policies on me. I think she always assumed I'd die first, and she'd finally hit the lottery."

"Do you want a beer?" I asked, already taking one out of the fridge for him.

"I think I'm going to quit drinking." His words were so quiet that I thought I misheard him.

"What?"

"That's what got us into this. Isn't it?"

"Not you drinking." I put the beers back in the fridge, even though mine was already open.

Gabe waved toward himself. "You're right. Give me a beer."

He drank three beers with me that night. Just enough to not feel the silent effort between us, but too few to be drunk. Drunk driving would forever be taboo for us. The way it should have been before the accident. We'd taken so many chances. One too many.

The important pile was the last to be packed. Josh always made fun of the pile, calling it the unimportant pile since papers and envelopes went there to die, but I eventually got around to all of it.

I sat at the kitchen island with the pile in front of me. I wasn't taking it to Rome with me. Part of my reason for going was to leave behind everything that used to seem important. The other part was about abandoning the woman I'd become. Josh's wife. His keeper. A woman obsessed with becoming a mother . . . no more. I was Anna Montgomery. A graphic designer who would sketch out the rest of her life while exploring the cobblestoned alleys of Rome.

My gaze slipped to the trashcan on my right and back to the pile. Surely none of this was all that urgent.

Josh's dental appointment reminder. Garbage.

Letter from the infertility doctor. I stared at it, knowing I'd probably never have a baby now. The ugly truth of my future was sinking in slowly as I packed away all my belongings. Josh's test results brought the bitterness back to the surface. *Exhale.* Garbage.

Benefits selection statement for the upcoming year. Keep. I started a pile to the left on the table.

Julie's and Mark's wedding invitation. The deep blue cardstock had a gold anchor at the top of it requesting the honor of my presence—our presence. Josh and I had been with them the night Mark proposed, I'd just forgotten that their wedding was coming up so quickly. I sifted through the contents of the envelope: directions, response card, reception information. The celebration immediately to follow at the Inn at Perry Cabin in St. Michaels, Maryland.

I tapped the corner of the invitation on the table. I hadn't seen or spoken to Julie since the funerals. She didn't know what to say. No one did.

I found Gabe's contact in my phone and pressed call. I'd say whatever he was saying.

"Hey," he answered before the second ring.

The sound of his voice hurt me. The deep loss in every tone was echoed in my own every day. "Hi." It was strange for me to call him, especially to say anything other than, "Where are you guys?" or some other logistical question pertaining to the four of us partying. But it was just Gabe and me left to do the talking. "How are you?"

"The same as you I'd imagine," he said. I nodded, ignoring

the fact that he couldn't see me. "Are you calling about the wedding?"

"How did you know?"

"Mark called to see if I was coming and asked about you. I figured Julie probably reached out."

"No." I picked up the invitation again. "I just found the invitation. We never sent a response back."

He paused, and my hope that he had all the answers diminished. "What do you want to do?"

"Well. I don't want to go." That I was sure of. The rest wasn't so clear. "But I love Mark and Julie."

"I don't want to go either. Where is it again? Isn't it far away? Do we need rooms?"

He forgot how Claire took care of everything. "It's in St. Michaels, and Claire booked us all rooms the minute the save the date card arrived." I sighed into the phone, not caring what it sounded like.

"We should go. I'll drive you down."

"My dress . . ."

"What?"

"It's fun. Flirty. The kind of dress you can get away with when you're already married."

"I'm not following you."

"Every single person there is going to be talking about how we're the two whose spouses died. I should be wearing something dowdy." I imagined a high neckline in my head. "With a veil, maybe."

"This isn't the Victorian era." The sound of his laughter took me back to a time two months ago. "How about you wear whatever you want, and we'll drink too much and make a scene." I'd missed his humor. "That'll give everyone something else to talk about."

"You're crazy."

"Like, falling-down drunk. What color is your dress?"

"Black."

"That's perfect."

I stared down at the invitation in my hand. Yesterday was the first day I'd made it through without crying. I was unquestionably *not* ready to celebrate someone else's wedding. I ran my hand over Josh's name on the outer envelope. He'd tell me to go. He'd say to wear the damn dress.

"Okay. You don't have to drive me, though. I'm not your problem."

"You are." I waited for the joke, but it never came. "I'm actually standing outside of a bar and it's starting to rain." I peeked out the window in front of me, but the sky was a clear blue.

"Where are you?"

"Chicago."

"Oh, I'm sorry. You didn't have to answer."

"I'll always answer. Just promise to keep calling." I nodded. "Anna?"

"Yes. I'm sorry. I was nodding," I said in a rushed voice right before tears filled my eyes. Josh should be calling him. Claire should be texting me. Plans would be made through a network of small conversations through the men and women until we all jumped into the car to ascend on St. Michaels for the wedding. "I'll let you go."

"Call anytime."

"I will."

The wedding was in a week and a half. It was a two-night event, and I was sure one night would be our maximum. I needed to check our reservations. Claire would have booked us for the entire weekend.

I inhaled and found Julie's name in my contacts.

"Anna." Apparently everyone answered on the first ring when it was a widow calling. There was the upside.

"Hi, Julie. I just found your wedding invitation. I'm sorry I never responded."

"Not another word unless it's to tell me you're coming. Please say you are. I'll totally understand if you can't, but I'd love to see you. Mark would love it, too." She rambled on. She was completely uncomfortable, and I couldn't blame her. "But if it's too much. Oh, Anna. I don't know what to say or do."

"It's okay. None of us know what to do." Because none of us were even thirty yet, so our spouses weren't supposed to die.

"Say you'll come."

"I'm coming. Gabe's bringing me down." I could hear something close to gushing on the other end. I imagined her motioning to Mark that I was coming, and him grinning, satisfied that they were making the widow leave her cave. "We're going to skip the Friday night festivities. Lay low, so to speak."

"That's fine. Whatever you guys need. I'll sit you together. Well, actually, you were always sat together, but now—"

"Okay." I couldn't let her go on and bury herself. "I'll see you a week from Saturday."

"Thank you, Anna."

"It's my pleasure. I can't wait to see your dress." That was the kind of thing someone would say to a bride. *You look beautiful. What a perfect night.* Gabe and I should practice some before we drove down. Maybe write some down and keep the list in my purse for those times when I just wanted to profess my hatred of human life. Maybe then.

15

Gabe

I PULLED INTO ANNA'S DRIVEWAY at exactly three in the afternoon, hoping we could miss the weekend traffic on the two-hour drive to St. Michaels. We'd arrive tonight, but stay hidden from all of the wedding hoopla until tomorrow. One full day of wedding fun would suffice for the two of us. Anna flung her bag onto the stoop and locked the front door behind her before I had a chance to knock. I peered at her, wondering if she was nervous about going or just didn't want me to come inside.

I walked over and lifted the bag onto my shoulder without saying a word.

"Are you sure you don't mind driving? I can drive."

"I'll drive." I always drove.

I put her bag next to mine in the back seat, and she hung her dress next to my suit.

"Have everything?" I asked. I answered back in my head, *everything but your husband.*

Anna took her new seat on the passenger side and shut her door. It wasn't until I started the car that she began to take tiny breaths to keep from crying.

"I know," I said and turned away from her. I backed out of her driveway. "It's just one more of the first times."

"The first time we've been in a car together since . . ." she said and wiped the tear falling down her cheek.

"First wedding. First day back to work. First time in Maryland. First everything," I said through a clenched jaw. Watching Anna go through this was worse than living it myself.

"I'm sorry," she said.

"What do you have to be sorry for?" I was still so angry. At myself. At Claire. At the whole fucking situation.

"You have nothing to be sorry for either. We had two cars. It happened sometimes. You couldn't drive us all around our whole lives."

I stared out the windshield.

"They're gone," she said.

That wasn't what bothered me the most. "How come two of us are still here?" I asked.

"Gabe, you can't keep doing this."

I didn't try to argue with her and just drove. The car windows stayed up, and I ignored the frigid air conditioning blowing on us until Anna pointed the vents away. There was no music. Just an endless road of silence between her house in Delaware and St. Michaels, Maryland. It was a mistake to come. Only a moron would have put the two of us in a car together and sent us off to a wedding.

I continued with that very thought until we reached the outskirts of St. Michaels. Every inch of Talbot Street, from the Carpenter Street Saloon to Justine's Ice Cream Parlour, felt different. When we pulled up to the entrance of the Inn at Perry Cabin, I was a million miles away from my life, which was exactly where I needed to be.

"It's beautiful," fell from Anna's lips. She was looking at the entrance of the Inn, but all I could see was her. I stopped and stared at her in wonder. Fear tightened my chest and overshadowed her as I realized my admiration for her was dangerously close to love. If not already.

I stood behind the valet as he helped Anna out of the car. Seeing Anna smile at him with the lightness of our summer lives was sobering. Her small gesture was a moment not wrought with remorse, and the first one I'd seen from her in what felt like forever. It was a start.

Our rooms were right next to each other. Of course they were. Claire had made the arrangements. The jokes that would have been made flew through my mind, and I kept them all to myself.

"How long do you need to get ready for dinner?" I asked as we both stood at our doors.

"Four minutes." Anna never needed much time. We all waited on Claire, but not this trip. "Come by when you're ready."

She left me standing outside my door. I'd stayed alone in hotels plenty of times for work. Work. Yes. I would think of this as work. One more arduous and slightly painful obligation. Appearing happy at Mark and Julie's wedding would be my job for the weekend. At least I had Anna.

I knocked on Anna's door and nervously waited outside like a prom date.

"Hey," she said and opened the door wide for me to come in.

"Is this awkward yet?"

She shook her head in answer, and I hated myself more. Anna's voice was gentle when she said, "I think we should try, for the whole weekend, to make each other laugh." I stood still and listened to her. I'd let her lead us through this weekend because I didn't know how to act. That wasn't actually just this weekend. I was a bit lost every day now. "Like that time we were on the Brandywine River and I kept ramming my kayak into yours every time you tried to start a story." I watched her as she spoke. She was holding me close to her peace. "Or that time you were laughing so hard you rolled off the bed in Vermont."

I almost laughed. "Like that?"

"Just like that." She walked by me into the hallway.

At dinner, we made a list of all the things people say at weddings, and Anna wrote them on a cocktail napkin from under her beer.

What a beautiful night.

We wish you nothing but happiness.

Your mother looks like a whore.

I think your father's drunk.

Have you heard about the bachelor party?

I might throw up.

By the time she wrote down, *I fucked the bride,* we were hysterically laughing. The waitress brought another round. To her, we were happy.

"I can't remember what anyone said at my wedding," Anna said, and I stared down into my beer. "Hey." I looked up, but was still lost in my own mind. She tilted her head to the side and asked, "What's the worst part for you?"

"Having no one to talk to when I come home."

She leaned forward and held me with her eyes. "You can call me."

"I should clarify that. Having no one to talk to when I really have nothing to say." That was all the time now. I had no words I wanted to share with anyone.

"You can still call me. I'd love to hear your useless thoughts." She almost sounded genuine.

"What's the worst part for you?" I asked her, but I wasn't sure I could handle her answer. If it were a lengthy dive into her and Josh's never-ending love story, I might jump off the dock and drown myself.

"Sleeping alone," she said. "Falling asleep alone."

I took a sip of my new beer and carefully replaced the glass on the table. "You took off your rings." I nodded toward Anna's hand.

She spread her fingers out in front of me, showing me the tan line where her engagement and wedding rings used to sit. "I'm going to Italy."

I stayed silent, watching her, studying her. I knew better than anyone still alive how much she longed to go. Josh had dragged his feet at even the idea of an Italian vacation. "When?" I finally asked.

"Next week. I put most of my stuff in storage." She looked back at her bare hand. "Including my rings."

"For how long?" I was afraid of her answer. I needed her here.

She sat back in her chair and finished her beer. "I'm going to work from there for a while."

I twirled my beer glass in my hand and stared into it. She was abandoning me in this nightmare. Just like that, things got worse.

I paid for dinner and made a point to offer her my arm on the fifteen-minute walk back. Anna hooked her hand into the crook of my elbow and stared straight ahead, somehow removing the absurdity of the gesture. We walked in silence until I delivered her to the room next to mine.

"Why don't you stay with me?" She didn't have to explain just as friends or imply the invitation was platonic. She was Anna.

"I can't." I rested against the wall next to her door.

She leaned into me, wrapped her arms around my waist, and let her head fall to my shoulder. She stayed still until I returned her embrace. Warmth spread through me. It was wrong to touch her, but I couldn't think about that. I needed her.

"It could feel like this all night," she said.

"I don't deserve to feel this way all night."

She stepped back and held my face in her hands. "It wasn't your fault." She tilted my head down to face her. "Are you seriously saying no to the tragic widow? Have you no heart?"

"It's too weird."

"Everything is going to be weird from now on." She unlocked her room. "Until the day it isn't." She took my hand in hers and led me toward the door. "Stay with me."

I took a deep breath and followed Anna. She turned off the light on the desk and walked into the dark bedroom. She pulled back the covers and laid down in her dress.

I sat on the other side of the bed facing the wall. When I laid back, my hands were clasped at my chest, my chin squarely tilted toward the ceiling. I could give this to her and take it for myself. We could have one night of peace . . . together.

She laid her arm across my stomach. I inhaled the sweet smell of Anna, and it took me back to when I could adore her from behind the camouflage of our friendship. Now, I had to stay away from her because the boundaries had died. She moved her hand up to my chest and left it there.

"Don't think about them. They left," she said. I reached up and wrapped my hand on top of hers. "Now there's just us."

I closed my eyes, and it was the first time I slept through the night in two months. The nightmares didn't terrorize me the way they had since we'd left the hospital. It was only supposed to be happy hour that night, but since then, none of the hours were happy.

16

Anna

WE ORDERED BREAKFAST AND ATE on my patio over-looking the Miles River. It was still early, not even ten, and sail-boats already filled the water and the sky was a brilliant, cloud-less blue. It was a picture-perfect wedding day.

"How'd you sleep?" I finally asked him after our breakfast had been delivered.

"Better than I have in a long time."

Me too, and I refused to feel guilty for eight hours of sleep. Surely Gabe and I deserved at least that. "After breakfast . . ." I leaned in and whispered to him over my eggs Benedict. "Let's take a nap together."

Gabe choked a little on his orange juice as he laughed. "You're serious?"

"Yes. The nights have been hard for me. I don't know if it is the location, or the mattress . . ." I forced myself to look at him, "or you, but I want more. I've been exhausted for weeks and—"

"Okay. We'll take a nap."

I sighed as I sat back in my chair. "You're too good to me."

"You know these rooms are seven hundred dollars a night. We could have saved a lot of money only getting one."

"If Josh had known how much they cost, there would have only *been* one."

"Well, Claire made the reservations, and money was never

an obstacle for her." He tipped his head and smirked as if Claire were sitting with us and he was still teasing her.

Claire had driven Josh crazy—Port for dessert, taxis for a few blocks, box seats, VIP everything. I'd secretly loved her for it. "How did the four of us get along?"

"We drank our way through it."

Gabe's words soured the whole meal. I set my fork on the side of the plate and stared back at the sailboats. Claire would have had us on one last night. I'd never heard a word of what Gabe wanted. He was always up for anything, but "anything" was always Claire's whim.

"What do you want to do today?" I asked.

He was surprised by the question. He pushed his plate toward the center of the table and rested his elbows in its place. Gabe didn't say a word, but he seemed to be examining me rather than searching for his own answer.

"We can do anything. What would *you* like to do?" I asked again.

His silence was closing in on us. I imagined the thoughts running through his mind. Fleeing, going back in time, dying. He might torture himself the rest of his life. I wanted to swim to the surface of our grief and bring him with me, but he was too heavy. "I want to take a nap." His expression softened. He didn't smile, but he was kind. "With you."

"I don't believe you."

"You're the one person I'll never lie to. I couldn't even if I wanted to. You know too much." His words were too much, and I looked away from him and toward a couple walking along the water's edge. The woman was laughing as the man pulled her along by the hand. He was rushing her to someplace, and the woman thought the whole thing was funny. *They're going back to the room to make love.* The way their hands were clasped as they moved told the story of the time they'd spent together.

They were one.

"Josh never held my hand," I said, looking back to Gabe.

His expression was filled with sympathy. My jaw clenched. His kindness was wasted on me. "I know," he said.

"Of course you do." He'd listened to me tease Josh about it for years. It was an inside joke the four of us shared. "Why do you think he didn't?"

Gabe shook his head. "I'm sure it had nothing to do with you." He stood and held out his hand. "I want to sleep with you."

So, for the second time in twelve hours, I laid next to Gabe in my bed. He slipped under the blankets first and held his arms open for me to crawl in. Without the darkness and exhaustion that I hid behind the night before, I felt awkward. I didn't let it show as I slid in next to him and let him drop the blankets over us. He was longer than Josh. I was tucked against his side, my head resting on his shoulder and his arm curling around my back so he could hold me. He was so warm, warmer than Josh was.

For years, I was always on the right side of the bed. Josh had insisted on the left. I stared across Gabe's chest at the sailboat picture on the side wall. I was on the left.

"I always slept on the right," I said and felt Gabe tilt his head down to look at me. "What about you?"

"It doesn't matter. They're gone, and now I'm here with you. On the right." He brushed his fingertips across the back of my shoulders until I shivered. Gabe pulled the covers up to my chin, and I fell asleep there. Under the weight of the comforter and out from under the loss. Just for a few hours.

The television blared as I got ready. Josh and Gabe would have gotten ready first and waited at the bar for me and Claire. We'd stroll in and kiss them both as they told us how beautiful we were. Josh would have said "pretty" because he never used the word "beautiful." He'd been frugal with his compliments, too.

I finished early and sat on the couch in my sitting room. I let the twenty-four-hour news cycle drown out my thoughts. Between the show's host and the news ticker running at the bottom of the screen, there was plenty to focus on. Entire villages being murdered or women being burned alive. There were people enduring much worse things than I was about to. I could do this. I was capable of attending a wedding without spewing hatred at everyone. I could go and smile and pretend. I took a deep breath and smoothed out the skirt of my dress, repeating over and over again that there were much worse situations than a wedding.

I'd almost convinced myself there was a chance of our survival when Gabe knocked. I wasn't ready. I had to be ready. So, I took a deep breath and opened the door. He looked a bit less tired than I'd seen him over the last few weeks, just a shadow of his old self returned. He stepped in, and I let the door close behind him.

"You're beautiful," he said. His words were light. *Beautiful* came easy to Gabe. He made me feel like the most gorgeous girl in the world.

"Like a pretty whore?"

"Kind of," he said. He shook his head. "Not at all. That dress is fine."

"It's the zipper that's the problem." I turned so he could see the exposed zipper down my back and faced him again. "And how low the front is." I looked down at my chest. "And the height of my shoes." His eyes fell to my feet. "And—"

"And nothing." He wouldn't let me finish. "You're beautiful." The heat rose up my neck to my cheeks. "Why are you blushing?"

"I don't know." I raised my hands to my cheeks to hide my

embarrassment.

"Don't lie." He moved closer to me and pulled my hands down.

"I haven't felt pretty . . . or anything else in a while."

"See what a good night's sleep will do for you?"

"And a nap."

He nodded. "And a nap."

"I've been practicing my smile since you left. I'm going to stay just like this all night." I grinned widely at him, and he furrowed his brow. "What?"

"You look deranged. Just act naturally. Julie and Mark want us here. We don't owe anyone anything else."

"Okay." I took Gabe's arm the same way I had the night before and let him lead me down to the water to where the ceremony was being held.

It had no impact on me. I barely swiveled to watch Julie come down the aisle. I didn't look at Mark at all. Instead, I busied myself with the sight of the boats on the river. When words were spoken, I hummed in my head.

"Till death do us part . . ."

Anger and guilt swarmed me. I pushed it all away and clenched my fists in my lap. If I'd had a nail file, I might have actually taken it out and used it. I completely detached from the situation for my own survival.

Gabe sat next to me the entire time in silence. He shifted in his seat during the vows, and I mentally hummed louder. If Gabe was dumb enough to listen to this, he wasn't going to take me down with him. He escorted me to the cocktail hour the same way he had to the ceremony. He was stronger than I was. I would have left.

We anchored a corner of space all by ourselves during the pre-dinner champagne and raw bar. Gabe found the bar and got us each a tequila and soda. There would be no celebration at our table. Only endurance, drinking, and pre-approved remarks.

We quietly watched the boats sail across the water.

"This would have been hilarious if they were here," I said so only Gabe could hear me.

"What would have?"

"I don't know, but everything was so funny when we were all together. Claire would have said something, and you would have made fun of her, and then we'd do a shot and laugh some more." I finished my drink. "We really were simple back then." It had only been two months, but it felt like a decade had passed.

The people nearest us left their posts for the tent, and both Gabe and I watched as one by one they picked up their seating cards.

"We should go," Gabe said and finished his drink, too.

"No dancing, right?"

"God no."

"Just checking. Nothing sadder than the two of us dancing."

"Just keep drinking," he said. "In fact, I'm going to find us another round to get us through the announcements. I'll meet you at the table."

"Okay. I'll be the widow in the slutty dress."

"Let's hope there's not more than one of you."

"Let's hope."

He walked away, and I made my way to the table to find our seats. I kept my head down and just hoped no one would try to talk to me, which they didn't. With our seating cards in my hand, I made a beeline to table six—close to the bar and far away from the bride and groom. The table was full of our replicas. Late twenties, professionals, couples . . . they were us two months ago.

A guy to my right stood when I walked up. "Hi. I'm Anthony."

"Hi," I said. Anthony appeared to be alone. "Anna."

"Have a seat." He motioned to the empty seat next to him, and I scanned the crowd for Gabe.

"I actually need two."

"Oh." Anthony did little to hide his disappointment. Weddings were such fertile hunting ground. "Well, there's two here."

I put my purse down above my plate on the table and relaxed as Gabe entered the side entrance of the tent carrying two large glasses of clear liquid. He'd talked someone into making him doubles. I shook my head at the sight of him.

Gabe put the glasses down in front of his seat and dried his hands on the sides of his pants. He extended his hand to Anthony. "Gabe Hawkins."

"Anthony Rydel. Nice to meet you."

"Likewise."

"You were smart to get provisions." Anthony nodded toward our drinks.

"This isn't my first rodeo."

With that, the bridal party was announced, followed by the bride and groom's parents, and finally, the handsome couple themselves.

Our table meshed pleasantly. Most of the girls were from Julie's sorority, and their husbands were bonded the same way Claire and I had been with Josh and Gabe's work partnership. Dinner was almost enjoyable. There was no sappy sentiment to dwell on. Just inappropriate stories of Julie's college days, or "daze" as they described.

"So, how long have you two been together?" the redhead with the large breasts across the table from me asked. The dance floor behind her was beginning to fill. The music had slowed. I wasn't sure who she was speaking to until everyone stared at Gabe and me.

"Oh. We're not actually together." I turned to Gabe. "Just best friends."

"I thought you two were *together* together," Anthony said, leaning forward a bit on his elbow and giving me a wide smile.

"No." I shook my head.

"Okay." Gabe stood, placed his napkin on his chair, and extended his hand. "We're dancing."

I looked from his hand to his face and back at his hand. "Okay." I placed my hand in Gabe's and let him lead me to the dance floor. He kept going past the outer fringe, navigated through the middle, and settled on a spot on the other side. There he pulled me close to him, and I let him. We were Gabe and Anna. No longer tied to Josh and Claire.

"I thought we weren't dancing."

"I'm not ready for some guy to hit on you." Gabe's teeth were clenched. His muscles were tight in his shoulder.

"Was that hitting on me?" I tilted my head to see him better and hoped he saw some humor in our current situation.

"It was about to be."

"It's this dress. The zipper." I nodded until I felt him relax beneath my hand. His grip loosened, and he took a deep breath.

Gabe left my side the rest of the night exactly once. We were seated near the bar, and he could easily get us drinks and keep an eye on me. When he went to find the bathroom, I tagged along and found him waiting outside the door when I emerged.

We kept our glasses full and ate whatever the waiters brought us. We indulged in everything but the emotions of the event. Those we left to the people around us who still had hearts.

"Can we get every single girl on the dance floor? We've got a bouquet to toss," the band singer said into the microphone. I took another sip of my cocktail and checked my phone for messages. There were none. "Every girl. We need all of you lucky single ladies out here."

"Aren't you going up?" Anthony asked, and I lowered my phone to my lap.

I'm single.

I was alone. Pissed off. Irate. Deathly sad and forsaken.

"No," I managed to get out before standing and excusing myself. "I'll be right back." I didn't look at Gabe or anyone else. The heat was unbearable under the tent. I needed air. I needed a door to shut behind me. I walked out and picked up my pace as I entered the hotel. When I finally reached my hallway, I ran to my room.

"Anna!" I heard him call behind me. "Anna, wait!" I didn't want to wait. I wanted to lock myself in this God-awful hotel room for the rest of my miserable life. "Anna!"

I opened the door and practically fell inside with Gabe behind me. I turned and faced him, pursing my lips together to stop the vile words that described my reality from leaving my mouth.

"What?"

I shut my eyes tight and lowered my head.

I'm lost. I'm alone. Nothing is the way it should be.

"What? Tell me."

"I'm never going to have a happily ever after. I'm not going to be someone's wife." The dam broke on the thought of my next words. It was what really bothered me. I blamed it all on Josh. Whether it was right or not, in my mind, he'd stolen the experience from me. "Someone's mommy."

Gabe pulled me to him. "You don't know that."

"I don't want to catch the fucking bouquet. I already had one!" I screamed the last sentence.

"Shhh. You did." He held me close to him. "Don't cry."

I lurched away from him. I didn't want to be coddled. I'd had enough sympathy to last me a lifetime. I wanted the rage.

I wanted to feel something other than sadness. "Don't tell me not to cry! Don't tell me anything!"

Gabe held my face in his hands. It was a gentle gesture, and it seared anger through me. Josh had been gentle. Gabe was fierce. Always. I craved it now, but he'd let it go in an emergency room over the summer.

I held his wrists in my hands, stood on my tiptoes, and kissed him. It was a hard press of lips against lips—desperate and savage. When I lowered myself and opened my eyes, he was just standing, still as a statue, and it made me even angrier. Without letting myself think, I reached up, threaded my fingers through the back of his hair, and pulled him down to me. I kissed him until he grabbed my arms and forced me to stop.

"No," he said, but I wasn't interested in what he wanted and tried to break his hold on me. "Anna, no." He was shaking his head, but I wouldn't listen. I could only transfer my pain to him.

I kissed him again until he held me away from him.

"Gabe. I need you to be the way you used to be for one night. I need you to be fearless and bold." He lowered his eyes, and I dipped down to meet them. "Make me forget."

He stood motionless in front of me. I would take the last shred of sanity he had for my own benefit.

"I need you to be a man. Not some drunk asshole."

"Fuck you, Anna." The breath caught in my throat. Gabe had never said an unkind word to me. Nothing close to what he just had. "You're so fucked up. *This* is so fucked up." He turned, grabbed the first thing he could reach, and threw the ice bucket against the wall behind me. "Have you lost your mind?"

Before he could consider it, I was in front of him again. He didn't push me away, though. With two quick strides he had me pressed against the wall, using his body to cage me. He ripped open the back of my dress, ignoring the zipper completely, and tore it off the front of me. The cool room air hit my naked chest and adrenalin coursed through my body. I wanted him more than any other man. My mind ran in circles of need, not letting me breathe or comprehend what I was doing.

I tore his jacket off his shoulders and yanked it down his arms. I threw it across the room and kissed him again. This time he didn't resist. He poured all his anger into me, pressing his lips to mine until I ached. I was on fire for him.

For something.

For someone.

"Tell me to stop, Anna." He labored the words into my neck as his lips dragged down to my collar bone. "Tell me, Anna."

My only response was to arch my back, offering my breasts for him to take.

When he bent his head and took my nipple into his mouth, my knees went out. His arm snaked around my waist to hold me up.

I was deranged.

I didn't care.

Gabe lifted me onto the desk. He kissed me while he took his shirt off, snapping the last two buttons in his hast.

I reached up to touch his chest, and he clamped his hands around my wrists. Energy seared through me from his touch. He pushed me onto my back and pushed my dress up to my waist. I inhaled sharply. Gabe was leading this, and I would let him . . . as long as he just kept kissing me as if he needed me to breathe, he could do anything. His tongue was in my mouth, his hands on my body, his heat pressed against me, and I was lost to him. When he hooked his fingers under the sides of my panties, I lifted my hips for him. There was no thinking and no consideration of consequences as I slid from the desk and dropped to my knees, lowering his pants as I went. I needed this more than I needed a friend.

I focused my mind on this one thing in front of me. All that mattered was the sounds he uttered when I took him in my mouth. He moaned, and the idea that I made another living being feel something other than anger or sorrow filled me.

He pulled my hair and pressed my face against him. Gabe was rough and uncensored, and I was enthralled. When he fisted my hair and drew my mouth away, I licked my lips and inhaled, letting him lift me from the floor and carry me through the suite and into my bedroom. He dropped me on the mattress before grabbing my hips and flipping me to my stomach. I didn't protest when he grabbed my ankles and dragged me to the edge. I didn't fight when he spread my legs wide. I didn't think as he entered me.

That was where I came the first time. The second, he was on top of me with my hands pinned above my head.

He bit my nipple. He shoved his fingers into me before the rest of him. There were no sweet nothings whispered in my ear and no promises of forever—just his hot breath that stole my own.

When he finished, our eyes met, and I thought he might cry. *How fitting.*

"Gabe."

He walked out and closed my bedroom door behind him. I listened as he put his clothes back on and walked out of my hotel room. I ran into the sitting room and heard the slam of the room door next to mine.

My image in the mirror haunted me. Makeup was smudge across my face. My hair was knotted and sticking up behind my head, but neither of those things scared me as much as the emptiness in my eyes. I was no longer who I thought I was. I was no longer Josh's wife.

I poured myself a glass of whiskey and burned my throat with the first sip. He wouldn't be proud of me. Josh wouldn't have even believed this was me, but he was gone, and I was alone—except for my one friend I could still love because he understood everything that I was going through. I'd just completely ruined that.

I slipped my nightgown over my head, wincing as the fabric fell over the nipple he'd bitten. The pain propelled me to inhale as I remembered his lips on me. The odds of him opening the door were slim. I'd pushed him too far, but he was Gabe. He was stronger than the rest of us. He didn't falter.

Unless I made him.

I knocked.

When he didn't answer, I knocked again, and finally he opened the door. He didn't make eye contact with me, but I walked in anyway.

"Sleep with me." Gabe stared at me as if he'd never seen me before. "I'm sorry, Gabe. Sleep with me."

He didn't move or speak a word. I crawled into the left side of his bed and rested my head on the pillow behind it. When the realization of what had just happened almost crept in, he came to me and laid beside me.

I rolled on top of him and closed my eyes. "Thank you," were the only words I could find. Gabe either had no words of his own or he hated me, because he only wrapped his arm around my shoulders and fell asleep beneath me.

17

Gabe

MY EYES OPENED TO A single thought: *My God, I've fucked this up.* Completely.

Anna was still asleep on my bed, and I sat on the veranda outside my room, disgusted with myself. I wasn't hungover or exhausted. I was mortified. *What the fuck, Gabe?* Anna—the one person I swore to myself I was going to take care of—I'd pretty much hate-fucked last night. I'd taken a perfectly nice weekend . . . the first peace either of us had felt in two months . . . and turned it into something out of a horror movie. Anna was going to hate me. She wasn't even going to be able to face me. If I had any remembrance of what it was like to be a gentleman, I'd hire her a car service to take her home so she didn't have to see me ever again.

I downed my coffee and started to stand when I saw her reaching for the door.

"Good morning," Anna said and stepped onto the patio. I stopped breathing for a second and tried to take in how beautiful she was. She looked like an angel in the hotel's robe.

"I . . ." *What? Say something, asshole.* "Got you a cup of tea." I moved the cup to her side of the table. "It's black." She nodded. "They didn't have green tea." *Now stop talking.*

She sipped the tea, which was probably cold. "How long have you been up?" she asked. The kindness in her voice hurt me. I didn't deserve it. I was a dick without a shred of honor.

"I'm not sure I ever went to sleep."

"I told you I was a whore," she said and laughed. It was in that moment that I began to worry about her.

I'd spent the morning trying to figure out what to say. How to apologize to my best friend for ruining what was left of our relationship. How to punish myself for taking advantage of her, but there were no answers. "I think we should get on the road."

Anna sat back and stared at me.

What would Josh say about last night? My best friend? His wife? He'd be appalled. Anna knew he'd be, too. Claire would be screaming, "I told you so."

"I'll go pack," she said.

"Wait." I reached out to stop her but pulled my hand back as if her skin was covered with hot lava. It may as well have been. She was as beautiful and dangerous to touch. "Of all the things I've done wrong in my life . . . I'm the most sorry about last night."

"I'm not." There wasn't an ounce of hesitation in her voice. Anna was solid with her words. Not stricken with guilt the way I was.

"How can you say that?"

"Because they're gone. Dead. No matter how much we want our old lives back, they're over." She leaned in again and lowered her voice. "And just for one night . . ." She swallowed and opened her mouth a little as she breathed. I wasn't sure if she was going to cry. "I wanted to feel something other than regret." She touched my hand on the table between us and waited until I looked at her. "We brought them with us . . . until you asked me to dance. You never would have done that if they were here."

"I would have done something if some guy was hitting on you."

She tilted her head to me. "Not that."

I couldn't argue with her. She knew me too well. I would never have asked her to dance if Claire and Josh were with us. Under no circumstances.

"If it was wrong, so be it. I'm thankful," she said.

"You're crazy."

"Possibly." She stood to leave and added, "The only thing I'm sorry about is the way you feel right now. I was selfish. I needed you more than I loved you. For that, I apologize."

She left me lost in everything she'd said and went into her room. I showered and changed and threw my stuff into my bag. I closed my eyes and remembered how strong Anna was. How insatiable she'd been the night before. With a hand on the wall, I supported myself as I went through every image in my mind.

I was going to hell.

I was losing my mind. This was some part of mourning. A breakdown around week nine. This was normal. They were all things I told myself so I didn't have to acknowledge that I took from her what I'd wanted all along.

Anna answered her door with her dress from last night in her hand. My eyes focused on the ripped zipper. I considered offering to pay for it. I should have, but I didn't want to bring up what happened. I wanted it to disappear from her memory. She couldn't hate me. I needed her.

She packed everything in the bag that sat on top of the writing desk. Her shoes and her underwear that I'd torn off her the night before were the last things to go in. My mouth watered at the sight of them, and I wished I had tasted her. She was torturing me. Sweat beaded on the back of my neck. She zipped the bag, and I picked it up without a word.

We waited for the valet to bring my car around. Julie's parents were walking up the drive and stopped to say goodbye.

"Gorgeous night," I said.

Anna added, "Julie was a beautiful bride."

We rode home with the windows up and the radio on and our fingers twisted together. I tried to decipher everything going on in my head, but the only thing I knew for sure was that I loved her.

At the Delaware state line, she let my hand go. I told myself the position was uncomfortable for her, but it wasn't her wrist that hurt. Last night—the wake of last night—was the awkward part, and the line we were crossing back over was to reality. We weren't lovers. We were Gabe and Anna, the widower and the widow. I should have stopped myself. It should have never have started. I shouldn't have taken her to Maryland in the first place. She wasn't my wife, and she wasn't my girlfriend.

I parked in the driveway of my late best friend's house the same way I'd done hundreds of times before. Anna rushed toward the house, as if she wanted to leave me by my car, but I stayed close. I needed to go in.

The old wooden door opened, and I wished I hadn't followed her. The furniture in the living room was covered in sheets. The short, stout ghosts rested in the exact positions they'd occupied when there'd been life around them. The house already felt abandoned, closed up tight.

I looked around, and the realization set in. Anna was leaving, and not just for a week or two. People didn't go to these lengths for a short vacation abroad. I placed her bag on the floor by the door and stepped into the living room so I could study the empty mantel. She'd packed it all away with every memory that still had the ability to hurt her.

"When are you leaving?" I cleared my throat. The words choked me.

"Friday."

"When are you coming back?"

"I bought a one-way ticket." The permanency of the

decision fell between us in the abandoned room. "I have no plans to come back."

"He would hate you going."

"I know."

"Claire would be jealous as fuck. It'd kill her. She'd have us on the next flight out." Dark laughter escaped from my chest and singed the end of my words. "She wouldn't stand for you outdoing her."

"Who gets the last laugh now?"

I turned to her. "Why don't you wait? We can go together sometime. Just for a few weeks."

She shook her head. We weren't going together. "Josh promised the same thing."

I inhaled deeply. I didn't like being compared to Josh, and I hated myself for being in this situation, but more than anything, I couldn't let her go.

"I've already been through all this with my parents," she said. "My sisters. Their husbands. The next door neighbors. I'm going to Italy, even though not a soul in my life thinks it's the right decision." She walked over to stand next to me. The whole scene was making me sick. "I'm choosing to ignore their advice because every single one of them is still married to a living person, and I'm not."

Neither was I.

"Call me if you need anything?" I asked as if we were separating for a few hours.

"Of course."

I moved toward the door. "Just keep calling."

"I promise."

I walked out, and Anna closed the door behind me. My chest tightened with every step toward my car. She was all I had left. She couldn't go. I'd never touch her again, but she couldn't leave me here without her.

I turned around and strode back into the house without knocking. She was standing next to the refrigerator as if she'd just closed the door. Her eyes lit up when she saw me. Without a word, I pulled her to me and kissed her. I forced the anguish and need onto her, and she responded the same way she had the night before.

Anna leaned into me, and heat poured over us.

"Don't go." The desperation in my voice scared me.

"I can't stay here."

"Stay for me. I need you. I hate myself for last night, but I'd rather hate myself for the rest of my life than have you leave." I caressed her cheeks with my thumbs. I wanted to touch her everywhere. "Don't go."

"I never went because of him." She lowered my hands from her face. "I can't stay here because of you."

Rage simmered just beneath my words. "Going to go fuck some Italian guys?" I couldn't help myself. I wanted to hurt her in the same way I was hurting.

"Is that any way to talk to your best friend?" Her words were flat. She wasn't even offended.

"Is that what we are?"

"I don't know. I don't even know what *I* am. That's why I can't stay here."

I walked out. The storm door slammed back against the jamb as I flew over the front steps. It wasn't even one in the afternoon. I drove home and fell into the bed Claire and I had shared. The one we'd bought when we'd found this house. I laid on the right side and fell asleep. I would've been fine with never waking up.

18

Anna

IT WAS MOVING DAY, AND I was just sitting around watching the time go by. If Josh had been with me, he'd be double checking every last detail. He wasn't here, and I'd already done everything. I stared out the window at the tree in the front yard. It'd been planted fifty years ago by the first family to live in the house. Four bedrooms and two and half baths must have been huge back then. The house was all brick. Unbreakable. It wasn't the wind or the rain that had cracked our foundation.

Gabe's Lexus pulled into the driveway, and he stepped out. My breath caught and I squeezed my eyes shut. All I could see was his naked chest again, and I willed the image away. *You're just lonely, Anna.*

Gabe stopped walking when he saw me watching him from the window. I waved to put him at ease, but there was nothing easy about any of this.

He was kind to stop by. A much better friend than I'd been to him. I took. He gave. He'd benefit the most from the Atlantic Ocean between us. The memories of our night together had kept me awake the last five days. I knew I'd only sleep well if he was beside me, but I couldn't take anything more from him.

I opened the door when he stepped onto the front walk. "Hi," I said, and he smiled as if it were six months ago and he was here to pick up Josh to go to an Eagles game.

"Hey. I'm glad I caught you." He stepped through the front door, and the area between his body and the staircase suddenly felt small. I stepped back into the living room to put some space between us. Distance was certainly the answer.

"What brings you by?" Those words sounded as good as any inside my head. I'd never had to think about what I was going to say to Gabe before. The tragedy of our new relationship continued.

"I just wanted to say goodbye." He was walking in a small circle by my front window as he spoke. When I didn't say anything, he stopped turned to face me. The sight of him backlit by afternoon sun took my breath away. "I wanted to beg you not to go."

"Gabe—" If he begged me, I'd stay, but I'd hate him for it.

"I'm not going to." He held up his hands in surrender. "If it's what you need, then I want you to have it."

"I think being away from me will be good for you, too." The words hurt me as I spoke them.

He shook his head. "That's not true." He looked down at the floor and back at me. "Although, I keep fucking this up."

"No, you don't. You haven't done anything." I went to him and wrapped my arms around his waist. Neither of us owed each other a thing except friendship and I needed him to believe me. The rest we'd leave in Maryland.

"I haven't figured out what happened the night of the accident. I can't stop thinking it was my fault."

"It wasn't."

"And then I try to take care of you and take you to Julie and Mark's wedding, and I end up . . ."

"You did take care of me." I shrugged, hoping to will my satisfaction with the night to my beautifully tormented friend.

"It's not funny, Anna."

I kissed his neck and returned my head to his chest. "It is a little funny, don't you think?"

"I can't believe I laid a hand on you. Josh would have killed me. I would have killed myself before he had the chance."

"If they were alive it never would have happened." I raised my voice at him. "They're not. We didn't do anything wrong, and we didn't do anything to them. Stop torturing yourself." I leaned back so I could see his face. "We're lonely and sad and kind of pathetic."

"Speak for yourself."

"And we drank a lot and had sex." Gabe winced. "We're not the first friends to do it." I held his face in my hands. "And as for that, you took very good care of me."

"Can we please never speak of this again?"

"No." I was on a roll. "You fucked me. It was semi-violent, and I loved it. No one's ever bitten me before. You're a fucking freak in bed in all the right ways." Gabe's face twisted in disgust, and he stepped back as if each word I spoke were a slap against his face. "You were hard as a rock, and I swallowed you whole. I couldn't think of anything besides putting your *dick* inside me." His mouth fell open. "Why is this so hard for you? It was a perfect storm. A once-in-a-lifetime chance that took my breath away. You're an amazing lover."

"Anna, stop!"

"That's what you told me that night, but I couldn't. I wanted you. What's the problem?"

"I wanted you, too." He was quiet. I'd beaten the fight out of him with my truths.

"See? It's not a big deal."

"No," he said, and I focused in on his words. "I have *always* wanted you."

I stopped breathing.

"Anna." I waited for him to explain. Gabe didn't mean what he was saying. He was all twisted up since the accident. "The big deal is that I always wanted you. Even when they were alive, I would—"

"Gabe, you didn't." My dismissal was firm. He needed one of us to be clear.

He stepped back, putting more than distance between us. "I know how this makes me sound, and I hate myself for it. But as long as we're both being honest, I need you to know that."

"Gabe . . ." I didn't know what to say. The hurt Claire would feel if she'd ever heard these words tore through me. She was a part of me, and she'd forever be between us. This was never part of Claire's plan. I couldn't think about how they may feel about this. They didn't have feelings anymore. "Gabe, I think you're confused. We were all in love. There were moments when I wanted to spend the rest of my life with Claire and hated Josh." I moved closer to him. He stayed still and let me touch him. "The four of us had something very special, and it was love. You have nothing to feel guilty about."

He shook his head denying my version. "Anna—"

"This is my fault. I changed what we had without asking what you wanted. I took from you what you never offered, and now I've got you thinking you were a horrible friend when you were the best one Josh ever had." Gabe lowered his head at the mention of his friendship with Josh, so I kept going. "Let this go. Let all of it and them go, Gabe, or else we'll be tortured forever."

He looked at me and moved toward the door. Gabe was still broken. "I'll try."

19

Gabe

YESTERDAY, I STARTED CRYING IN the shower for no reason. I couldn't figure out what exactly was happening. The last time I'd cried, I'd invaded a hornets' nest when I was nine. I'd choked up the night I came home from Claire's funeral, but I hadn't shed any tears. Since then, I'd been able to put my feelings for my deceased wife into two boxes. Guilt and relief, neither of which required any crying.

I rolled over instead and turned the channel on the television that still hung too high to be comfortable to watch. I reached into the bag of Cheetos on the coffee table and dumped the last few into my mouth before tossing the empty bag. It landed next to drained beer bottles and a handle of Captain Morgan with only a shot left in it. If I never finished it, I wouldn't have drunk the entire bottle.

My phone rang, and I knew it was my mother. She was stalking me since Claire died. She assumed I was depressed because what husband wouldn't be? I perused the sticky and sad buffet in front of me. No depression here.

The name on the phone caught my eye. It wasn't my mother.

"Anna."

"Gabe. How are you?"

"Are you here? Did you come back?" She'd been gone nine

days and it'd felt like a year.

"No. I'm in Rome, but I wanted to talk to you."

"About what?" I straightened the empty bags in front of me, as if she could see through the phone and would judge me.

"Nothing. I just wanted to hear your voice."

I stopped and let my head hang low. Her words were like a warm blanket. "Call anytime, Anna. Day or night."

"How are you?"

I looked down at my underwear and then the rumpled blankets I'd slept under the night before. "I'm hanging in there," I lied.

"I've been reading a book about mourning."

"That sounds fun."

She laughed a little, and I wanted her to come home. "It's got some good information about what we're going through. You should read it, too."

"Why don't you just call me every day and tell me the highlights?" I carried the empty chip bags to the trash and went back for the beer bottles.

"It says we have to take good care of ourselves."

I let go of the bottle and stood up straight. "That makes sense."

"Yeah. I know you run and work out a lot, so I probably don't have to tell you that one, but I needed a reminder. Less wine. More walking. Fresh air. Sleep whenever it will come. All of that."

"Of course." I straightened the cushions on the couch and swore to myself I'd sleep upstairs the next time I was able to actually sleep.

Anna was silent on the other end of the line. All the way from Italy, I could hear the sadness in her breath. "I'm so lonely it hurts," she finally said and started crying.

"Come home." I wanted to scream it at her, but I was gentle.

"Come home, and we can get through this together."

There was another pause. I needed her in front of me so I had some clue as to what she was thinking. She should have FaceTimed me. I remembered my hungover and exhausted body and was thankful she was only on the phone.

"I was cleaning the sink today," she said.

"Yeah?" I just wanted her to keep talking.

"I remembered Claire told me once she used to clean her sink every night before she went to bed." If Claire did, I didn't remember it. "She said she cleaned off the island, organized the mail, and cleaned her sink every single day."

"You're losing me, Anna."

"I didn't do that." I stopped moving to concentrate on what she was saying. I wanted desperately to understand. To be the one who heard her. "I still don't."

"That's okay."

"Is it? Do men expect that? Do you think Josh was disappointed that the mail piled up all week until the weekend?"

"He didn't care." I was shaking my head.

"On the weekends, I'd go through it all and put the important stuff in an important pile, but nothing really became of those items either. They just weren't thrown out." She was crying harder now. "And our sink was dirty, I guess."

"Anna, listen to me." She sniffed. "Are you listening?"

"Yes."

"Important piles full of not-really-important stuff are fine. Dirty sinks don't matter. You were a great wife, and Josh knew it. He never complained. Not once. Nobody gives a flying fuck about the last time their sink was cleaned." She laughed a little, and I kept talking, not wanting her to sink again. "Men only care about sex and food. You could burn the house down, and we wouldn't care as long as you were standing naked in front of it holding a pie."

"It's nice though. I'm looking at it right now, and the sink is lovely."

"You're losing it." She laughed and I loved the sound. "You need to come home immediately."

"Thank you."

"And if sink cleaning is what you're calling taking care of yourself, we need to talk about that, too. Working out, cooking fresh food . . . get some gelato, masturbate for God's sake, but don't clean your sink."

"Claire used to do it every day."

"So she claimed," I said. Anna had to agree that Claire's reality wasn't grounded in the rest of the world's.

"I'm going to go. I'm sure you're busy. It's Saturday."

I looked around my disgusting house, trying to remember when the last time I ran the dishwasher was. "I've always got plenty of time for you. Keep calling."

"I will."

"Or come home."

"I love you, Gabe."

"Love you, too."

Anna hung up, and I fell back onto the couch. This life sucks ass.

20

Anna

I STARED AT THE BOOKS I stacked on the only table in my apartment. It wasn't exactly a kitchen table, since my apartment was a studio. There were sheer curtains hung from the ceiling to differentiate my sleeping area from the living area, but there were no other separations of space. The studio apartment was supposed to feel bright and cheery, but it only seemed cold and stark to me. I blamed that on myself. So much was my fault these days.

My notebook, highlighters, and Italian dictionary were strewn around the self-help books. I'd purposely bought each one in Italian, and when I wasn't working, I was translating them to practice the language. I thought it was a brilliant plan, until I actually wanted to know the advice the books offered. My impatience with my spiritual healing must have been a sign of grieving as well. If I could read the damn books, they'd probably have some information on exactly that.

I wondered if the books said anything about having a shocking realization that you'd always secretly loved your best friend. Or, in Gabe's case, your best friend's wife. Your wife's best friend. This was fun. I could go on and on defining the relationships that made Gabe's declaration of "always wanting" me hugely inappropriate and wholly impossible.

He was in crisis and falling apart. My going to Italy was

truly for his own good. Gabe wasn't one to openly discuss his feelings, but he loved Claire. I assumed he told her late at night. That he whispered it in her ear when Josh and I weren't paying attention. That when he held her hand, he squeezed it tight to the beat of the music or when he made love to her, he told her he couldn't live without her.

I'd already found the section of the book that discussed the need for comfort. It took over two hours for me to translate enough to know it was warning me that I was emotional and needy, and I'd likely search for a shoulder to cry on. In my case with Gabe, it turned out to be a dick to ride on.

I sat back in my chair and wallowed in the disgust I had for myself. Gabe would have never acted on his feelings for me had I not thrown myself at him. I'd practically dared him to. I was despicable.

He was lonely. He was alone. I'd played the part of supportive shoulder to cry on for him, and he'd actually started believing that he'd wanted me all along.

I needed to apologize to Gabe. I'd completely taken advantage of him. A knock startled me, and when I opened the door, a petite brunette was standing there. Her hair had purple streaks in it, and she smiled with a grin so wide it appeared to cover the entire lower half of her face. My guard went up immediately. I didn't want a new friend. I wanted my old one back.

"*Caio,*" she said and handed me a bottle of wine. "*Parli Italiano?*"

"*Si, Sto ancora imparando.*" I told her I was still learning.

"No problem." She easily switched to English.

"Oh."

"I'm Sophia. I live below you." Even in English, she spoke unbelievably fast.

I slowed my words, hoping she'd mimic me. "I'm Anna."

"Nice to meet you." She nodded and walked past me into my apartment.

She was forward and comfortable and a bit alarming. I was left in her wake to wonder if everyone in Rome was like her. "You, too."

She surveyed the apartment's décor, none of which I had picked out. "What do you do for work, Anna?"

"I'm a graphic designer. I work with product packaging." I waved my hand in front of the large computer screen at the back edge of my table.

"Oh. How nice. I'm an artist, too."

I perked up. Someone to talk to about work and not my life. "What kind of artist?"

"I'm a photographer. I take photographs for travel magazines and websites."

"That sounds wonderful."

"It is if you don't want to make any money."

I only worked so I'd have a reason to get up in the morning.

"Do you have a boyfriend . . . or a girlfriend?" she asked, and the joy was sucked from the room.

I shook my head to try to save the conversation, which had turned personal very quickly. "No. I was in love back home, but I'm here now." I left it at that. I wasn't about to open up to a complete stranger about Josh and Gabe. I could barely decipher it in my own head. Lately, I was having trouble remembering even one thing that I liked about Josh. I looked back at the computer to avoid Sophia.

"Oh, don't worry," Sophia said. Her smile was kind, her eyes knowing. She slowed down for me. "*A tutto c'è rimedio, fuorchè alla morte.*" I worked through the translation in my head, desperate to understand what she was saying. "Everything has a cure . . ." she added to help me out.

The rest of the phrase I managed. It would forever be stuck

in my head.

"Except death," I finished for her.

"*Si.*"

Sophia left me to consider an invitation to have dinner with her friends the following night. I couldn't say no or else I'd sit in my apartment and think of that phrase for the rest of my life. There was no cure for death. I was going to have to find a way to live with it.

21

Gabe

JOSH'S REPLACEMENT WASN'T A BAD guy. He did his job well. He put up with my impatience, temper, and newly formed hatred of most people. For that, he deserved some type of co-worker medal. What I probably needed more than an excuse to be a dick, was someone telling me to straighten my ass out.

No one did, though. My wife had died. She'd been in the car with my best friend. That was over two months ago. Someone should have told me to snap out of it already. Surely I knew someone heartless enough for that. Anna came close, but she'd moved to Italy, so I was left to wallow in self-hatred and loneliness as much as I wanted to.

"This is Amara," Tom said with a dirty smirk that Amara couldn't see since he was standing behind her. That was the other thing about Josh's replacement. He forced me to go to bars and assumed the best drug was found beneath the clothes of whatever woman was standing next to us.

"Nice to meet you," I said and ignored Tom.

"You, too. I've heard so much about you." I could tell by her sympathetic expression that she'd heard I was a widower. She leaned into me and stood up straight, putting her enormous tits on full display. Everything about her posture swore she'd suck my dick until I forgot my wife. It wasn't my wife I was thinking about, though.

I eyed the bar—my exit from this situation—but as soon as my sightline abandoned her boobs, Tom handed me a beer and her a mixed drink. I was entrenched in stupid conversation about nothing I cared about for the next hour.

I drowned my intellect in beer and whiskey until Amara excused herself and Tom suggested, "You should fuck her." It almost sounded logical.

Amara returned from the bathroom and wrapped her arms around my waist from the back. I lifted my arms and examined the clutched grip of the sad little creature behind me.

How did I get here? And how do I get out?

She came around to the front of me, grinning as if I'd just proposed. Tom handed her another drink, and she clinked it against my glass to toast our union. Amara drank hers down and tapped her pointed, red-painted nails on the sides of the glass. She winked at Tom to signal she needed another.

"Maybe slow down," I suggested. It was completely hypocritical. My daily goal was to remain just sober enough to work until I could get home and drink myself into my tortured sleep that would only last a few hours.

"You're the sweetest guy I've ever met."

Wow, this was easy and terrible, and as she licked her top lip, gross.

"I just think . . . did you drive?"

"No. I need . . ." She paused for effect and tilted her head toward me. "A ride."

I looked over her head for Tom. He seemed like the perfect driver for her, but he was nowhere to be found. "Where do you live?"

"Downtown. A few blocks up. That's what I love about Wilmington. Everything's so close." I nodded and checked the time on my phone. Eleven. It felt more like seven. I was losing concept of time. My life was slipping away. "Where do you live?" she asked. Her chatter did save me from myself. My thoughts, at least.

"Chester County."

"Oh. It's nice up there. In a house?" She was timid with her question.

"Yes. In a house." I left unsaid, but understood, that it was the house I'd bought with my wife. The one she'd picked out and decorated. The one with the television hung too high. "I'm going to head out. I can drop you off if you want."

She leaned into me and pressed her boobs against my chest. "Let's go."

Amara directed me to a high-rise right off Delaware Avenue with her hand between my legs the entire drive. I didn't want her hand there or Amara in the car, but a warm heat I hadn't felt since Anna, spread through my body. When I stopped at a light, I glanced down, and the flashes of nail polish moving back and forth over my zipper had an appeal. My dick was hard before we reached her street.

She unbuckled and practically climbed onto my lap. "Do you want to come in?"

No. I didn't want to be doing any of this, but my dick was throbbing under her touch.

"Um . . . I'm not sure," I said and placed my hand flat on her back as she kissed my neck. I'd stopped at the front door, and when a group of people walked out of the building, I moved the car into a more secluded spot near the back of the lot.

"Here's fine," she said without looking up or having any idea of where we were.

"Good."

That was my last real input. Amara unzipped my pants and yanked on them until I raised my hips and pushed them down some. She worked my dick like I was filming her for an Academy Award. I assumed this wasn't Amara's first time with her head down in the driver's seat.

I wasn't kind. I pushed her head until she took almost all of me in, and then I pulled her hair to raise her head back up. I controlled her movements until I forgot it was her down there. Until I forgot how long it'd been since anyone had been down there.

A junior associate I recognized from work walked by with his girlfriend and raised his hand to wave. I pressed her head lower, ignored the way she gagged a bit, and waved back.

I didn't care if he saw or didn't see. Not really. I didn't know Amara. I barely knew myself. I tilted my hips and pressed Amara's head down again. Farther. She couldn't take me in far enough. I inhaled the thick smell of her shampoo as her head rose and fell, and I let my head fall back. I forgot. Everything.

Some guttural sound fell from my lips as I came down the throat of a girl I'd just met. Amara might be a genius. She'd known what I needed better than I had.

"Yum," she said and wiped her lips.

My genius.

"Do you want to come up?"

I peered out the window at the apartment building. It was the polite thing to do, but I couldn't. "I know it's horrible of me, but I can't." The only non-cruel way to escape this was to throw the widower card. "I'm just not ready."

"Oh, I understand. I'll give you my number, and when you *are* ready, you can call me."

"Thanks." It was as dead a statement of gratitude as my wife.

I drove home and jerked off to the thought of Amara sucking my dick. I wasn't sure why, because I could have just stayed at Amara's, but I preferred to be alone than with her. I didn't even want to see her again.

A bit of her lip gloss was stained on my underwear. I rubbed it with my thumb and wondered if it'd ever come out. Claire had been in charge of all stains. I didn't know the first thing about fabrics. She probably didn't know much either, but in my past, I would have just pointed this out to her. I laughed. *Hey, Claire. Can you get this girl's lip gloss off my underwear? It was all over my dick from when she gave me a blow job.* Insert explosion sound. Insert gun shot. Insert knife jabbed into my man parts.

I turned down the television and called Anna. It was six thirty in the morning in Italy, but I wanted to hear her voice. Even if it was just on her voicemail.

"Are you okay?" she answered.

I swallowed and shut off the television completely. Anna was too good for the current state of my life. "Yes. You?"

She exhaled. "I'm just lying here, listening to the birds outside my window."

"Yeah?" I just wanted her to talk. I didn't care about what.

"There are maybe two. We had so many birds at our house in Delaware. They'd sound crazy just after dawn. It was as if it was their job to wake up the rest of the world." Her sweet voice telling me about birds brought me back to civilization. "But here there are only a few."

"What color are they?"

The sounds of her sitting up came through the phone. "Uh . . ." She moved around some more. "They're both gray. Like a rainy day. They sound pretty, though."

"I can hear them."

"It's going to be sunny today. What is the weather like there?"

"Dark."

We both laughed. "Oh, I forgot. Sorry." I could hear her moving again and imagined her resting back on her pillow. "Why are you calling me so late on a Friday?"

"I just needed to hear your voice."

"Rough week?"

"Rough month, but I'm fine." She stayed silent and waited for me to divulge something more. "Really."

"One of my books said it's important to talk to caring friends. Call anytime."

"Is that what we are? Caring friends?"

"For now. What would you call us?"

"I want to call you my friend who moved home from Italy to be with me because she was the only thing that truly made me happy."

Silent pause again. I allowed her the time to choose her words carefully.

"Another person can't make you happy. We've got to figure some of this out for ourselves or else we'll just end up hating each other and our situation."

"We're calling it a situation now?" I was nasty. She'd dismissed my not-real, off-handed invitation for a relationship, and I was going to pout and take it out on her.

"Gabe, what do you want from me?"

"I want you."

"There's nothing left of me to give you. I need time, and so do you."

"I'm going to go. I shouldn't have called."

"Yes, you should have. Caring friends—"

"How much did you spend on all of these books?"

"One hundred and fifty-three euros plus a pound of self-esteem as the cashier stared at me pitifully."

"I hope they help." I did. Anna and her books were all I had to work with. They had to help.

"I love you, Gabe."

I closed my eyes and lowered my head. I wanted to yell at her for saying it, but the words warmed me, and I couldn't deny the effect. "Love you, too."

22

Anna

THE DINNER OUT WITH SOPHIA and her friends became many dinners. Happy hours, drinks, parties. She was the perfect person to live above if you wanted to go out and meet people. I would have thought God had sent her specifically to me for this reason, except I didn't want to meet anyone.

I liked her, though. She was kind. Not just to me, but to everyone she'd ever met. There was nothing overly exciting about her, but also nothing sinister. It was a peaceful combination that was as much as I could handle in the friend area at the moment.

I accepted about every fifth invitation. Every time I said yes, Sophia jumped for joy and held her hands clasped at her chest as if solving my reclusive behavior was a puzzle she was close to cracking.

Tonight's dinner was especially difficult. I'd been crying more often over the past months. I'd hoped Rome would interrupt the random tears, but the last few weeks had been the same here as they were in the states. The books had said there'd be peaks and valleys. I assumed I was at the bottom of a ravine and tried to be patient until I could pull myself back out. The bizarre thing was I didn't miss Josh, at least I didn't think I did. Most of my dreams were of Claire. Some were of Gabe or, more specifically, his body. I tried to forget them as soon as I woke up, but those were the ones that stuck with me.

I said my regrets in Italian, and everyone clapped at my perfect diction. They were an obliging group. When I stood to leave, a guy named Lucca stood as well and said he'd walk me home since I was on his way.

Being alone with him made me nervous. He was my height with warm eyes and dark skin. He watched my lips as I spoke, as if he were imagining kissing me. It'd been months since Gabe had touched me, and the only man before that for *years* had been Josh. I convinced myself I was overthinking the walk until Lucca grabbed my hand and held it in his. I stared at him with a stiff, dead expression, trying to convey my discomfort, but he only smiled and swung our hands as we strolled onto my street.

We stopped in front of my building. I was thinking of something appropriate to say in Italian. A gracious thank you or a joke about abstinence. There were too many factors to put together before he took my face in his hands and kissed me.

I froze.

Like, actually stopped all involuntary movements, including breathing and eye contact. I stiffened right there in his hands on the sidewalk. I wasn't sure what would happen next.

Lucca leaned back and examined me.

I burst into tears and ran inside.

I locked my apartment door behind me and threw myself on my bed. I cried from need and despair and utter embarrassment. I didn't want to be here any longer. When I couldn't cry anymore, I laid on my back and stared at the ceiling, and then I did the most selfish thing I could think of. I called Gabe.

"Hey," he said as if I'd just called to see what time we were meeting later.

I tried to inhale, but my lip quivered.

"Anna. Are you there?"

"I'm here." I sounded pathetic, mostly because I was. "I'm

sorry to call."

"Can you please never apologize for that again?" I nodded and sniffled. "What's going on?"

"I shouldn't have come here." The dam I'd been holding up since I'd moved cracked. "It was a huge mistake. The books said not to make any big changes, and I've screwed this whole thing up. I'm ruining my life." I turned over and crushed my face in my pillow. I leaned up just enough to say, "I'm so sorry, Gabe."

"Hey." He was calm. His voice was soothing. I knew how much effort this took for him. "You're doing great. Stop reading those books. They don't know you. I do, and I'm impressed."

My short laugh was mirthless. There was nothing impressive about me.

"Believe me. I haven't changed a thing, and I'm falling apart. It's not Italy. It's not you. This whole thing is going to take time."

"I cry all the time. It's getting worse." I started to cry again. I was pathetic.

"Anna, I want you to come home more than anything. More than any other person walking around on this earth, I want you to be near me, but I think you should stay in Italy for now."

I wiped my tears and focused on his words. "Are you just saying that?"

"Yes." He made me laugh again. "I hate you being there. It's killing me slowly. I'm selfish and unhappy, and I want you to come home and make me feel better."

"I love you," I said. It was the only truth I still believed.

"Stay in Italy. Let your heart heal. Hurry." I closed my eyes and could see him in my mind. "I'm waiting for you to come home. I'm here each day hanging on you and the stupid books you're reading and the fact that the two of us are still here for a reason." I took a deep breath and exhaled into the phone. "I need you to be strong," he said. "Even stronger than you were that night Josh and Claire got into a fight because he caught her cheating at rummy."

I curled up in my bed and laughed at my beautiful friend. "I thought you were going to have to pull them apart."

"I was only acting like I cared to help you. I think that was the first time I ever really thought they deserved each other," Gabe said.

I could barely stop laughing at the memory to ask, "Why?"

"Because Josh had drunk too much. Claire was cheating. I wasn't listening, and you were mixing the two of us drinks as they went at it." Gabe laughed, too.

"She only cheated because you guys underestimated her."

"That makes no sense."

"It does if you know Claire." I raised my eyebrows as if he could see me.

"Josh loved the moral high road, and Claire loved to speed down it with her top off and middle finger in the air."

"Oh my God, you're right. They drove each other mad, didn't they?"

"I've been thinking about the four of us a lot. You and I were often just watching or managing them," he said. I crawled under the covers on my bed. He was like home. "It's time to let them go, though. We don't have to take care of them anymore."

"I feel haunted." I didn't tell him that it was more than Josh haunting me. It was my feelings about Josh and the emptiness left behind. It was also Claire and the memory of the last time she'd hugged me before getting into the car that would in a few minutes kill my husband. I didn't tell Gabe any of it.

"It's going to get better."

"I love you," I said.

"I know. You're my favorite stalker. Go to sleep."

"Eat something healthy," I said.

"Drink some wine. I love you, too."

I hung up and held the phone to my chest. I slept through the night and only dreamed of him twice. At least only two times that I could remember. I wouldn't tell him about either.

23

Gabe

IT WAS THE WEEK OF Thanksgiving, and everyone was festive and jolly. When I said "everyone," I was, of course, not including myself. I left work on Wednesday at noon and drove straight to the Philly airport. My sister, Rita, told me I was spending Thanksgiving with her, her husband, *and* their two kids in Florida. Well, "Told me" wasn't exactly correct. She sent me a link to a flight reservation already booked in my name.

I had a carry-on, a backpack, and barely a shred of my former self with me as I boarded the plane. My seat was on the aisle in row twenty-six of an oversold flight. The woman in the seat next to me reminded me of Anna. It was her hair. Except this woman's hair was brown. And shorter. And when I looked at her objectively, she was nothing at all like Anna.

I pulled out my phone before I slid my backpack under the seat in front of me. Anna's last text to me read: "I love you." That was the way she ended every conversation. Claire and Anna had tossed the phrase around the way Josh and I had said, "See you," but now, coming from Anna, it was a life preserver thrown to me. Whether it meant a thing to her or not, it was keeping me afloat.

Words didn't come to me. Nothing witty was typed into the text screen. I hit the off button on the phone. I'd promised myself I wouldn't fall into texting her. Anna deserved a phone call, and the sound of her voice had some kind of healing effect on me that I couldn't quantify.

I thought of her the entire flight to Tampa. When the plane landed, the need to talk to her was overwhelming, but I had to wait as the twenty-five rows in front of me deplaned before I could call her. My sister, who I was sure was stationed just past security, would have to wait. It was after ten in Italy. She'd be tired. Maybe even sleepy sounding. Her voice was softer that time of night. I loved it.

"Hello," she said full of energy.

"Hey. Happy Thanksgiving."

She sighed into the phone. "You, too. How are you?"

"Shitty."

To that she said nothing. In the background, I heard music and then a male's voice say, "Anna, where's—" He was cut off, probably by some gesture Anna made that I couldn't see all the way from Florida. My eyes closed as the pain sank down my body and spread through my stomach.

"Gabe, can I call you back?"

"Of course," I said instead of, "You're dead to me," because I wasn't sure I could live without her.

I hit end on the phone and rolled my suitcase to the nearest bar. I ordered three shots of tequila, paid for them, and downed each of them one after the other.

Rita's house was full of love and warmth. My contribution was the stench of liquor and some slurred words. She kept my glass full and the sympathetic expression glued to her face. Her husband seemed less impressed, but he, too, kept his opinions to himself.

I settled into their couch with the remote in my hand and pretended that it was just me, in my house in Pennsylvania, with some additional people tiptoeing around. It almost worked too, but Rita's daughters, Mia and Lia, they were merciless.

"Uncle Gabe, why do you look like that?"

"And why do you smell like that?"

"Would you rather be a unicorn or a panda?"

"Can I brush your hair?"

"You're white. You should go outside more."

I nodded. Once in a while I made eye contact, but mostly I tried to ignore their voices. Until Lia asked, "Do you think Aunt Claire's in heaven?" She'd moved between my legs and was staring right at me when she asked. She kind of reminded me of her Aunt Claire.

"I do."

"Was she a good girl?"

Claire's death certificate had listed the cause of death as pending. When I'd called the coroner's office, they said they were still waiting on the toxicology report. No skid marks. No evidence of mechanical failure.

Was she a good girl?

"Uncle Gabe! Was Aunt Claire good?"

Rita came in and refilled my glass with whiskey. "Of course she was," she told her daughter. Rita was a good sister. "You two need to get to bed."

Mia put her hands on her hips and raised her eyebrows at me. "What about him?"

"What about Uncle Gabe?"

"He needs to go to bed, too."

"Mia, it's not for you to decide when adults go to bed."

She scrutinized me with more attitude than one would think possible from such a tiny human. She was definitely my sister's daughter. "Somebody needs to."

"Mia! Bed. Go get ready, and I'll be up in a minute to tuck you in."

Lia kissed me on the cheek, followed by Mia. She leaned back two inches and stared into my eyes. I opened them wide, hoping she could see something inside me. She backed up slowly, and I smiled at her. She scared me a little. Just like her mom.

24

Anna

THE PARTY IN THE APARTMENT below mine was a bad idea. When Sophia had invited me, I'd declined. Without any hesitation, excuses for why I couldn't walk the dozen stairs down to her apartment had come flying out of my mouth. I'd eventually warmed up to Sophia enough to tell her about Josh. I wished I hadn't. The knowledge made her look at me with pity. I only had what was left of me to work with, so I couldn't really find it in myself to care. She should count herself lucky. The old Anna would have made her cry.

Sophia had kindly accepted my decline, but her lack of argument was explained when she sent up her hot friend, Alex, to get me. She was good like that. Always smiling. Gabe had called right after I'd answered the door. I'd promised myself I'd never not answer, but I feared he'd heard Alex before he'd hung up.

I had been flipping my phone between my fingers for what felt like hours. I didn't want to interrupt his Thanksgiving dinner. I knew he looked forward to it every year, and I didn't have it in me to spoil it for him. It was after one in the morning when my resolve broke. If I didn't call him, I'd fall asleep and not wake up until Thanksgiving was over, which would have been my preference.

He answered but didn't say hello.

"Gabe?"

There was still silence. I checked the phone. The timer on the call was counting forward. He was on the other end.

"Gabe. I'm sorry." I wasn't exactly sure what I was sorry for. Having another man in my apartment? Not having time to talk to him? Having sex with him in St. Michaels? Yes, I could add that one in. It felt right to apologize.

"Happy Thanksgiving, Anna." He slurred his words. He was drunk.

"Gabe—"

"It was our first holiday alone," he spewed. "Why didn't you come home?"

He was breaking my heart or what was left of it. "Gabe—"

"Why, Anna? Are you avoiding coming home? Or me?" The idea that I was hurting him tore through me. Life could be cruel, but I could not. At least not to Gabe.

"Because here, it's not a holiday. It's just a Thursday." I glanced at the clock hanging above the television. "A Friday now." I took a deep breath in preparation for my truth. "I wasn't ready for a holiday."

His laugh was dark and short. "I'm obviously handling it fine. I could have helped you."

"I'm so sorry."

"For what, Anna?"

"For ruining whatever it is we had left of each other."

There was movement on the other end of the line. I imagined him sitting up. "Anna, you didn't." He was alert and stern. "Don't regret what happened at the Julie's wedding. Please." He pleaded with me. I couldn't deny him a thing. I owed him too much.

"The moment we had sex, we stopped supporting each other. We let go and took what we needed from one another. There was barely anything left as it was."

"You're wrong. I'd do anything for you. A year ago. That

night in St. Michael's. And right now. You're the only thing left in this world that I care about, Anna."

"I know . . ." I'd hurt him more if I had to. Neither of us could go on like this. "I need you to do something for yourself first. I need you to take care of yourself, because I can't pull us both through this. You're becoming weak."

"You make me sound like a dead weight you're dragging behind you into the bright sunny day."

"You're not, and God knows I'm crawling into the daylight inch by inch, but I need you to . . ." I listened to his breathing. I wasn't sure if he was still awake. "I need *you*, Gabe."

He was silent for so long after that I thought he had passed out. Just as I was about to hang up, his voice sounded—slurred and soft and full of pain.

"I hate you," he said. "Come home."

"I love you, too," I said, and Gabe hung up.

I put my phone on my nightstand and closed my eyes. Without Gabe, there was nothing left to be thankful for. There had to be something else out there. For both of us. This couldn't be the end.

25

Gabe

MY THROAT BURNED AS IF the air I was forcing into it were tiny drops of acid. A pain in my shoulder sent a prickly tingle down to my forearm. I feared the last mile of my run might have triggered a heart attack. Outside my garage door, I bent at the waist and rested with my hands on my knees. I was more out of shape than I appeared.

I considered falling on my back in the center of the front lawn, but it would be a horrible place to die. I'd rot there until the kid across the street rode his bike by and noticed me. It could be days if he was staying at his dad's.

I straightened and trudged through my garage, noting how my car was covered with the road salt from the season's first snowstorm. Claire would've been pissed. She hated when it snowed before the New Year. She was the only person I'd ever met who didn't love a white Christmas. Anna had agreed it was an inconvenience, but I could tell by Claire's expression, she knew Anna was just being nice. The way Anna always was.

The house was warm. I let the water from the kitchen faucet run until the cool stream penetrated the heat on my fingertips. The photographs on the fridge haunted me even with my back to them.

Claire's refrigerator wasn't a messy mix of pictures and reminders. It was a precisely placed collage of photographs I'd always felt she looked better in than I did. Claire had referred to the composition of the pictures. How her photo selection and placement was the perfect artistic representation. I'd dwelled on the content. She'd ignored me. I'd stopped discussing it, and then, after a while, it had rarely come up unless Anna and Josh had been here and we'd all found something funny about Claire's art show.

I turned and faced the photographs armed with my steadying heart rate and cold glass of water. The bottom row had one large photo of the four of us at the Kennett Brewfest. The picture next to that one was of Claire from the same day. Her arms were above her head as she reached for the stars and sang to the rest of us. I'd blamed Anna for encouraging her, but there had been no stopping Claire. We'd all known it and had happily climbed onboard the crazy train with her because, without her, we'd all have been bored.

"I must have been hideous," Josh had always said about the picture in the top row Claire had cropped him out of. He called it, "The one I was too ugly to be in."

"You should have cut me out, too," I'd told her. There was something strange about my expression. I almost looked confused.

"You hate it because you look guilty," Claire had quipped back, dismissing the idea that the picture should be replaced.

"About what?"

I studied the picture now. Without Josh, it appeared like my arms were around Claire and Anna. To the outsider, it'd be impossible to tell which woman was my wife.

Claire and I didn't seem like a couple in the picture beside it either. We were sitting next to each other on the beach, but we were facing opposite directions staring into the distance.

I sipped the water in my glass and took a step back. Without Claire's voice in the house swearing the collage was artistic, I saw it in a new light. The picture of Claire and me at the beach was positioned in such a way that it looked as if she were staring at the picture of the three of us. She was almost angry at the sight.

"We should call it the marriage shot because it looks like you two can't stand each other," Anna had joked of the center picture. She never spoke that way, though. She'd drunk too much that night, and the tone of her words was dark. It was a place I'd never seen her sink to. She was always light and positive and usually sober enough to take care of her drunk husband.

I didn't seem angry in the center picture, though. I was enthralled with something, but I didn't know what. My face showed the same wonder as a thirteen-year-old boy hearing "Welcome to the Jungle" for the first time. To the left of the picture was one of just Anna, who was back lit by a bright sun.

"You look like an angel," Josh had said and laughed as if the observation were ridiculous.

"She is an angel," Claire said and walked away, leaving no place for anyone to disagree.

I was always terrified to look at Anna's picture. Afraid Claire might catch me and the damage would be too great to repair. As I stood there, all I could see were Anna's eyes. She was completely honest. When Anna cried about never being someone's mommy, the day she'd told me she had to leave me to find herself, and when she'd said she loved me, it was all I saw—the truth in her eyes.

Claire had sworn the pictures weren't random and that they told a story. Without beers or the laughter or Claire, the tale was easier to see. It was my love for Anna on full display, and Claire was in the middle of it just watching.

She knew . . . Claire *knew* how I felt about Anna before I did.

I let the guilt mix with anger inside me until the familiar disgust for my wife returned.

I took a picture of it, making sure it was clear enough that someone could see the positions of the pictures as well as the details. Not that anyone would ever believe what I was saying. Anna would tell me I was crazy. Claire would be pleased that I'd figured it out. She'd accept my understanding as a statement of love, even if it came with a joint realization that I wanted someone else.

I tore all the photos off the fridge and dropped all but the one of Anna into the trash. I couldn't bring myself to throw it away. Claire was right. She was divine.

I breezed through the house removing every personal photo from the walls and the shelves. "Goodbye, Claire."

It was time to sell the house.

26

Anna

I HAD TRIED TO DRINK wine only after four in the afternoon. I'd justified it because no one needed happy hour more than I did, but since it was giving me crazy dreams, I dropped it to only drinking wine on the weekends. Wine, along with everything else, only managed to upset me since I'd moved here. If I had a euro for every time a waiter gave me a free glass because I was crying in it . . .

I had also stopped eating with Sophia and her friends. After the third time I'd excused myself because I was in tears and needed to collect myself, I figured it wasn't worth the embarrassment.

I talked to Gabe yesterday, and he had done nothing but complain about the cold. Here it was nearly sixty-five degrees, and I smiled just a bit as I tilted my face to the gentle sunshine. Claire would have been pissed about the early snow. Snow was rare in Rome. I'd miss it.

A stroller stopped on the street right next to my table. The baby was bundled up in pink. Her tiny nose, closed eyes, and pouted lips were the only things visible. I wondered if she was too hot. If her mother sang to her. If her father always hoped he'd be her daddy.

The mother—I assumed she was the mother by the way she made sure the baby was blocked from the day's breeze—looked up and smiled gently at me. I was staring, but I couldn't stop.

"Stella," a man called and walked up. He kissed the woman and then bent to kiss the baby. I watched them until they disappeared around a corner, and then took a long, deep breath.

I was alone, but I wasn't crying. I picked up my phone to call Gabe again so I could tell him about this milestone in my despair. I still felt depressed, but I was getting stronger. I scrolled through my contacts and realized I'd gone too far when Josh's name appeared. The letters on the screen left a strange, empty feeling where my love for him used to be. He'd left so abruptly. I was trying to figure out when I'd stopped loving him. I wanted to know the exact day, as if I should add it to the back of our wedding album.

I'd ruined us, and I think by the end, I'd hated him, but I couldn't deny the role I'd played in our relationship. We'd stopped talking or we'd refused to listen. I was as guilty as he'd been. I wouldn't do the same thing to Gabe. I'd always tell him what I wanted and what I needed. Although, he already seemed to know the difference without me saying a word.

Josh always made time to talk to me when he'd been at work. I'd left him the saddest message the last time I'd gotten my period. He hadn't even called me back and Josh always returned his calls. He'd been meticulous, but that day, he'd left me alone with my grief. The same way he had now.

The tragedy of the whole thing was that I knew he wouldn't call back. Josh had been loving and, at times, affectionate, but there had been a part of Josh that was cold. I only ever caught a whiff of it, and it usually only happened when I needed his warmth the most.

"Does he know how much you hate that?" Claire had asked and tilted her head toward Gabe, who was helping Josh into the passenger seat of his car. He'd drunk too much, which was becoming the norm. As was me taking care of him.

"Of course he does." I'd sighed and looked on as Gabe leaned against the car door he'd just shut. He was able to stand. Walk. Drive. Josh was slurring in the passenger seat.

"You're too good for him," she'd said. By the time we'd reached the car, we'd settled into a giggle. I'd forgotten that my husband had, once again, left me to take care of us.

He hadn't apologized the next day for getting so sloppy drunk. I'd stopped bringing it up years ago. When I'd finally realized he was drinking to escape, I'd been too afraid to ask him what he was running from. Terrified it was me he'd been trying to avoid.

I found Gabe's number in my contacts and called him. He answered after the first ring.

"Good morning." His voice was deep, as if he'd just woken up. Maybe he had. I shifted in my seat as my body responded to it.

"Hey." The air touched my skin differently since I heard him. I was more alive.

He was quiet, probably waiting for me to start whining about something, but for once, I was okay.

"I'm coming home for Christmas," I said.

"Really?" I could feel him smiling through the phone. One beamed across my face in response. "You're not toying with me? You're really coming home?"

"Yes." I was nodding and smiling. People around me were probably mistaking me for someone who was genuinely happy. "I want to see you."

"When? Anna, when are you coming?"

I took a deep breath. I hadn't gotten that far yet. "Um, I don't know. I'll stay through the holiday, though."

"I can pick you up at the airport. Drive you around. Whatever you need." He stopped short of offering me a place to stay. I didn't dwell on that. I'd never sleep in Claire's house without her there.

"I have to let my parents know. I'm sure they'll be eager to drive me around."

"Oh. Of course." I'd hurt him somehow.

"I want to see you, though." He needed to know it. I wouldn't hide it from him. "You're the reason I'm coming home." My cheeks heated at the admission. It was different from a friend telling another friend something. This was more personal.

"I want to see you, too." He was quiet again, and the silence felt a bit sad. "Call me as soon as you know the date."

"I will." I smiled again. I wasn't sure if it was at the thought of going home or because of Gabe. "I love you."

"I love you, too."

27

Gabe

IT WAS MY FIRST GLIMPSE of actual joy since Anna'd left in October. I shouldn't have let her go. I could feel myself decaying with every step I'd taken away from their house that day, but nothing I'd said had swayed her. Not that I'd had many words to utilize. Her husband was dead, my wife's driving had killed him, and Anna had wanted to move to another country. It was hard to defend a position on the matter when all I'd really wanted to do was follow her wherever she was going.

Her voicemail with her flight numbers and dates, *that* was something different. It wasn't a message checking in. It wasn't just a light interruption to my endlessly brutal days. Rather an actual invitation to spend time together. With Anna's return came the possibility of my sanity coming back, even if she was staying with her parents in Chadds Ford.

I'd spent twenty minutes figuring out whether to invite her to dinner or drinks. A movie. Perhaps something to do with the holidays.

"Are you home?" I asked in lieu of a greeting. Her last message was from the airport terminal in Rome. The sight of her name on the screen of my phone when it was already in my hand sent energy coursing through me. I could have run ten miles.

"I am. God help me. I've spent the last two hours with every relative in my extended family. I haven't had a minute alone since I got here."

She didn't sound excited. Her voice was raspy, and I assumed she was exhausted. I exhaled the disappointment. "We can do this another time. It doesn't have to be tonight."

"No," she said without hesitation and gave me hope. "Seeing you has been the only thing I've been looking forward to. Please don't cancel."

"I won't." There'd be no cancellations. "What do you want to do? I'm going to leave work early so I can come get you." I wasn't sure what time to say. I could not go in at all and go get her for lunch. "Maybe around three?"

"Oh, wow. I didn't realize you'd be ready that early. I still have some gifts to buy." Again, her words tore me down. This conversation was taking too long. I could be at her house in a half hour. "How about I meet you at Pizza by Elizabeth's at five?"

"Uh . . . sure." I wanted to go shopping with her. Spend the day driving around in the chaos of the season with Anna by my side, but I didn't want to scare her away. I'd wait, knowing this day would feel sixty hours long.

"You look tired." She was being nice. I probably looked like shit. How could I not? I'd stopped running, working out, and eating right for months. I'd replaced all of those things with Scotch. It was a gentleman's drink, so I thought it'd be okay. Based on how tight my pants felt, it was a chubby man's drink.

"Thanks." We both laughed.

"Don't worry. You're still as strikingly handsome as you've always been." She was kidding, but I chose to take her seriously.

Anna read the menu over. We'd been here a half dozen times before with our spouses, but this was our first time at a table for two. She knew exactly what she was going to get. She'd order the Davis Pizza. She always did. "I'll have a glass of the Cetamura Chianti."

"How Italian of you." I'd never seen Anna drink wine before. I wanted to change like she had. "Cancel my Scotch. I'll have the same," I told the waiter.

"It's like water in Italy. I drink wine every day."

"It must agree with you. You look amazing." I wasn't just being nice. Her hair was the same golden blond I pictured in my mind every time I closed my eyes. Her eyes were the same warm green. Whereas I had the complexion of a verging alcoholic who sat in an office every day, Anna's cheeks were pink, as if she'd just returned from a stroll down by the river in a brisk breeze.

"It's been a rough few months," she said. I stayed quiet and let her collect her thoughts. "I knew going to Italy wasn't going to change anything. It's not like I thought I could outrun the accident." Our drinks were delivered, and our waiter ran off to check on another table. "But I was hoping I was wrong. That somehow being in a new place would give me a new life." She sipped her wine and held the glass near her lips, waiting to take another.

"Staying here wasn't the answer. It's miserable. At least you're not in the same house you lived in with Josh."

"What's going on with your house?"

"It sold. I have to be out in sixty days." Saying it aloud excited me. I couldn't wait to leave it. It was a prison, and Claire would always be the guard.

"Come to Italy." She tipped her glass and took another sip.

I engaged in a small, awkward laugh.

"I'm serious. Come to Italy. They need managers there, too."

"Of what?"

"Of me." The lights dimmed in the restaurant, and neither of us said anything as the hostess stopped by our table to light the candle between us.

"I feel like I'm floating through my life. That if I don't find a connection to the earth, I might disappear forever. I need an anchor," Anna said, watching the hostess as she moved to another table.

I drank my wine. Like, half the glass. "I'm not sure I'd be hired as an anchor these days, but I'll consider it."

"I got you something."

"Today? I hope I wasn't the gift you still had to buy." I'd rather have just spent the time with her. Whatever was in the box she'd just taken out of her bag couldn't compare to sitting somewhere with her and talking.

"No. This I brought from Italy." She handed me the box, which was wrapped in green foil.

I had something for her, too. The tickets to the Rockettes were in my pocket. It was a selfish present, wholly designed to make sure we spent more time together. I unwrapped the paper, balled it up, and tossed it onto the booth seat next to Anna. She didn't flinch, which I loved about her.

"A scarf?" I asked and hoped more than anything that was what it actually was and I wasn't insulting her somehow.

"Yes. I made it."

"What?"

"I made it."

"You've never made anything."

"I made you dinner once." She'd burned it and we'd ordered sushi, but I guessed that counted.

"How could I have forgotten? Well, it seems you're even better at . . ."

"Knitting." She nodded.

"Knitting than you are at cooking." I wrapped the scarf

around my neck. It was soft and warm. The green stripe down the center reminded me of Anna's eyes. I hoped she'd chosen it because of that.

"This winter is going to be a hard one." She sipped more of her wine, and then the smile drained from her face. "The book I'm reading on grief said the first everything is difficult. First dinner alone. First Christmas. First winter. It's supposed to get easier once we survive them."

I twisted the ends of the scarf around my palms and cinched it tight around my neck. "I should be fine. I've got this great scarf." I bounced my eyebrows at her to remind her to be happy. I needed her to remember how it used to be between us. Easy . . .

"I thought of it like a hug." She stared down into her now-empty glass of wine. "In case you might ever need one."

I wanted her. That was all, but I'd take the scarf. I'd take whatever scraps of this life she'd give me. "Oh, I need one. Like, twenty. Each day." I rubbed my hand down the length of the yarn. "I still can't believe you made it. It's really well done."

"It took me three tries. I cursed you through every one of them." She reached across the table and tightened the knot of the scarf. "But it was worth it."

"Of course."

"Julie called me yesterday. She heard I was home." Anna watched for my reaction.

"Asking if the rumors were true that we fucked and I bit you?"

The waiter was back. He took our orders. The Davis for Anna and the Montgomery pizza for me, and we both ordered another round of wine.

"No, actually. She didn't bring it up. Do you think people know?"

I shook my head. "I doubt it. How could anyone imagine . . . that?"

"I've been picturing it quite a bit."

My dick perked up, and I wanted to beat it down with the bread basket. I was barely holding on to my sanity. "What does that mean? What are you doing, Anna?" I wasn't even sure these were signals to identify as mixed, and I couldn't figure out what was going on. I could barely evaluate myself, let alone my best friend's widow whom I'd fucked.

"Do I have to know?" She was so solid sitting across from me. None of this seemed to be freaking her out the way it was me. Her lack of guilt was as unnerving as the crime.

"Yes. I kind of need you to. Because I'm a bit lost these days."

"That's okay."

"No." I was stern with her. "It's not. Not with me."

Anna reached across the table and covered my hand with her own. "I know I'm no longer married." She looked down at the table. "And neither are you." Her eyes returned to mine. I wanted to stay forever there. "When we were both alone, we were together. And now I think of that night often."

I studied the light pink polish on her nail tips and the lack of jewelry adorning each finger. "I do, too." I rested my other hand on top of hers and lightly moved it back and forth across her soft skin. "About that night . . ."

She started to pull away, but I stopped her. "You don't have to say anything," she said.

"I do. I need to tell you lots of things about it, because my guilt doesn't rest solely with Josh and Claire." I looked up from our hands. "It's not even just about that night."

Our pizzas came, and the aromas of both calmed the words brewing in my mind. We were out to dinner. In a restaurant in Greenville, Delaware. This wasn't the place to apologize for fucking biting her. Sweat covered the back of my neck at the thought of her breast in my mouth.

"Your Christmas present is tickets to the Radio City Christmas Spectacular. I want you to spend the night in the city with me." The words just fell out of my mouth without thought or filter, and I was positive she would turn me down.

Then, just like that, Anna whispered, "Okay." She cleared her throat and then looked me in the eyes. "When is it?"

"It's on Wednesday. I was hoping we could go up in the morning and spend the day in the city before the show."

"And then have sex that night?"

I dropped the slice of pizza I was holding onto the plate in front of me. "What the hell is that?"

"I don't know. I'm trying to figure this all out. Is your intention that we might be able to have sex while I'm in town? Is that why you got us tickets to a show in Manhattan instead of Philadelphia?"

"I got tickets to the show in Manhattan because it's the most famous holiday show in the world."

"Oh." Anna was detached from the painful jabs she was hurling at me through this dinner. I didn't feel like I knew her anymore.

"Maybe it's a bad idea." I suddenly doubted everything, but it's not as if I had a great grip on it to begin with. It was wrong to come here . . . to believe Anna's return to the States was going to erase everything that'd happened to us.

She leaned across the table, looked to our right and left, and then focused squarely on me. "What do you say we finish this pizza and go have sex somewhere tonight?"

I swallowed. I couldn't breathe. My tongue might have been swelling in my mouth. This was some sort of allergic reaction. "Wh-wha—"

"I don't want to have to 'figure out' what's going on with us.

I just want to be with you in whatever form that takes."

"Anna . . ."

"Not drunk. Not completely heartbroken. Just two people who think of each other often. Dare I say, love each other, even if it's just as friends. Maybe we are just friends."

"Are you—"

"Clothes off. Eyes up. Fully aware of what's going on. That should be what we do after dinner. I think it might answer a lot of questions for both of us."

Stand.

Sit.

Run.

Drag her to my car. Thoughts of what I wanted to do to her invaded every inch of space left in my mind. I waved down the waiter. "Check, please," I said when he arrived at our table.

"Is everything all right?" He was surveying our barely touched pizzas.

"Fine. We're going to need these to go and the check." I stared at Anna the entire time I was speaking to him. The corners of her mouth tilted up toward the light in her eyes. She was pleased with the decision to leave.

My mind flew in twenty different directions as we walked out of the restaurant. "I'll drive," I said and led Anna by the elbow toward my car.

"I can follow you."

"No. I'll bring you back for your car."

"Are we going to do it *in* your car?"

Josh's death had affected her more than she'd let on. She wasn't the same Anna, which was good because I wasn't the same Gabe either. "No." I opened her door and waited while she sat in my car and reached up for the to-go bag.

I drove south on Route 52. I should leave her at her mom's.

A real friend wouldn't even take a chance on this, but I had nothing, and she was the only thing I wanted.

"Where are we going?"

"To the Hotel DuPont."

"In Wilmington?"

"Yes."

"For the whole night?"

"For as long as you want." I left off the part about how it could be a week if she'd have me that long. "I'm not going to fuck you in the back seat of my car." I was still disgusted at myself for St. Michaels. Even if she never wanted me again after tonight, I was determined to show her I could be gentle. I would take my time. I inhaled and exhaled slowly, stamping down my need to be with her.

"Don't overthink this, Gabe."

"Right. As opposed to last time, when I was completely prepared."

"Last time was my fault." She wasn't apologizing. Just stating her contribution. "I was so incredibly selfish." I didn't like the way she spoke about it. She was detached.

"This time I want it to be your choice," I said and pulled up to the valet stand.

"Checking in, sir?"

"Yes. Hopefully."

"Last name?"

"Hawkins."

He tore off the end of the valet ticket and handed it to me. I met Anna on the other side of the car and took her hand before walking into the hotel lobby. The front desk employees stood at attention, all smiles and professionalism.

"Good evening, sir. How can I help you?"

"I'm hoping you have a room available."

"Do you have a reservation?"

I should have plenty. "No. Is that a problem?"

"It shouldn't be. We're not booked."

Anna walked away from me and stared out the windows that looked out on to the street. She and Josh had never stayed here to my knowledge. They'd gotten married somewhere in Pennsylvania, but I couldn't be sure. I studied her for any signs of recognition, but she looked peaceful. She couldn't have stayed here with him. "One king okay?"

"Perfect. Thanks." I handed her my license and credit card.

Anna turned toward me right as the woman handed me the keys and pointed to the elevators. I walked toward them, and Anna met me halfway.

"All set?" she asked.

I could only nod. I was having trouble being near her and not ripping her clothes off, but I stayed on task. Elevator buttons. Holding the doors open. Opening the room. It wasn't until we were safely locked inside our room that it hit me. She was going to take off her clothes. How many times over the last few months had I thought about this? Jerked off to this? Dreamt of this? I stood straight, holding my breath until she looked at me with those beautiful eyes.

"Are you okay?"

"I think I might be a dick. Certainly a horrible friend," I answered honestly. I was jealous she didn't feel the oppressive guilt that always came with my desire for her. It was because she'd never wanted me the way I wanted her. She'd been innocent until she was no longer married.

"Look at me." Anna's voice was quiet. She was serene. I craved her peace as a nervous energy spread through me.

I raised my gaze to meet hers.

"You're my favorite person in the entire world," she said. "That's got to mean something."

"I think it means you're a horrible person, too."

"Then thank God we've got each other." She raised her hands to our surroundings. "Is it this? Because we don't have to do anything. I just feel like St. Michaels hangs over us every time we talk."

I was supposed to say something . . . the voice of reason . . . the tirade of strength. I didn't know what, but I knew I wasn't supposed to abandon her in her statements. Instead, I kissed her, and the taste of her lit me on fire. I pulled away and caught my breath.

Steady, Gabe.

Anna unzipped her parka and draped it over the chair by the desk. She untied the belt on her long cardigan and took that off as well. So many clothes. I swallowed. I didn't know what I should be doing and watching her was better than anything I could think of.

"Still okay?" Anna asked, and I nodded. I might have lost the use of speech.

She took off her shirt and jeans. Anna stood before me in a matching set of black lace underwear and bra. It was as if she knew this may happen and chose the perfect set. She rested her hands at her sides and faced me. With the lights on and without a care in the world.

I let my eyes cover every inch of her. If it were possible, I would have sworn she was more beautiful this time around. Hot energy coursed through me. If I moved at all, I'd rip those two tiny pieces of fabric away from her body and make her mine. I wanted this night to be different—slower.

Anna didn't let me think too long. She came to me, wrapped her arms around my neck, and kissed me. I clenched my fists at my sides as her hands fell to my shoulders and flat on my stomach. She stared up at me and placed her hand on my dick and rubbed it through my jeans. I inhaled the touch of her after the three long months without it. My dick throbbed with anticipation.

"Don't leave me here alone, Gabe." She unbuttoned my jeans and lowered the zipper. "Make me remember this time."

I couldn't forget. I'd tried everything to erase that night in St. Michaels, but nothing released it from my mind. I pulled my shirt over my head and threw it behind her. Her bra was gone and my hands and mouth were on her before I thought about it. Between the slippery fabric and her clit, my fingers explored her wetness. Anna wanted me. Her head fell back. I let my tongue move up her neck as my finger slipped inside of her.

"Hmm," she moaned, and I moved two fingers in and out of her. She was moaning for me. I could have come at the sound of it.

I ripped back the comforter on the bed and threw the pillow on the chair. "Come here," I said. Anna came without hesitation. My heart was pounding against my chest, mimicking the throbbing of my dick. "I'd love to force you down on this bed and fuck you until you can't walk, but I also want to be gentle. Maybe caress you until I ask if you'd like to be on the top or the bottom." My fingers circled her wrist and I lost myself there. Anna touched the side of my face. She was gentle. I was not. "But I need you on top of me." My voice was low, barely tunneling from the depths she lowered me to. I ground my teeth together, seeking some control. "Is that okay?"

"That's perfect."

I sat down and slid back on the mattress. Anna climbed on and straddled me. She sat on my thighs with my dick pressing against her and stared at me for a moment. I couldn't look away from her body on top of mine.

"Look at me, Gabe." I stared into her green eyes. This was the most open I'd ever been with a woman. It was raw and sober and enlightened. The reality made every touch of her skin against mine electric.

I raised her up by the waist and forced her down onto me. A wave of pure satisfaction rushed through me.

Anna picked up the rhythm and rode me. I reached up and pinched her nipples. My blood coursed through my body and pounded in my dick. I was on fire for her. Ready to explode. I threaded my fingers in her hair and thrust up into her every time she lowered. I fisted my hands and pulled harder, and she didn't fight me. If anything, she moaned a bit louder with every tug of her hair. I wanted her to come first. I wanted to come in her mouth and on her tits. I wanted to take her from behind and in the shower. I wanted to fuck her a thousand more times.

I rolled her under me and thrust into her. I raised her leg up against my chest and rested it on my shoulder without ever breaking eye contact with her.

"That's it, Gabe. Fuck me." Her words pushed me over the edge. I couldn't have stopped if a bullet had hit me. I let my weight fall against her and continued. "I'm going to come."

"Do it," I said in her ear, barely able to breathe. "Come, Anna."

She shook beneath me and tightened around my dick until I thought it might refuse to come out of her. Every muscle in my body clenched as I came inside her.

I inhaled and dropped my head to her shoulder.

Peace filled me.

Anna kissed the side of my face and my neck and right by my ear. Tiny kisses each time. She ran her hands through my hair and caressed my shoulders with her fingertips. I wanted her to touch me everywhere.

"I'm sorry," I said.

"For what?"

There was so much to sort out. I started with, "I needed you more than you loved me."

"Impossible," she said, and I almost believed she meant it.

I dwelled on her words as Anna got out of bed and went to the bathroom. She walked through the lit bedroom as if it was no big deal. It wasn't, after all. I'd just had my dick in her and her nipple in my mouth. I felt pretty close to her body. No need to hide it.

While she was in the other room, I raided the minibar. Jack. Absolute. Petron. A tiny bottle of Macallan 12 hid toward the back. I opened and inhaled the sweet smell of the whiskey before pouring it into the two glasses on the tray.

Anna walked out and dove into our bed. I handed her a glass and crawled in next to her.

"We're going to need more liquor," I said.

"We are. I think we need to talk."

"I knew you were going to say that." My head hung low, and she kissed the back of it. I buried it next to her breast. If only I could stay there forever.

"I've read six books on grieving, and they all pretty much agree we're fucked up."

"Great. I'm glad I skipped educating myself on the process."

"I'm serious, Gabe. I think we need to talk through all of this or we're going to end up hating each other."

I was going to say it was impossible to be worse off, but she was smiling as she lifted the whiskey to her lips and she was completely naked in my bed. I was in better shape than most men would ever be. I rolled onto my side and faced her, resting my head on my bent arm. "Okay. What do we need to say?"

"How was that?" she asked, shifting gears and leaving me at a loss for words.

"That?"

"Yes. Us together, having sex. How was it?"

Her candidness was disarming. I silently compared what I'd wanted it to be with what it actually had been. The contrast was disturbing. I'd wanted to be gentle. Hold her. Add some romance in, not order her to climb on top of me.

"It shouldn't take this long to answer," she said.

"Sorry. I'm embarrassed about the way I was with you in St. Michaels." Anna looked confused. "I wanted the next time I touched you to be . . . sweet." At least I didn't bite her. "But when I'm with you." My voice was gruff. "I don't feel sweet."

"I don't want you to ever control yourself around me. That sounds like the worst sex ever. Take what you want from me, and if it's ever too much, I'll let you know. I, for one, wouldn't change a second of either time we've been together. You're a fantastic lover."

Of all the girls I'd been with, Anna's opinion was the only one that mattered. "Really?"

"Really. You're strong and powerful. I feel you even when you look at me. Don't ever change—not for me or anyone else."

Claire tried to invade my thoughts, and I threw her out of my head. "That wasn't even some of my best stuff, you know?"

Anna laughed at me.

I shook my head, admonishing her. "It's not good to laugh when discussing a guy in bed."

"Sorry."

"Besides fantastic, how was it for you?"

Anna only stared at me. I braced myself for what she would say. I couldn't take any regret from her. "You feel guiltier about Claire than I do about Josh," she finally said. "I'm callous."

"I feel guilty about Josh. Claire has nothing to do with us."

"That's impossible. Of course she does."

I shook my head. "No. She doesn't. Not for me, and I feel guilty about that. I can't be with my friend's wife, but I can be with my wife's best friend . . ." I looked away. "In some ways, I felt freed by Claire's death, and *that* I should feel bad about."

Anna's eyes closed and a tear slipped between her eyelashes.

I pulled her against my chest and held her close. We laid in silence until she fell asleep in my arms. I stared at the ceiling of the hotel room. I was falling in love with her or, worse, I was in love with her already. I sought the comfort of her. It couldn't just be because of what we'd been through.

Hours later, I kissed her shoulder and neck until she stirred.

"What time is it?" she asked in a sleep-filled whisper.

"It's eleven. Do you need to call anyone and tell them you're not coming home?"

Anna rolled over and rested her chin on my chest. "Am I not?"

"Maybe not ever."

"Then yes. I should call someone." She stood and dug through her purse, which she had dropped just inside the door when we got here. She texted someone, waited a few seconds, and responded to a text she received. "It doesn't feel this late," she said, looking around the room. Her eyes found me. A heat flowed through me from her attention. "Let's take a bath."

"A bath?"

"Yeah."

"It's only been twenty-five years since I've had one. Why not."

"I'll run the water." She left me alone in our bedroom. The toilet flushed, and the water turned on. I rested on my hand behind my head. There was so much I didn't know about Anna. Man-woman stuff. All the things I never could have asked her before because she was my friend's wife seemed important.

"Ready," she called from the bathroom, and my dick got hard. Just like that.

I walked in, and her eyes slowly perused my body, stopping at the evidence of my arousal. I looked down at him, too.

Looking good, as usual.

"Do you always walk around with a hard-on?"

"I haven't had sex in three months. You're lucky I didn't meet you for dinner with one."

She shifted in the water, sitting up and leaving me enough room to climb in on the opposite side.

I lowered myself into the hot water and adjusted my legs so they rested on each side of Anna. She put hers on top of mine and touched my stomach with her toes, the feel of her smooth skin against mine was intoxicating. It left me unaware of where I was or where I should be.

I tugged her ankles until she lowered deeper in the water and was closer to me. I wanted her with my hands and my mouth and my dick, which was already throbbing under the bubbles floating around us.

Savoring every inch of her, I slid my fingers up the insides of her thighs until I reached her body. I sat up straight and rested a hand on her stomach while I pressed a finger into her. Her head fell back. Her mouth opened as she inhaled a shaky breath. She wanted me.

I watched the rise and fall of her chest and moved my finger in and out of her, replacing it with two and stroking her clit with my thumb. When the little glimpses of her nipples rising and falling in and out of the water became too much to ignore, I slid my free hand up her body to cup her breast.

"How's that?" I asked.

"A . . . ma . . . zing. Don't stop."

I wanted to kiss her and feel her bottom lip between my teeth, but I couldn't move for fear of her eyes opening and her position changing. She was happy, and it was because I was touching her. I wouldn't stop for anything.

Anna arched her back. Her breath caught in jagged inhales. I squeezed her nipple and felt her come around my fingers inside her. I didn't stop, though. I kept moving my fingers in and out until she shuddered from my touch and squeezed her knees together. She blushed and covered her eyes with her wet hand.

"Thank you," she said.

My breathing was heavy. My dick throbbed in front of me, seeking her out in the tub. "Anna, are you on the pill?"

"Kind of. Fuck me, Gabe."

I didn't stop to figure out what she was talking about or to ask any questions. I shifted my weight until I was on top of her, and her ankles locked around my back, pulling me against her. I rested there, fully seated inside her as I kissed her neck, but I couldn't wait long. I pulled out and thrust into her again. She was wet and silky in the water beneath me, and I wanted to pound into her until she couldn't walk.

I started to say her name, but nothing came out. My hips moved without my direction. They sought her. Every fiber of me wanted her, and I kept grinding into her until I came.

I could finally think, but all I thought was *I love her . . .* and *I love fucking her . . .* and *I'm not letting her go.*

I breathed heavily in her ear. Anna reached up and held my face above her with both hands. She looked from my eyes to my lips and back again. Her breathing matched my own. She kissed me. Her tongue took what I didn't think I had left to give, but my body would always meet her where she was. I let every bit of myself feel Anna beneath me.

I dropped my head to her shoulder and inhaled deeply again. There I rested until she shifted, and I realized I was crushing her between me and the tub. I sat back and let my euphoria spread through me. I was weightless and happy.

"I'm not on the pill," she said. I listened to every word, letting them break through my peace.

"No?" I barely cared that she wasn't and that she hadn't told me. I just wanted Anna.

"Josh and I were trying to get pregnant, and it never worked."

"What?"

She shook her head and stared down into the water in front of her. The bubbles had gone and left a window to see through. "We tried for two years. Josh was tested, and he told me that there was nothing wrong with him. That the problem was me." She looked up at me. "I hated him for it. The night he died, I hated him."

"I'm sorry, Anna." I barely knew what I was sorry for. I'd only heard random snippets of conversations of marriages being torture through infertility. They were my aunt, the older guy I worked with, and my college roommate's now ex-wife. He'd said the disappointment had been more than their marriage could survive. "I had no idea."

"I know. We didn't talk about it."

"Not even to Claire?" I couldn't believe Claire wouldn't have told me about it.

"To no one. Not even my mother." She looked up. The hurt in her eyes threw me. "I was too ashamed."

I moved her around and sat her so her back rested against my chest. I couldn't look into her eyes anymore. She was flawless, and the idea that she wasn't was ridiculous to me but not to her. I kissed her cheek and ran my fingertips down her chest and back up again. "You're perfect."

I fell asleep with Anna in my arms. It was the first time I'd slept through the night since St. Michaels. I needed her for my sanity. She was good for my health. Even more than either of those things, I just wanted her to be with me.

She slipped out of my arms and headed to the bathroom without a word, grabbing the room service menu on her way back. I was getting used to her without clothes on. The guilt over seeing my friend's wife naked was gone. She was Anna without clothes, which was pretty much my favorite way to have her.

"Eggs or pancakes? Or do you want to leave our cave?" she asked as she perused the menu.

"I don't want to go anywhere. What we eat is up to you."

She looked at me over the menu. "I'm really looking forward to going to New York with you."

"Yeah?"

She nodded. "That is, if we ever leave this room."

"This room is perfect, but New York will be good, too."

"No awkwardness, right? We'll just be us."

"I'm going to hold your hand and make love to you," I said and ran my fingers across her thigh. "I want us to laugh as if we've never been sad before."

"And then I'll go back to Italy."

Her words broke through my daydream and left me cold. "Why?"

"Because I'm not through this yet. It's only been four months." She threaded her fingers through mine and raised our hands to her lips. "If we pursue this today, at best, it'll be a disappointment." I shook my head in disagreement. "At worst, we'll be a tragedy."

"You don't know that. All those books you've read don't know us."

"I know I still burst out in tears for no reason—ordering coffee, matching socks, watching television. I'm not right."

I wasn't sure what to say, but I had to find the words to make her stay with me. My chest was tightening at the thought of leaving this room. I couldn't even think about how I would feel having to watch her get back on a plane to Italy. Again. "Anna—"

"I don't know if we have a future, but I do know, it doesn't begin now."

28

Anna

"MY MOTHER WANTED TO KNOW if we were going to have separate rooms tonight," I said when Gabe climbed into the driver's seat.

He paused before he started the car. "What did you tell her?"

"I asked her if it mattered." I'd thrown her with the question. She'd asked, but my mother never would have suspected Gabe and I were sleeping together. "She said she guessed it didn't." Gabe looked out the windshield and stewed on that. "But she stopped asking me questions, so that was helpful."

He backed out of my parents' driveway and onto the street. We were going away for the night. Hundreds of thousands of people were doing the exact same thing. Traveling to New York City to see the tree and a show. The city would be packed with men and women who hadn't spent one moment of their trip considering whether it was okay to be with the person standing next to them.

He turned on the radio, and Christmas music flowed throughout the car. "Christmas carols?" he asked, confirming I could handle them.

I let the words of "Silent Night" penetrate my thoughts. They didn't hurt. There was no reminder of Christmases past with my now-dead husband that I couldn't bear. "It's nice," I said, and Gabe held out his hand. I rested mine in his.

By the time we reached New Jersey, I'd almost forgotten that the trip should have been weird. Gabe wasn't as comfortable. He squeezed my hand and said, "When I'm not with you, which is far too often, I think of what a horrible person I am. The worst friend in the world to Josh and you. A man without honor. Every wife's worst nightmare." He tried to pull his hand away, but I held it tight. "I'm ashamed of myself for wanting you."

"Gabe—"

"But when you're near me, I don't care about any of it." He didn't look at me. I didn't think he could face me. "And that makes me feel like an even bigger dick."

"You're not a dick." Gabe raised his eyebrows and finally glanced my way, disputing my opinion. "Let's say that you actually did have feelings for me when we were both married." He turned away immediately. "Over the years we've been together . . . we've seen each other naked." He laughed. "You've carried me when I couldn't walk. We've passed out together. I saved your life in the river."

"No, you didn't. I was fine."

"I'm the reason you're alive." He laughed until his shoulders shook. "We've been alone a thousand times at least, and you never once did or said anything that wasn't something a true friend would do or say. In fact, that's what makes your claims so unbelievable. If you really had feelings for me, you wouldn't have been so good at just being my friend."

"I'm not a complete asshole."

"You're not even close to one. If they were still here, would you have ever even told me how you felt?"

"Never."

"Would you have kissed me?"

"I'd have cut my dick off before I touched you."

"See?"

"That doesn't mean I didn't feel that way, though, Anna. I was planning on ending our friendship after our vacation."

Fear and hurt of what could have been shot through me. Gabe couldn't leave me. Even if I kept boarding a plane to Italy, I wasn't really leaving him. I was just going away for a while. "What?"

"It was getting worse. I hated myself. I was going to tell Claire that working with Josh and hanging out with you guys was too much." Gabe stared straight out the window leaving me alone beside him. "That I wanted some distance from the two of you."

"You wouldn't have."

"How could I not? I wasn't going to act like your best friend when I felt differently. That's not the guy I am, and I wasn't going to hang around in hopes I ever had a chance with you, because I never wanted one." His own pain settled into the creases in his forehead and the hard edges of his jaw. "We were friends. The consequences to being more than that were outside the realm of possibility for me. Too many people would be hurt." He rubbed his thumb across my hand. "Mainly you."

My chest was tightening. The guilt was creeping back in, and I wouldn't allow it. Not today. Not this weekend. The thought of losing Claire without her dying was inconceivable. "I want to talk about something else."

"Me too," he said, but we rode all the way to the Lincoln Tunnel in silence.

The Radio City Music Hall Christmas Spectacular made it hard to think about anything more than how wonderful this time of year was. I tried to lose myself in the show, but the twin girls seated next to me, with their fur-collared coats and their light-up toys, stole my attention. Together with their parents, they were every dream I'd ever had of children and the holidays and a family for me and Josh. I couldn't ignore them anymore than I could my past. If Gabe noticed, he didn't say anything. What was there to say?

At the conclusion of the show, Gabe and I stayed in our seats. We let the twin girls and all the other families file out before us. We were in no hurry. Liquor poured over ice cubes and a dinner somewhere were all that awaited us. More questions. Less answers.

"Anna?" The soft voice came from behind me. I turned my head and looked over my shoulder to find Gina, Conrad's wife, standing a few feet behind me.

"Gina. Oh my gosh." I stood and moved to hug her. "I haven't seen you since—" Since Josh's funeral. I swallowed hard and watched as the awkwardness crept across Gina's face. She didn't know what to say. "It's okay." I shook my head and smiled. "Really. I'm okay."

Gabe was behind me, ready to catch me if I fell. Gina peered over my shoulder. Her eyes lit up a little at the sight of him. It was easy to forget how attractive he was. To me, he was Gabe. To other women, he was striking.

"Do you remember my friend, Gabe? I think you guys met at the wedding."

"Sure, and your husband . . ." Gabe said and tried to remember Conrad's name. "Conrad."

"I can't believe you remember."

"I'm good with names," Gabe said, which wasn't true. Something about Conrad had left a mark on Gabe that night. I thought back to the cocktail hour. Hadn't Claire said something?

"Anna!" Conrad said as he walked up and lifted me off the ground into a hug, which sparked the memory.

Claire had said he was more excited to see me when his wife wasn't around than when she was. At the time, I'd thought it was odd. Conrad lured me to the edge of the balcony and spoke quietly to me. Gina and Gabe stayed behind, as if they sensed we'd need a moment alone. Gina was probably used to it, since Conrad was the most social person I'd ever met, which is probably why Claire didn't seem to care for him.

"How are you?" he asked.

I nodded deeply to emphasize the, "I'm fine," that came out of my mouth. "Really. I'm pulling it together."

"Wasn't his wife in the car, too?" He tipped his head in Gabe's direction.

Gabe was smiling and nodding at Gina, but his eyes were squarely fixed on me. "Yes. Claire died also." It sounded even more tragic when I said it out loud.

"So now what?"

I turned my attention back to Conrad. "What do you mean?"

"You two go to shows now?"

"Conrad?"

He rubbed the back of his neck and drug me farther away from Gabe and Gina. "I know this is going to sound crazy, but I was hoping you'd reach out to me after Josh's death."

I blinked . . . and then blinked again. I was having trouble understanding. "For what exactly?"

"For whatever he's providing."

"Conrad—"

"I know you've always felt the same way about me. We were never at the same place at the same time in life. I just thought you'd call."

"We were at the same place. We were friends. Now, I don't know what place you're in—"

"Anna, don't. Call me as soon as you can. I'll leave Gina in a second for you."

I pulled away, repulsed. I didn't want him to leave Gina. The touch of his hand on my skin was making me sick. I moved my arm farther out of his reach and banged Gabe in the chest with it.

"Everything okay?" Gabe wasn't speaking to me, though. He was giving Conrad the stare I'd seen him use a few times before. It was an alert to whoever was on the receiving end of it that this might be their last day on earth.

"Fine."

"Anna, you have to come up to the city and stay with us. I thought you were in Italy." Gina was completely oblivious to the offer Conrad just made. I shouldn't have judged. Up until a few minutes ago I was, too.

"I'm only home for a few more days. Thank you, though."

"How's Rome?"

The usher motioned for us to exit. Gina led the way with me by her side. When we reached the hallway, I noticed Gabe and Conrad weren't behind us. I was uneasy about their absence. I wasn't sure who I was more worried about . . . or for.

"Anna?" I turned my attention back to Gina. "How's Rome?"

"Sorry. It's amazing. I'm not quite as great as it is yet, but I'm coming along."

She rubbed my back, and Gabe walked through the door. Every late night and hungover morning with Conrad flew through my mind. Drunken talks. A million laughs, but never one moment of anything but friendship. How had I been so blind? Conrad followed Gabe, looking exactly like the weasel he was.

"Thanks."

"And keep in touch," Gina said before hugging me. I didn't touch Conrad. I wasn't even sure I could without vomiting. Gina didn't seem to notice the new distance between us. Gabe was content and pleasant as he took my hand and led me onto 51st Street.

"You okay?" he asked when we were seated in the last two

open bar stools at Capital Grille.

I rubbed his thighs with my hands. I was careful to stay near his knees, but touching him anywhere on his body affected me. "I'm confused, but fine."

"Life is strange." Gabe took a sip of his martini. He placed it on the bar and put his hands on top of mine. "Stick with me. I'm easy to understand."

"Simple, one might say," I added in agreement.

He lifted his glass again and tipped it to me. "To simplicity." I toasted him as well. "You laugh, but we've had enough drama for four lifetimes. What we need is some peace and quiet."

I yearned for it, too. We ate at the bar and instead of walking around the vibrant city, I asked Gabe to take me back to our room. I wanted to lay down with him and feel the quiet. I wanted not to be alone.

We fell asleep with me on top of him. Josh never liked to cuddle when he slept. He'd give me a kiss and roll over. Gabe wanted to be touching me whether he was conscious or not. Sleeping with him would be the hardest thing to leave behind. Gabe held me tighter against him as if he'd heard my thoughts and argued that *he'd* be the thing I missed the most. Every bit of him.

I woke up first and sat on the edge of the bed with the putrid memory of Conrad fresh in my mind. Josh had been right about him, and even when Josh and I were still dating, the subject of Conrad's friendship had always been a sour one for him. I had lots of guy friends, though. I'd never used Gabe as an example to dispute his argument. I wasn't willing to open our foursome to any scrutiny when it came to the boundaries of relationships.

Josh had also been right about the house we'd bought. I'd wanted something bigger and closer to the water. He'd convinced me to buy the one we had because it was more modest and a closer commute. He'd been right about our cars, our retirement, the wedding . . . maybe. He'd wanted the big party. I'd fought for eloping. He'd won, and both our mothers had been grateful, but it wasn't really what I wanted.

He'd been strategic and cautious and would never have considered moving to Italy the way I had. I stared at the windows of the building rising up next to our hotel. I was rebelling against Josh as much as I was exploring Rome and healing. I exhaled and pushed that thought down.

What I would never accept was that he'd been right about not trying to have a baby. He'd said he was saving me the heartache of not conceiving, but he'd been only protecting himself.

"What are you doing up?" Gabe asked.

I inhaled with my eyes closed. When I let the air out, I let the anger go, too. "I was just wondering if you ever truly know someone."

"Does this have anything to do with your old friend Conrad telling me to back off?"

I turned to him. The sheet was around his waist, and the glimmer from the lights outside caressed his chest. He was beautiful. My rock that somehow made me laugh and feel safe in this fucked-up world, which made him just that much more stunning. "Conrad's not my friend anymore."

29

Gabe

"MY SISTER'S COMING. WE'RE GOING to get Claire's stuff together to donate," I said into the phone as I continued to load the dishwasher.

"I can't believe you haven't done that already." Anna was just being nice. She could believe it.

"I've been dreading it, but it's time. I don't want to live here anymore." It wasn't living. It was existing.

"The sister I met at your housewarming party? The one from Florida?"

"That's the one. She's been on me since the funeral to do this. It's strangely satisfying for her that I've actually listened to her suggestion."

"She's older than you, right?"

"Three years. How'd you know?"

"Because I can imagine you'd grate on an older sister."

I closed the door on the dishwasher and smiled. My sister liked Anna because she didn't put up with my shit either. "She's lucky to have me."

"Gabe, you dressed?" Rita stuck her head in from the garage door that I'd purposely left unlocked.

I hurried off the phone with Anna and faced my sister. "Of course I'm dressed. It's two in the afternoon."

"In case you haven't noticed, you've been a bit detached the last few months." My sister saw everything when it came to me. I used to call her "the hawk" when we were teenagers. She was always weighing in on who I hung out with and what girl I dated. I hadn't even introduced her to Claire until I'd known I was going to marry her. Rita had been silent on the subject from the minute they'd met. Even after I'd proposed, she'd never said a word.

"That's all changing. I went for a run this morning."

She put down the empty boxes she'd hauled in and let the relief relax her body and expression. "You did?"

"It was just a run." I shook my head, but not even I could dismiss the significance.

"Nothing is ever *just* anything. That's awesome, Gabe." She looked around the house, which was much cleaner than the last time she'd been here. The absence of bachelor-cave syndrome pleased her as well. "How's Anna?"

Her name threw me a little. "Anna?"

"Yes. Your friend . . . also lost her spouse . . . Anna."

"She's good."

"Why are you acting so strange?"

I relaxed. Nothing to hide here. "No reason." I moved about the kitchen with a fake purpose. "I don't see her that much. She's still in Italy."

Rita put her hand on my shoulder and gently said, "I'm sorry." She'd known without my telling her that there was a reason to be sorry. "Let's get started. This is going to be the last awful thing you do."

"Promise?"

"Promise."

I followed Rita to my bedroom. There were two walk-in closets, and Claire's, which was on the left, hadn't been opened since Anna closed it all those months ago.

Rita paused for a second in front of it. She didn't turn to me or say a word. It was as if she was communicating with Claire. She opened the door and walked in.

The closet was as orderly as Claire had kept our house. Not cold or sterilized, but neat and tidy. Everything seemed to be exactly where it was designed to be. I moved toward the shelves and reached for the Louis Vuitton bag she'd asked me to get her for Christmas the year before. She'd never used it. She'd hugged it Christmas morning and told everyone about it. Then she put it in the dust bag and placed it on its shelf.

"Nice," Rita said.

"Do you want it?"

"I couldn't." Her eyes widened as I opened the interior to her. "I do want it, but it's too weird."

"Someone at Goodwill is going to be very excited."

Rita lined up pairs of shoes on the bottoms of the boxes. She was careful to keep each with its mate. "What did you do with her rings?"

"Claire picked them out. I offered them to her mom, but she couldn't bear to take them so I had them buried with her."

"What a waste."

"She was only twenty-eight. Barely an adult."

Rita nodded. "By your standard." She took sweaters off the top shelf and put them in a trash bag by her feet. Rita reached up to the back of the shelf and pulled forward a turquoise-blue porcelain box. "What's this?"

"It's another treasure Claire insisted on having. That box"—I pointed at it—"I carried back from St. John practically in my hands so it wouldn't break."

"Your honeymoon?"

"Yes. She had to have it. When she saw it in the window of the shop, she just started to cry." I looked as oddly at the box as I had at Claire that day. It was a box, and there was no question she could have it. She'd waited outside for me to buy it and bring it to her. I'd never seen it again after we'd gotten home.

"She was a little strange." Rita's voice was quiet. She was testing her weight on the ice of the subject of my dead wife and suggesting with her wide eyes that the box contained the finger of Claire's first boyfriend or the brain of her childhood pet.

"Yes."

Rita's eyes met mine. She knew there was more to the subject, but the box in her hand was more appealing than the conversation. She lifted the lid and tilted her head as she examined the contents.

"What's in there?" I asked.

"All sorts of stuff." She rested it on the shelf closest to her and rifled through the pictures and papers that were inside. Rita lifted a picture close to her face and turned it over, reading the words on the back. "Who's Cole?"

I shrugged. I'd never heard of a Cole. She handed me the photograph and looked around my shoulder as I studied it. It was Claire as a young girl, and she had her arms around a young boy who resembled her.

The back of the picture read: "Claire and Cole, 1997, Lost Lake" in her mother's handwriting. There was something different about Claire in the picture. She was lighter, and her eyes sparkled like they rarely had when I'd been with her. I'd only ever seen her come close to this picture, and that was when she'd been laughing with Anna.

"What else is in there?"

"Ticket stubs, receipts, rolling papers." Rita held them up as noteworthy. Claire had smoked once in a while. It wasn't a big deal to anyone but Rita. "And . . ." she unfolded several sheets of paper, "letters." She read the papers. Her brow was furrowed in confusion. She looked up at me for some explanation, but I didn't have one.

I held out my hand for the papers Rita was holding. One

read: "Never is a fictional place." Another read: "You're the only one I believe." They were all written in the center of the paper and had been folded in eighths, as if handed under a crack in the door or behind a teacher's back. Rita dug through the contents to the bottom of the box and held up the last paper. It was folded into thirds. The color vanished from her skin as she stared at me over the top of the note.

This one says, "I don't want to be here anymore."

Rita took the first load to Goodwill by herself. She said she was leaving, and I nodded without taking my eyes off the picture of Claire and the boy. They were too young to be boyfriend and girlfriend. At least in the picture. He could have been a family friend. I went through each letter and note. There was no hint as to his last name or whether my wife had been in love with him.

I closed the lid on the blue box and carried it down to the kitchen counter. I opened my laptop and searched the Internet for Claire's name in the state of Minnesota. Her image popped up. Several, in fact, which surprised me. I hadn't thought of Claire ever having done anything noteworthy enough to be captured by a photograph and put online that she hadn't told me about. Most of the pictures were general community stories. Claire and a bunch of other kids at the prom. One of her doing a local race to raise money for victims of crimes.

I hit the back button and returned to the web entries. A few articles highlighted the life of Claire before I met her. I scrolled through every listing and skipped through pages two and three listed for my search. The entries started to fragment with either Claire's first or last name, but not both. I was coming to the end of Claire's online personality. The last one that used her full name was only a mention in another larger story.

It was an obituary written in 2004 for a Cole Tyler Heller.

He had died tragically at the age of sixteen, leaving behind Claire's mother and father . . . and his twin sister, Claire Heller. It made no sense. I searched for Cole Tyler Heller and muddled through tiny bits of information until I was forced to concede to the truth. Claire had a brother.

Claire always finely orchestrated the information she shared, but to not mention a twin sibling. Rage crawled up my neck and lodged in the back of my throat. What the fuck had she been thinking? She was twenty-two when I'd met her. This hadn't seemed like a significant entry in the get-to-know-you book of dating? Or when I'd asked her if she had any siblings. Or what her family was like?

"A broken band of freaks," was what she should have said. The catatonic look on her mother's face at our wedding suddenly made perfect sense. The way Claire discussed her childhood with an eerie detachment could finally be explained. Her complete refusal to ever step foot back in Minnesota.

I picked up my phone and dialed her mother's house.

"Hello," my ex-mother-in-law said. The frailty in her voice calmed me enough to keep from screaming at her.

"It's Gabe."

"Hello, Gabe." She didn't sound surprised by my call, almost as if she knew my sister and I were sorting through Claire's stuff and my call was scheduled.

"Claire had a brother?" I wasn't interested in polite conversation.

Claire's mother breathed into the phone. I imagined her starting to cry and looking around the room for support from her husband, who never really held anyone up, including himself. "Yes," she finally said.

"A twin?"

"Yes."

"Why didn't anyone ever tell me?"

She stayed silent, and the rage took over.

"Answer me!" I yelled into the phone.

Through her sobs, Claire's mother said, "Since the day he died, Claire wouldn't let us speak a word about him."

"That's so sick."

"I know, but she loved him so much. More than herself, really. They were inseparable since birth, and we didn't want to hurt her more than she was already."

"Did she talk to anyone? A counselor at school, pastor, a close relative?"

"Not that I know of."

"Your brother doesn't just die and you stop acknowledging that he ever existed."

"You do if you're Claire."

With that one sentence, she made me understand. Claire could do anything, and she often had, whether the rest of the world thought it was okay or not. I took a deep breath and found myself empathizing with my mother-in-law. Both of her children were dead.

"How did he die?"

"He shot himself in the head."

I closed my eyes as if the bullet had just hit me between the eyes. "I'm sorry."

"Claire found him. We thought the two of them had gone together down to the river behind our house, but he'd gone alone. Claire came running home screaming at us to help her. She was covered in blood." Her words caught. "When they put his body on the stretcher and wheeled him away, Claire fell over. I swore she'd died, too."

"What the . . ." My head was spinning. A sweaty sheen covered my back and clung the fabric of my shirt to my chest. I pulled it away, seeking some type of relief.

"She was never the same after that. We'd lost both of our

kids with one shot from a gun."

I couldn't stomach another word. I was going to throw up if she kept talking. "I'm going to go. Sorry to bother you."

"Gabe—"

I ended the call and placed my phone on the counter next to my computer. I wanted to call Anna and tell her all this. Tell her that Claire had lied to us every day she'd known us, or at least that she hadn't told us about her brother. I wanted to betray Claire—to tell her secrets that she'd never shared back then.

30

Anna

IT WAS DIFFERENT THAN WHEN I'd come to Italy in September. Gone was the weight of destruction I'd carried with me then. I'd practically sunk under it. Italy was a cave I'd run to and hidden from the light inside of. I'd told myself and everyone else that I belonged there. The city of Rome had called me to it my entire life, and with end of Josh's, it had been logical for me to go. I wondered if any of that actually made sense.

The world kept moving forward as if Josh and Claire had never even been a part of it, but they had been. They were real for a short time. He was a part of me. Claire was part of Gabe. But Gabe and I were left here without them to figure out how to love each other, even if each of us was missing a half, or two-thirds depending how I looked at it. What exactly was the mathematical definition of your best friend and your spouse being erased from your existence all in the same moment? It was the type of question Claire and Josh would have argued about.

I inhaled and listened to the birds outside my window. I imagined a blue one among the flock of gray that sang to the sun while it rose every morning. Even in the cold of January, they were out there and would stay until all of Rome was awake.

My phone rang and I answered it without looking. I knew

was Gabe. He was the only one who called at this time. My mother usually called during dinner. She had a knack for finding the most inconvenient time for me to speak to her about how I was ruining my life. Gabe had the gift of always calling when I was in bed. Either dreaming about him or sometimes Claire or Josh. I opened my eyes and reached for the phone.

"Gabe?" I said, and he didn't answer. There was nothing but silence on the other end. I sat up to see if it affected the connection. "Gabe?"

"I'm here." His words were somber.

I checked the clock on the bureau next to my bed. It was after midnight at home. "What are you doing up?"

He exhaled into the phone. I pulled the comforter up closer to my ears and settled into the sound of Gabe's voice. "I'm lying here staring at the ceiling."

"Oh," was what I said. I'd been in the exact same position a hundred nights since I'd moved to Italy. There were never any answers written in the cracks of the plaster above me.

"Did you know Claire had a brother?"

I stopped breathing and moving. I stayed very still and let his question form in my mind. Did I know? How did Gabe know?

"She did?" I was noncommittal with the question tone. I didn't want to lie to Gabe, but I wouldn't go searching for answers that would only hurt him more.

"Oh, yeah. Not just a brother. A twin."

I thought he might be drunk. "Gabe—"

"You know what pisses me off the most about my wife having a brother she never mentioned to me?"

"What?" The words were soft, leaking from around the fear clogging my throat.

"The fact that all the years we were together, I tried . . . so hard, I tried, to figure out what was fucking going on with my wife. What would make her happy. What had made her sad. I spent so much time wondering which of my actions or words affected her it drove me almost mad. But the whole fucking time, it had nothing to do with me. I could have been sitting back and drinking a beer. Whatever I did never changed a thing."

"Gabe, I'm sure that's not true."

"How do you know what's true?"

"Because I knew Claire, and there's not a doubt in my mind that she loved you."

"He killed himself," Gabe said. His words were filled with disgust. I wasn't sure who it was directed at.

I sat up in my bed. "Gabe, this isn't helping." I wanted him to let all of it go. He had to find a way to leave the past in the past or neither of us was ever going to have a future. "You've got to let her go."

"Let her go?" he practically yelled. "If she were here right now, I'd kill her myself. Crazy bitch. She—"

I didn't want to ask. The words wouldn't stay down. Like bad seafood, they came rushing out. "She what?" I closed my eyes and prayed for Gabe's next statement to not ruin us.

He sighed. In my head I could see his chest rising and his face relaxing as he exhaled. Gabe was calming down. "Nothing," he said.

I didn't ask any more questions about Claire and her brother. They were both gone, and Gabe and I were still alive. We could only be together if he stopped questioning the past. "Gabe, I need you to move on. I know it's easy for someone to say to another person, but this is me—not some book or some stranger at work. I was there the whole time. When you loved her and when you lost her. I was there. You've got to trust me on this."

"I love you, Anna." I started to respond, and he added, "But you don't know what it's like. Josh never had any secrets. He was a good man entitled to all the love, respect, and mourning that's surrounded you since he died. He was worthy. Claire wasn't."

My stomach churned. I wanted to punch him in the face. Gabe was wrong. "Claire was beautiful. I loved her, and so did you." There were times when I stared at my ceiling and the only thing I was certain of was that Claire might have saved my life. At least what was left of it. I wasn't going to let anyone, especially Gabe, demean her memory. "If you're going to talk this way, or even feel this way, you can't call me anymore."

"Anna . . ."

I closed my eyes. I couldn't lose him, too, but I would. I'd choose Claire over him, even today, when there was nothing left of her but a memory.

"I'm sorry."

I exhaled and fell back onto my pillow. "Gabe, I love you. Let's leave it at that. Let go of the accident. What's it going to change now?"

"I don't know." He was calmer. "I've been working out. Trying to live again. I clean and buy groceries and do my laundry." I hung on his every word. "But the accident is haunting me. She's haunting me."

"She would never do that."

"This is the last thing I'm going to say about her, because I know you loved her. When I first met Claire, she was exciting and surprising and unlike any woman I'd ever known. She wasn't just beautiful; she was fascinating." I thought of all the ways Claire had enchanted me, too. "She changed, though. Sometime in the past few years . . . it was as if something flipped inside her and she was different. I could predict how she'd feel about things, but I'd never know how she'd react. Some days it was so bad, I hardly said a word."

I knew exactly what Gabe meant. Claire had been enticing

but dangerous. She'd demanded a complete level of control that no one else in the situation even had known was possible. When something had fallen out of her reach, she'd struggled. None of this mattered now, though.

"In the last few years she became more . . . difficult."

"I'm done."

"Anna—"

"It can't be me. I'm not the person you can talk to about this. I'm sorry. I want to help you, but I don't want to talk about them anymore. I'm finally doing better. I feel better. I'm eating and sleeping and walking and breathing. I look at the sky, and I don't cry. I talk to people, and they make me laugh. I can't keep doing this with you. I won't."

"I'm sorry, but doesn't the accident still run through your mind? That night? Isn't it always somewhere near you?"

"Gabe, I've really tried to put this all behind me."

"They said she hadn't been drinking, but I bought her drinks. Claire was always drinking."

"Gabe—"

"There were no skid marks. Josh wasn't wearing a seat belt." He was getting worked up again. "None of it makes any sense. Why the hell was she in the car with him in the first place? I stopped for gas. That was all. We weren't supposed to be doing anything except going home to party more—"

"Stop!" I screamed at him. Things I should have said to make him stop kept running through my head. If he kept asking these questions, he was going to ruin everything. He had to just let them go. "I can't keep going back to this."

"I'm sorry." He exhaled into the phone. "I'll stop."

"You will?" There was no other choice.

"I promise. Holding onto this isn't worth losing you. I'll try to let it go."

I wanted to tell him what Claire had told me in Josh's car

the night she'd died. That this was all going to seem like a few horrible months and then it'd be over. I was afraid to say her name. I'd never say it to Gabe again. He couldn't see her clearly, and her words wouldn't make him feel better. I clung to every syllable of them, knowing that she was right. I just had to get through this. "I love you, Gabe."

"I love you, too. Come home."

STAGE III

ILLUMINATION

31

Gabe

IT WAS VALENTINE'S DAY. I only knew because, even though I didn't watch television anymore or talk to many people, it was all over the radio. Even satellite radio. It was impossible to escape. The year before, Claire, Josh, Anna, and I had all huddled together in a dive bar, drank shots, and passed out at Anna and Josh's house. Anna hadn't needed a big declaration of Josh's love and Claire had just wanted to be with them, so I'd been off the hook, too. I'd still had to get her a card and a present because Claire thought the no-present part was insane.

I remembered the jealousy I'd felt when Josh had told me he hadn't had to run to the mall at lunch to join the rest of us in our last-minute search for a gift.

"Call Anna," he'd suggested. He'd said it so flippantly, as if it wouldn't cause some seismic rumble beneath the surface of my day. It was *that* easy for Josh, though. Anna was pleasant and reasonable and not jealous. Josh had no idea how uncomplicated Anna was.

She would know exactly what to get Claire, but if Claire ever found out I'd called Anna, she'd be pissed. Somehow, I was magically supposed to figure out the perfect gift for a woman who'd never once gotten me one. Claire's gifts to me had always been veiled representations of her own needs. Like the new bathing suit—for Valentine's Day—which was the predecessor for a lengthy conversation on what tropical island we should go to. I didn't even think that in her own head Claire had realized what she'd been doing. When she was alive, I tried not to spend too much time thinking about the inside of her head. I found myself dwelling there quite often since Rita had found the blue box.

I didn't call Anna. I wasn't even sure Italy celebrated Valentine's Day, and if they didn't, I wasn't going to be the one who reminded her of it. I'd mailed her a note. Not some horribly cheesy, bright shiny red heart card, but just the stationery I'd taken from the Hotel DuPont when we'd been there. It was inside the leather folder with the room service menu and other amenity information. I'd pushed it to the side and wondered if anyone ever made use of the hotel stationary provided, and then I'd taken it with me.

If Anna wasn't going to let me keep her, I needed something. It felt crazy, but I had to have something to remember her by. When I'd addressed the envelope to her Italian address, I'd laughed at how stupid I'd been. A piece of paper from a hotel wouldn't make her come home, and it would never fill the need I had for her. Only Anna could do that.

I closed the garage door and shut out the night's darkness before turning off the engine of my car. I needed a hobby. If I weren't going to drink myself to sleep every night, I needed to do something to feel as if I were actually living this life. Skiing, fishing, painting. Maybe I would cultivate an interest in Civil War reenactments . . . although, history was my least favorite subject.

I mindlessly carried the mail into the house and put it on the island with the stack from the day before. In my refrigerator, I found two grapefruits and a takeout container from the Italian place by my office. Eating healthier was more work than my fall diet of Doritos and IPAs, but I was determined not to sink any further. Working out again kept my body healthy. My hope was that my mind would catch up.

The mail was an endless pile of circulars I never opened, catalogs I never read, and the last remaining bills that I couldn't pay online. I flipped through them to make sure nothing important was missed, and stopped when I reached a letter from Anna. I pushed everything else to the side and stared at it in the middle of the counter. It wasn't a card. It was an old-fashioned letter that was addressed in pen with her handwriting. I wanted to call her, but the intelligent thing to do would be to read it first. What if she was telling me she never wanted to see me again? No. I dismissed that fear. Anna wasn't the type of person to do that and the timing seemed cruel.

Gabe,

Of all the first holidays, Valentine's Day approaching is hitting me the hardest, which is crazy. It never meant a thing when Josh was alive. Last year, the four of us spent it together, and now this year . . . we're all alone.

Here they celebrate La Festa Degli Innamorati, "The Day of Lovers," and it makes me think of you. Husband, boyfriend, provider, partner were all Josh. He meant so much to me and the family we didn't yet have.

Lover, though, that is only you.

This is the first holiday since they died that instead of missing them, I'm missing someone— something—else . . . you. I've decided it doesn't matter if we started as friends or if the only reason we ever met was because someone sacred to both of us initiated our introduction. I'm even convinced they'd want us to be together. I know you're laughing, but there's a strong possibility they would. When I walk through the ruins here of societies long obliterated, I read all the stories of romance and deception. The Romans were a sordid bunch. Claire would have loved them all, and Josh would have loved us for making him come here, even though he never would have actually found the value in the expense.

If it were us instead of them . . . if a thousand years from now, someone were to read our story, would it seem so horrible that we continued to love each other in a new way? If it were Claire and Josh, I'd want them to make a life together. I swear I would. Although, if it were Josh and Claire, we both know they'd kill each other. Her salon appointments alone would drive him to the brink of insanity.

The man who works at the coffee bar down the block told me that February 14th is Valentine's Day because on this day, male birds choose their partners. In further evidence of his claim, the birds outside my window have been eerily quiet today, as if something very big is happening in their world.

I want you to choose me if you'll still have me.

I hope you're well.

I miss you.

Love,

Anna

I exhaled and realized I'd been holding my breath the entire time I read her letter, as if I were afraid of Anna. The only thing I feared was losing her. I'd experienced the possibility of that loss the last time we'd spoken on the phone. Her letter was different. It was a new approach to us. I'd get over Claire's lies and the accident. I'd leave it all behind for a future with Anna.

I replaced the letter in the envelope, set it on top of my keys and phone, and sorted through the remaining stack of mail. Most of it was junk, but then I picked up a thin envelope without the usual markings of promotional garbage. The sender was the Chester County Coroner's Office. I tore open the envelope and was faced with the toxicology report I'd requested months before.

I skimmed through the details of my wife and skipped through the list of drugs qualitatively tested for. Amphetamines, barbiturates, benzodiazepines, cannabinoids, fentanyl, the list went on and on. Drug families I'd never even heard of. Finally, I found alcohol. The result was negative.

When the police had told me at the hospital that Claire had no alcohol in her system, I'd sworn to myself that they'd been wrong. I'd practically demanded an autopsy. The fact that I'd been admitting to her guilt and forcing an investigation into a car crash the police had already deemed an accident hadn't mattered to me. It was as if Claire and I were still having an argument, and she was winning from her grave.

I scanned the rest of the report. Negative, negative, negative. Once in a while, a normal would show up, but there was nothing out of the ordinary. Claire crashed Josh's car into a tree on a beautiful, clear night, without any trace of alcohol or drugs in her system. The idea of suicide tried to creep into my thoughts, but I couldn't let it. My head ached with the effort to keep the truth away, and I grabbed Anna's letter and went to bed without eating.

32

Anna

"YOU'RE ABOUT FIVE MONTHS ALONG."

"What?" The same deep shockwave that soared through me when he'd told me two weeks ago that I was pregnant returned. I'd come home from the doctors to the letter Gabe had written to me on Hotel DuPont Stationery. It'd been the happiest day of my life.

At the time, I'd been reeling from the realization that I was in love with my best friend. That was enough. Gabe was more than I thought I'd have after Josh's death, and this was just . . . everything I'd ever wanted.

"Five months. What were you doing last October?" Dr. Russo was teasing me.

"I was at a wedding. Back home."

"Well, it must have been some affair, because you left with the *mother* of all favors." I looked over at the ultrasound screen next to me. "Literally," the doctor added. "Do you want to know if you are having a boy or a girl?"

I couldn't take my eyes off the baby inside me. It was a miracle.

"Anna?"

"Oh. I'm sorry." In all the years I'd wanted a baby, it never mattered if it was a girl or boy. "I don't know. I haven't even told the father."

The doctor sat back in his chair and stared at me. He let the ultrasound wand slide off my belly. "Do not do this alone if you do not have to."

"It's not that. It's just all so sudden. I'd been trying to have a baby for years, and . . ." *And what, Anna? You haven't even told the father, and you don't think he wants children, so you don't really want to share this with someone who's not going to be happy.*

"Tell him," were the doctor's last words on the subject. He printed pictures, wrote some things on a piece of paper, and sealed them all in an envelope. "If you want to know the sex, it's in here." He handed me the envelope. "I'll see you back next month. Until then, call if you have any questions."

"I will." I held the envelope in both hands. I was going to have a baby. "Thank you."

I walked home from his office, knowing it wasn't the doctor I should be thanking. It was Gabe. I owed him for so much more than this baby, but it was the only thing that mattered now. All of the anger and confusion and sadness had slipped away. It was replaced by tiny hands and twinkle toes.

I could give this to him, too. If Gabe had ever thought of having a child, of being a father, then he'd want to know about this. I could take away his pain the way this baby had taken away mine, or I could further ruin his life with the burden of a child he never wanted. I shook my head. This baby would never be a burden.

In my heart, I knew it was a girl.

I slipped the envelope into my underwear drawer as soon as I got to my apartment and called Gabe. It was six thirty in the morning at home. He'd be on his way to work.

"Good morning," he said.

I wasn't sure there was a time I could call him that he wouldn't sound like he was expecting my call. "Hey. How are you?" I glanced around the room, searching for something to calm the nervous jitters infiltrating my body.

"Good for a Monday. What are you doing?"

I stared at the drawer with the envelope. "I was just out for a walk."

"Oh, the life of you Europeans. Just walking around in the middle of the day."

Gabe was winding up to make fun of me, which I would normally love, but I interrupted him with, "Will you come to Italy?"

"Huh?" The radio in the background of his car turned all the way down.

"I want you to come to Italy."

"I was hoping you'd just come home."

"I know." He'd asked me every single time I spoke to him, and he signed every email with, "Come home."

"But if you're not, then I'm going to have to come to Italy, I guess."

"You'll come?" I was as relieved as if he'd told me he wanted me to have his baby, which he hadn't and maybe never would. My mind was swallowed with possibilities. If he didn't want anything to do with me or the baby, that was fine. I'd have it alone, and then I'd never be alone again.

"I'll come." Gabe's voice was smooth, and the tone sent waves of need across the surface of my skin and deep down into my core. I lowered my chin and raised my shoulders, seeking to control the lustful frenzy I'd never felt before. I wanted him here immediately. "When do you want me?" He was taunting me.

"Can you come tomorrow?" Two could play this game. "I'm ready for you right now."

He paused, and I used the seconds to catch my breath. "Let me see what I can work out."

"Okay," I managed to answer, but I was already lying on my

bed touching myself to the sound of his voice.

"I'll email you later when I know something." I arched my back. My forearm rested on my belly. I closed my eyes and let his voice warm me with my hand. "Anna, you okay?"

"I'm fine." *As long as you keep talking.* My eyes closed as I let myself be lost in the touch of my hand. Ripples of quiet need rushed from my fingers to the muscles of my legs, and then I could only feel one spot on my body as my face was covered with heat. I moved the phone away from my mouth so he couldn't hear me panting. "Call me, though. Doesn't matter what time."

I thought of Gabe inside me.

He'd be here soon.

"I love you," he said.

"I love you, too." He hung up, and I dropped the phone on the bed next to me and came to the thought of Gabe's hands touching me.

33

Gabe

I KNOW I PROMISED TO let it go.

I tried. I really did. The dreams kept coming. I'd bolt up in my bed, sweating, my heart racing. All because I thought my wife had murdered my best friend. In the nightmares, Claire did it with a knife or a gun. Sometimes she pushed Josh down a flight of stairs. In every dream, Anna and I just sat and watched them the same way we'd watched them argue for years.

Claire and Josh had a special relationship. Josh would have called it an annoyance, but he tolerated her. God love him. He put up with all Claire's antics as if he'd married her himself. I thought that, deep down, he kind of liked her. At the very least liked the fact that she not-so-gently pushed him to do things he never would have on his own, but I might have just been telling myself that.

I was fucking his wife. The least I owed him was to find out how he actually died. I wished Anna wanted to know, too. This would all be so much easier if I could talk to her about it, but the last time I'd tried, she threatened to cut all contact with me.

The Kennett Square Police Department looked like an old firehouse. I parked across the street. I had the toxicology report, the autopsy report, the police report, and Claire's death certificate in my hand. When I glanced down at the evidence of her innocence, I started to wonder what I was doing here.

To me, though, the documents were proof of her guilt. The police didn't know how she'd drunk or, worse, had acted like she'd been drinking. They didn't know she'd had a brother who'd committed suicide. They didn't know she'd scared me.

"Can I help you?" the officer behind the front desk asked.

I looked down at the name on the police report. "Yes. Is Officer Reeves here?"

She nodded over her shoulder to the officer who showed up at my door the night of the accident.

"Mr. Hawkins." He had spotted me and was already making his way to me.

"Yes." I stood up straight. I had to know the truth about what had happened before it destroyed me. "Do you have a minute?" I held up all the reports. "I have a few questions."

"Sure. Come on back."

I followed him into a room with a small table and four chairs around it. The walls were mostly brown. I was mostly nauseated.

"What can I do for you?"

I laid out the reports in front of me. "Every single one of these documents state that my wife wasn't under the influence of any drugs or alcohol."

He didn't ask to see them. "Yes."

"But when I came home that night, she had a glass of wine in her hand. When we went out, she was drinking."

"Do you think *all* the reports are wrong?"

Deep breath. "No. I believe my wife was sober." The officer looked confused. "But I don't think it was an accident."

He sat very still for a moment. He understood exactly what I was saying, and unlike, Anna, he could stand to hear it. "Mr. Hawkins, you knew your wife better than anyone, but what you're suggesting—"

"Is horrible. I know. It's also haunting me. I need to know

the truth. It wasn't just my wife in the car. It was my best friend, too." Officer Reeves studied me, probably making sure I wasn't the crazy one. "I'd underestimated my wife in the past. Not anymore. I need to know what you saw. What you thought that's not included in this report."

He leaned his forearms on the table between us and exhaled loudly. He looked me in the eye. "When I arrived at the scene of the loss, my first impression was that alcohol or drugs were involved. There were no skid marks, no signs of averting the loss," he said. His voice was steady. "But impressions aren't evidence. We can't rule out mechanical failure, animal, driver distraction . . . there are many factors to consider in an accident." He had more to say. There was more to it.

"Go on. Please. I'm the only one still asking questions."

"The passenger . . . your friend . . . had been ejected." Breathing was suddenly difficult. I'd been so engrossed in Claire's role in the accident I'd let myself ignore Josh. At least, as much as my subconscious would allow. "We transported him to the hospital, but it was clear he wasn't going to live."

"And my wife?"

"Unbelievably, she was breathing. I waited with her until EMS arrived. Her injuries were extensive, but she was alive."

"Claire would be the one to decide when she'd die. Not a tree." Bitterness crept up my throat.

"She moaned several times and I thought she said, 'I don't want to be here anymore.'" My heart stopped. I wasn't breathing anymore. "At the time, I thought she was talking about the side of the road, but now that you're here, I'm assuming it means more to you than I'd originally thought."

"Yes," I thought I said. She killed him. She killed herself and took Josh with her. Sick bitch.

"Mr. Hawkins?"

"Yes. Sorry. What does this mean? If Claire killed herself

and Josh, what does it mean?"

"Unfortunately, we still don't know for sure exactly what happened on that road." But I did know. "And even if we did, she's gone. He's gone. I'm assuming the insurance has settled all the claims based on her liability?"

"They did."

"Then that really is the end."

I had to tell Anna. She had to know. She was going to hate me and Claire and would never want to see me again. She'd run as far from the truth as possible, including her relationship with me. Maybe that was why she wouldn't talk about it now—she already knew . . .

"Can I ask you something else?"

"Sure." The way he treated me made me feel fragile.

"Would you want to know?"

He thought for a moment and said, "I think I'd be just like you. I'd have to know."

Anna had to know.

34

Anna

I WAITED AT THE BAGGAGE claim. The bench hurt my back, but most things did these days. It had been forty-eight hours since I'd called Gabe, and somehow, he'd made it so he could stay a week.

Josh would have never even considered it if he'd been in Gabe's position, but he wasn't. He was dead. I stopped thinking about it and went to the bathroom again. I shifted to the side in front of the mirror. The coat I wore hid my belly well, but still my hands had a way of finding the small bump. I faced forward. You couldn't tell I was pregnant at all. A little extra weight in my face, but I was in Italy. Pasta, pizza, wine. I was eating my way through a huge life change. A few pounds were probably expected.

I walked out into the bright sunshine coming in the windows of the airport. My eyes adjusted just as I saw a new group of people entering the area. My breath caught. Gabe was near. I could feel it.

Mothers, fathers, couples, grandparents flowed into the room, searching signs for which conveyor belt held their bags. I looked at each person as they passed, afraid I might miss him in my haste. He must have been on the back of the plane.

I walked closer to the crowd. My heart fell as the last few passengers made their way in. It wasn't his plane.

"Anna." His voice behind me touched me from my head to my toes.

I exhaled and turned around.

Gabe was holding a bouquet of flowers. He was bigger than I'd imagined him in my bed the past few weeks. A glorious beast with a sweet smile and roses in his hand. The sight of him threw me emotionally, and without a word, I launched myself into his arms and kissed him. I didn't care who was standing near us or that my purse had fallen and was painfully swinging off my elbow. I wanted him to press me against the wall so I could wrap my legs around his back. I wanted Gabe to fuck me.

As if he knew exactly what I was feeling, he responded with the force that was everything I had remembered. His tongue in my mouth. His arms lifted me closer to him. His smell. His hair. All of it was taking me over.

He placed me back on the ground in front of him. I rested my head on his hard chest. He was back in shape. Back to how his body was before the accident. I laid my hand flat over his heart, and I watched as I ran it down to his stomach.

He caught it with his own. "Let's get out of here." His voice was thick with the same need building between my legs.

I'd thought we'd go out to eat and I'd be able to tell him about the baby in a civilized manner. Then, I'd hoped, we'd go back to my apartment and make love. My body had other plans. It wanted Gabe naked more than it wanted food. The pregnancy hormones had rendered me hornier than I ever thought possible.

"I have a car waiting." I stepped back from him and collected my thoughts. "Did you check a bag?"

"No. This is it." He had a backpack and one carry-on suitcase.

I took a deep breath. This was really happening. "Let's go."

He held out the flowers. "These are for you."

It was sweet and romantic. I waited for the Gabesque joke about them, but he only seemed pleased with himself as he held them out to me. They were pink roses surrounded by greens and smaller purple flowers.

I inhaled their thick scent without considering the queasiness it might bring. All I felt was love. "Thank you," I said and took Gabe's hand.

We walked to the waiting car and got into the backseat together. Gabe took my hand and kissed it. Italy felt different with him here. It'd been this enchanting, wondrous place where I'd always wanted to live, but with Gabe here with me, it felt like home.

We rode in silence the whole forty-five minutes. I sat with a giant grin on my face and my head on his shoulder, and Gabe stared out the window at the city I'd fallen in love with. When the taxi stopped in front of my building, Gabe pulled out his wallet. I stopped him and paid the driver. "*Grazie*," I said. Neither of these men could possibly comprehend how thankful I was.

He looked up at my building and picked up his suitcase. His flexed arm made me want him to carry me instead. "Nice place."

"Thanks." I unlocked it and the door inside the foyer that led to the elevator. At the fifth floor, I led him to my loft.

Gabe stepped inside and left his suitcase and backpack by the door, seemingly taking in every inch of my mostly white and a bit drafty apartment.

I had to say something or my clothes would be off in a minute and my stomach would say it all. "Thank you for coming." It was all I could come up with. I'd practiced this speech with us at a restaurant. First we'd order, and then I'd tell him. After he'd had a big glass of wine. "Do you want some wine?"

He shook his head and stared at me until I swore he could

see to the bottom of my soul.

I ignored his answer and walked across the room to the kitchen. I opened the wine on the counter and poured him a glass. He laughed as I worked, moving so close to me that I could feel the shaking of his body and the heat he emitted. He moved my hair to the side and kissed the back of my neck. I closed my eyes and leaned on the counter in front of me. Three months had been too long.

"I need to talk to you."

"And take this coat off," he said.

I looked down at the only thing still hiding my secret. "Yes." I handed him the wine. "Drink."

He took the glass and gave me a foot of space to breathe. He drank the wine, never taking his eyes off me.

The fear of him being angry or, worse—wanting to leave— rushed through me, leaving in its wake the realization of how much I needed him.

"Gabe—" The words didn't come. None of them.

He unbuttoned my coat and slipped it off my shoulders. He placed it on the chair next to us. With my face in his hands, he kissed me until I nearly forgot what I was supposed to tell him.

His lips moved to my neck and he said, "You're even more beautiful than I remembered, Anna."

"That's because I'm pregnant." The air was sucked from the room as he froze with my face still in his hands.

Relief flowed through me. I'd told him.

"What?" Gabe stepped back, and his hurt-filled eyes studied me.

I straightened my back and ran my hands over my belly. It wasn't as far out as my boobs, yet, but I was obviously pregnant. "I'm going to have a baby."

He only stared at my stomach and then stared back at me.

"Your baby."

His expression changed immediately. The lost torture was replaced by wonder. He inhaled sharply. "My . . . baby?"

I nodded and closed the small distance between us. I took his hand and put it on my stomach. "Yes. Our baby." A million thoughts flooded my mind, but I let him have this moment.

"How?" He kissed me, pulled back, looked me in the eye, and then kissed me again. "When?"

"At Julie's wedding."

His head dipped down as the words sunk in. "You were pregnant at Christmas and didn't tell me?"

"I didn't know. My periods have been off for a while, and with the accident and the move, everything's been off." Nothing would ever be the same. "I finally went to the doctor's two weeks ago, and he told me I was pregnant. I just found out when I called you that I'm five months along."

"When are you due?"

"July ninth."

"How?" He shook his head. "Do . . . do . . ."

"It's yours." I was hurt, but I didn't deserve to be. I was the one who kept leaving him. "I haven't been with anyone else."

"I wasn't going to ask that." Gabe lifted my shirt over my head. He kissed me again, and I melted into the idea of this being our baby. He unhooked my bra and took my breast in his mouth, and I had to hold on to him to keep from falling. The sight of his tongue on my nipple almost made me come. I wasn't the same woman I'd been before the pregnancy. I was insatiable. Especially when it came to the man standing in front of me.

"I've missed you," I said and let my head fall back.

He got on his knees and ran his hands over my stomach, peppering the baby bump with kisses before pulling each of my shoes off and then my leggings.

I throbbed. It was probably everywhere, but I could only

feel the pounding between my legs. I fought to breathe as he slipped his hands in my underwear and touched me.

"Gabe." I rocked my hips, unable to stop myself.

My jaw dropped in protest when he moved away and stood, but he silenced me with a kiss as he picked me up and strode through the small space of my apartment. My bed was soft, but I wanted his hard body against me

"Tell me this isn't a dream." He was standing there looking at my naked body in complete and utter adoration.

"Take off your shirt," I said instead.

He took off all his clothes and climbed on top of me. Before he let his weight fall, he moved to the side.

"It's okay. You can't hurt us."

"My dick is so hard right now that I might break you in half." His breathing was heavy. Every inch of his body was strong and strung tight with anticipation, but the look in his eyes was vulnerable.

I leaned down and took him in my mouth. He was larger than I remembered and rock-hard. I sucked him until the wetness between my legs no longer cared about his needs. I climbed on top of him and rode him for a few seconds before I came. I was selfish, but I could get away with it. I was pregnant. I took it all in. Gabe's dick, our baby . . . a life for a life.

I was still coming down from my climax when Gabe flipped me with one smooth motion. He pulled me to the edge of the bed and thrust into me. I ran my tongue across the inside of my top lip and studied his chest. I closed my eyes and focused on the sensation of his body touching mine, and when the tightness started to build again, I arched and took everything he was giving. He didn't say a word. Just kept fucking me until we both came with him inside me. But he was already inside me. The thought made me smile as he tried to regain his breath.

I stole a minute to be thankful. For Gabe and this baby.

35

Gabe

I OPENED THE BATHROOM DOOR and looked out as I dried my body. Anna was lying on her side facing me. "Did I wake you?" I whispered as if there were anyone else to wake.

"No. The absence of you did." She stared at my chest. "Are you coming back to bed?"

I flung the towel over the door and crawled between the sheets, pulling her close to me and inhaling her scent. "I have a lot of questions," I said. My mind hadn't stopped since my eyes had opened.

With her head on my shoulder and her hand on my chest, she said, "I have just one."

I played with her hair. "You go first then."

The moment of reckoning. Things were about to take a turn. *Their* names were going to be brought up, because no matter what Anna and I ever did in our lives, Claire and Josh would somehow always be with us. They would haunt us until I told Anna the truth.

She rolled over more until she was almost on top of me. Her chin on my chest, and she stared at me. Her eyes were bright against her soft skin. "Claire told me you didn't want kids." Some sliver of guilt tugged at my mind. She knew. Claire had known I'd been avoiding the subject. I stayed still, waiting for Anna. "So if you feel trapped or disappointed or forlorn . . . I want you to tell me. Because this is the best thing that's ever happened to me, and I can do it alone."

"Anna—"

"You always take care of everyone else. I don't want you to be here just because this is your responsibility."

I kissed her. I could barely keep my hands off her, even when she sounded like an insane person. "This is going to be cruel to hear, but I need you to know the truth." She stayed very still in my arms. I was going to sound like an asshole, but she needed to know. "I didn't want to have children with *Claire*." The warmth inside me was replaced by a nimble chill at the mention of her name. It slid down my back, and I pulled Anna closer to me to ward it off.

"Why?"

"I loved Claire. When we first met, I just wanted to be around her. She made everything brighter somehow."

"I know what you mean. I loved her that way, too."

"But the longer we were together and the more I came to understand her, I realized there was something wrong. That light wasn't always on, and when she slipped into the darkness . . ."

"Claire could get into a mood, but she was still Claire."

"She scared me."

"What?" She sat up and faced me.

"There was something very wrong with her, and the thought of her and I raising a child scared me."

"There was nothing wrong—" Anna stopped and stared at the wall to our left. She was lost in her own thoughts.

"It's okay. I know you loved her and you were never anything but loyal to her. I just needed you to know how I felt. You have to believe me, you and this baby are the only two things I want in this life."

She nodded and faced me again. "I do believe you. I feel the same way."

Anna struggled to button her jeans, and after a few minutes of not being able to, she grabbed a rubber band, hooked it through the buttonhole, and then twisted it around the button. It was cute, but then she looked at me in defeat.

"What do you say we go buy you some maternity clothes today?" I asked. I pulled her toward me so I could rest my hand on her stomach. It was a slight contour but could still be hidden if I hadn't kept her naked as much as possible. I ran my hand over it in amazement. My baby was in there.

"Because I'm a fat cow?"

"You're not a fat cow."

"Big-boned?" she asked.

"Husky maybe." I nuzzled my lips into the side of her neck where it tickled her. "You'll feel better if your clothes fit."

"I'd feel better if the clothes I already own fit."

"Getting fat is the best part of this."

She laughed at me and pushed me down on the couch. She straddled me and kissed me. "You know what the best part is?"

I forgot what we were talking about.

"I can't get enough of you. Of it." She rubbed my dick until it was hard. "I just want to fuck you all day long." I can't imagine what my face looked like. Pure exaltation. Shock.

I kissed her again and took off her shirt. "Clothes will be a good investment."

"For four months?"

"You're getting pregnant again as soon as this baby delivers." I took her breast in my mouth. It was bigger. Swollen. Her nipple protruded farther than it used to. I sucked on it until it was rock-hard between my tongue and my lips. "Does that hurt?"

Her head was tilted back and her breaths were coming in

short little pants. "No."

I slipped my fingers up the leg of her shorts and moved her panties to the side. Anna lifted up a little, letting me press a finger into her.

Her breath caught. "That doesn't hurt either," she said.

"No?" I kept my finger moving as I kissed her neck. I could feel her heartbeat race as I moved my lips from her shoulder to her ear. With my other hand I squeezed her nipple. Hard. I wanted her to come. "Eyes up, Anna." I wanted her to see me while she came.

She was wet. The touch of her sent my blood coursing through my body as it settled and throbbed in my now hard dick. Anna lifted her head. I pressed two fingers inside her, moved my thumb to her clit. I touched her there until my heavy breaths matched her own.

I played and pressed and kissed her until she moaned again. I didn't let her breathe until she collapsed on top of me.

"Promise you'll never leave me," she said and tightened her arms around my neck.

"Never." I laid her down beneath me.

We walked. Apparently everyone walked around Rome. It was sixty degrees and the perfect weather to explore the city. At home, winter was still lingering. The temperature had been thirty-eight degrees the day I'd left, and I'd been bundled in a winter coat and the scarf Anna had made for me. Now, I was walking around this ancient city with her and wearing only a hoodie.

She browsed through the stores, stopping to touch something or pick up a trinket. We wandered through the streets with their lumpy pavements of stones and shops and cafes everywhere, and we held hands almost the entire time. On the rare occasion I was more than three feet from her, I watched her in awe. She was mine and carrying my baby. Five months along. A few times, that night in St. Michaels tried to break through my thoughts, and I pushed the memories aside. Anna was pregnant because it was meant to be. Even if it had begun in a torrent of anger and sadness. None of that was still between us today.

Faire Dodo was the maternity store Anna's friend had recommended. Anna thought the name was French and meant to sleep, or sleep tight in English, but she'd laughed and said she was just guessing.

"Don't listen to me," she said and opened the door to the store.

"Why? I think you're doing pretty well with Italian." She stopped walking and stared at me with anticipation. "What?"

"Are you making fun of me?"

"No!"

"I'm terrible. I still have to ask everyone to slow down."

"Well, at lunch I had no idea what was going on. When you and that waiter were laughing, I just assumed it was at me."

She leaned into me and rested her hands on my chest.

I kissed her. I couldn't not. When she touched me, I had to have her.

"I would never laugh at you."

I raised my eyebrows at her.

"Well, maybe sometimes, but never at your expense or with a waiter."

I kissed her again before remembering what we were even doing in this store instead of in her bed or her shower or on her countertop. "Let's get you some clothes."

She moseyed through the store without much interest. The saleswoman came over and talked to her in Italian and smiled at me. She led Anna to the corner of the store where the denim and casual shirts were. While Anna lingered there, the woman selected dresses and other items and put them in a dressing room for her.

I was immersed in baby. There were baby clothes, lotions, toys. The store felt pure just because of its contents. The bright walls and pastel colors hid the late employees and missed shipments and shoplifters. Anna left me sitting in a chair while she pulled the curtain of her dressing room closed.

"Your first?" the saleslady asked in English when she left Anna.

The reality hit me. There would be more. Anna and I could have six kids. Maybe some of them conceived in a relationship. I nodded before managing to get out, "Yes."

"She's lovely." We were normal. This lady was acting like we were adorable even.

"Yes."

Anna tried on a bunch of things and finally emerged wearing a pink sleeveless dress with a low cut V-neck. There were ruffles around the collar that made it even sweeter than the color.

"You're beautiful."

"Where would I wear this?"

"To a wedding."

"Oh God, please tell me we don't have any of them to go to for a while."

"Maybe ours," I said.

Anna stopped playing with the ruffles and stared at me. It was only for a second. She broke into a smile and laughed as if I were joking. The idea was far from absurd. Baby . . . marriage . . . slightly out of order, but not ridiculous. Anna's reaction made a wedding seem farfetched. She was right. Maybe we should start with a date instead.

In the end, she selected two pairs of jeans, three leggings, four shirts, a cardigan sweater, and the pink dress. The lady bagged it all up, and I paid for it.

"You don't have to do that," Anna said as I signed the credit card receipt.

"I want to."

We carried our bags and bought hot chocolate to drink while we sat on the Spanish Steps. The sun had dipped low in the sky, and the evening felt more like March than the day had. Anna huddled close to me and let out a large yawn, which she tried to cover.

"I'll carry you home," I whispered through her hair.

"People will stare." She nuzzled in closer.

"Let them." She slipped her hand in mine, and I held it between my legs. Her nearness was making it impossible to be in public. I rubbed her hand against my inside thigh and moved it back to rest it on my dick.

Anna moaned a little near my ear. "You're naughty, Gabe Hawkins."

"I know. Let's go home."

She stood and pulled me to my feet.

I held out my arms. "Last chance."

She just laughed and shook her head before leading me down the stairs. We dodged couples and families every few feet who were just sitting, watching, or talking as if they didn't have a care in the world.

We turned down an alley covered in stones with a step down every ten or fifteen feet. Green vines covered the tops of the buildings and climbed down the walls. Some almost touched the ground. I pressed Anna against the wall of one of the buildings and kissed her again. The day had overtaken me. Her, the city, a new version of vacation, maternity shopping . . . it was all changing the makeup of my life, and I couldn't resist it.

"I love you," she said when I finally let her go.

I stood up straight. "I love you, too." Then the guilt just about stole the breath from my chest. I needed to tell Anna that her husband was dead because my wife had killed him. My wife who thought I'd felt something for Anna. I shook my head. Who *knew* I'd felt something for Anna. She deserved to know, even if she didn't want to. The truth was going to take every moment like this from me.

"I need to talk to you," I said. I bowed my head and let the fear of losing her ground me.

Anna stood on her tiptoes and kissed my cheek. "I need something other than talking." She took my hand and led us toward her apartment.

"Anna."

"I'm pregnant, remember? You have to let me have my way." She stopped and rubbed her hand over my dick. It hardened at her touch.

I let go of what I had to tell her and let her lead the way.

36

Anna

HE WANTED TO TALK AND kept bringing it up. I would have sex with him until he forgot Claire and Josh ever existed and whatever was weighing on his mind that he was so hell-bent to share with me took its rightful place—forgotten.

I needed Gabe to be strong, not just for me now, but for the baby, too. I stepped out of the shower and wrapped myself in a towel. The baby liked showers . . . or hated them. I wasn't sure, but she moved more after a shower than she did the rest of the day. I reached down and rested my hands on my growing belly, waiting for the movement I knew would come.

Nothing.

I moved my hands around my stomach and unclenched my nerves. I ignored the terror and told myself, "She's fine." This baby was strong. I dropped the towel to the floor and closed my eyes. My hands laid flat across my stomach as I willed her to move.

"Are you going to take all day?" Gabe said from the other side of the door.

The baby kicked as if she were answering his question, and I finally exhaled. She was fine.

"Gabe, come in here."

He opened the door. "Well, okay." He was still undressed.

The sight of his body threw me a little, but then the baby

kicked again, and I refocused on the reason I'd called him. "Feel this," I said and nodded toward my stomach.

Gabe paused. He stared at me with a satisfied expression and then his gaze fell to my stomach. He walked over, and I took his hand. I placed it under mine and held it there.

"What am I supposed to feel?" he whispered as if we might wake the baby.

"She just kicked."

He leaned back amazed. "She . . ."

"Kicked or moved."

"I can't feel anything."

"You have to wait." I sounded too authoritative, so I softened it with a smile.

He placed his other hand on the other side of my stomach and kissed me.

I reached up and pulled him down, letting myself get lost in him again. When he touched me, he stole every thought from my mind that wasn't him. Thank God.

He jerked back as the baby kicked against his resting hands, and I smiled as his eyes darted between my eyes and my stomach.

She kicked again.

"I told you. She's strong."

"How do you know she's a she?"

"I'd tell you if I knew. It's written in an envelope if you want to find out."

With his hand still on my stomach he asked, "Do you want to?"

"I already know it's a girl. I can feel it." He watched me as I spoke. The same way he used to monitor Claire. "I don't feel sentimental. I feel powerful. It's the kind of thing only two women in one body could produce."

Gabe laughed. "One woman is certainly enough."

"Do you care if it's a boy or a girl?"

"I only care about you." He leaned forward and pressed a sweet kiss to my lips. "And this baby. Boy or girl." His expression was naughty. I braced myself for his torment. "Although, I think it's a boy."

"Really?"

"Boys can be powerful."

"Interesting."

"And strong." Gabe made a muscle, and I reveled in the sight of it. "And strategic." He picked me up and carried me back to our bed. "And loving." He placed me in the middle and climbed in next to me. He kissed my neck near my ear and whispered, "And . . ."

He didn't finish his thought. At least not aloud before I finished. Gabe was a brilliant lover. Why was I still here? With him? Gabe was funny and sexy and he loved me. Why me instead of Claire?

I couldn't let her go, not even the thought of her.

"Let's go see the Pope today," I said.

"Oh, did I miss his invitation to stop by?" Gabe was finally dressed and drinking a cup of coffee. "This coffee is terrible."

"I know. I think it's the coffee maker. I usually just buy it down the street."

"I thought you only drank tea."

"Now that I know I'm pregnant, I don't drink any of it, but before, I had coffee once in a while."

He feigned appalment. "It's like I don't even know you."

His words hit me harder than they should have. "Let's go to church. You're Catholic, right?"

"Born and raised. If I see the Pope, my mother will love you forever."

His mother . . ."When do you think we should tell people about the baby?" I wrung my hands and scanned the room for an answer that wasn't there.

Gabe walked over and hugged me. "We can tell them whenever you want. I'm not ashamed."

I rested my head on his chest. "I'm not either. It's just . . ."

"Your husband died, and his best friend knocked you up?"

I leaned back to see him. He wasn't wavering in the least. Gabe had abandoned his debilitating guilt about the accident. "You're over the accident?" I asked, knowing Gabe would know what I meant without us having to talk about whose fault it was again.

"This baby's here for a reason. For now, I only want to look forward and not back." I held my stomach at his words. It was just going to be the three of us. It would be perfect. "You and him." I laughed, knowing this debate would continue until I gave birth unless we opened the envelope in my underwear drawer. "You're the happiest I've ever seen you."

Gabe hadn't been with me the nights I'd cried because I'd gotten my period. He'd never known the devastation of wanting a baby and failing month after month. I'd kept that from him because he hadn't been my husband, and I'd kept it from my husband because he hadn't been kind. He'd left me alone with my pain. I wasn't alone anymore.

"I am. I'm so happy."

The security checkpoint created a bottleneck and made the crowd seem worse than it was.

"St. Peters Square is huge. We'll be fine," I said to convince Gabe this wasn't crazy. He still didn't believe we'd actually *see* the Pope.

Every Sunday that the Pope was in Rome, he spoke from his apartment window to the thousands of people who gathered to hear him. It was only fifteen to twenty minutes long, but for some people it was the highlight of their entire lives. I'd been twice before since I'd moved to Italy. I wasn't Catholic, but I was a fan of the Pope and I was amazed by the adoration of those who stood on their tiptoes to see him.

The curtains separated, and the Pope stepped to the podium as the crowd around us screamed and cheered. The woman to Gabe's left pointed so her son could see from his father's arms. She was crying. I, too, was overcome with his presence, or was it the presence of the Lord?

"*Buongiorno,*" the Pope said. He continued to share greetings in other languages, only a few of which I could translate.

When his speech moved smoothly into Italian, Gabe took my hand in his. He was mesmerized by the Pope's image on the television screen in front of the columns surrounding the square.

I let my mind stop translating and become lost in the Pope's cadence. I prayed.

Dear God, thank you.

I inhaled deeply.

For this baby and Gabe . . . and the chance to be a family.

I kept my eyes closed and lowered my head.

And take care of Claire. Thank her for me. Make sure she knows that I love her and miss her and I'll never forget her.

Claire would never tolerate being forgotten. I hoped she and Josh were together somewhere. She'd take care of him.

Where would I be if we'd never known them? If Josh hadn't taken the job at the bank? If Gabe had settled out of the service in the Midwest somewhere? Where would I be?

Gabe reached over and squeezed my hand. I leaned my head on his shoulder and that is where we stood until well after the Pope left the window and the crowd began to disperse.

"Thank you," he said.

I knew he meant for more than just bringing him to Vatican

City before lunch.

I thought I was going to cry and beg him to stay, but I held it together. I didn't say a word until we were seated at the first bar on the way home. Gabe stared at me and tilted his head as if he were searching for something.

"Stay," I said. The word was barely audible, but it silenced us as if I'd yelled.

Gabe leaned back in his chair. He didn't move toward me or take my hand in his. I was asking the impossible. Moving to Italy wasn't his dream. It wasn't going to be his happily ever after. He'd want me to go home. He'd take me back there where the memories would swallow us alive.

"I can't." I held back the tears. "I have to go back and get some stuff," he explained with a glint in his eye.

I exhaled the breath I hadn't known I'd been holding. Every muscle in my body relaxed at the thought of him with me. "You're terrible."

"Did you really think I'd say no? That I could leave you here?" He leaned in and looked me square in the eye. "Now?"

I could only shake my head. The words wouldn't come. He was going to stay with me.

"I'm going to be wherever you are, Anna."

Before I could thank him, Gabe sat back. His gaze dragged around the street and the tables surrounding us as he mindlessly observed them.

"You okay?" I asked. I was terrified he'd change his mind. Say he wanted to move and then realize it wasn't what he ever wanted.

"There's a lot to figure out. I'm going to need a visa. My job. Money." He raised his eyebrows at me.

"I have plenty of money."

"I'm not really the kept-man type."

"Maybe you'd like it."

A little smile broke through the tension. We weren't used to navigating finances beyond a dinner bill, which he almost always paid. "If you deliver the baby here, he'll be an Italian citizen?"

I nodded. "*She'll* have dual citizenship since both her parents are from the States."

Gabe exhaled.

"What else are you worried about?"

"I'm not worried." He was strong again. "I'm just thinking."

That was what scared me. The thinking. I'd been trying to avoid it since August.

37

Gabe

IN MY HEAD, IT WAS one of those heart-wrenching scenes in the movies where the man unlocked his arms from around the woman's sunken shoulders and walked into the airport, only looking back once. In reality, a tear fell down Anna's cheek, and I practically died inside.

"I'm coming back."

"When?" We'd talked about it a hundred times. I needed to put some things in storage, talk to my parents, and do something about my job. Anna had assumed I'd quit it, but it seemed so final.

"Two weeks. Tops."

She groaned a little. "I know I'm being horrible. It's just—"

"You can't live without me. You'll lie awake at night missing my body."

Her face scrunched up in the cutest way as she laughed a little. "Something very close to that."

"It's not too late. You can hop on this plane with me and come back for a few weeks."

Anna's head shook in terror. "I don't want to go back there." She was like a little kid paralyzed on the high dive, getting Anna to consider a future in the United States was going to take an act of God himself. I couldn't stand to see her hurt right before I left, though.

"Just wait for me then. I'll be back before you've really had time to miss me. I'll rush through everything, causing significant mistakes that will haunt me through my professional career and personal business affairs for decades to come."

"Thank you," was all she said.

I kissed her and got in line for security. I didn't turn around. There was no point in torturing either of us. I flipped through my phone and found my boarding pass on it. A message popped up from Anna.

I already miss you.

I looked back at the spot I'd left her. She was gone.

*

The flight I'd booked was fifteen hours long with a two-hour layover in Philly before finally arriving in Florida. Everyone spoke English. I could read the signs. I understood the nuances of human communication that were somehow lost to me in the Italian accent.

The moment the plane landed, I pulled up an app on my phone and ordered a car service to my sister's. The United States made sense to me. I was a smart guy, though. I'd traveled half the world in the Army. I could figure out Rome or wherever else Anna needed to be. Italy was the least of our worries.

"You're early," Rita said when she opened the door, waving me in.

"I know, but I feel like I left Italy six days ago. It's a long flight."

"It's a long way." I followed Rita into the kitchen, where she handed me a beer out of the refrigerator. "How's Anna?"

It was the question Rita was dying to ask me every time I texted or emailed with information of my visit. She'd shown great restraint in not picking up the phone and interrogating me over the last week.

"She's pregnant," I said. I took a sip of my beer and placed it in front of me.

"I knew it!"

"What?"

"I knew it. I *knew* she was pregnant when you said you were going to see her."

"I'm in love with her."

"I knew *that* when you were a wreck at Thanksgiving."

I winced at the memory. Anna and I had both come a long way from the previous year.

"Do you think I'm an asshole?" I asked. Rita didn't smile. "You can tell me."

"Oh, I know, and I would tell you." She opened a beer for herself and took a seat next to me. "I think you were both grieving and now you're not. I'll bet this happens more often than you think."

"I need to tell you something," I said, and she just waited. "I had feelings for Anna before Claire and Josh died."

"What kind of—"

"Let me tell you everything before you ask any questions. Okay?" It was only the second time in our lives I'd seen Rita silent. The first was when our mother had told us she had colon cancer. Rita had the same expression that night, too.

Rita nodded without a word.

"I never did anything. Never said a word to anyone. In fact, I spent most of the time telling myself I was crazy and I didn't even really like her. She was just different from Claire. Anna's peaceful and calm. Claire was . . ."

"Difficult."

"Yeah. She was a handful for sure." I took a sip of my beer, seeking courage in the brown glass bottle. "Facts of the accident don't add up. Claire's blood alcohol level was zero, but she had been drinking when I came home from work that night. She'd also ordered drinks at dinner and at the bar."

Rita leaned back to the refrigerator and took out two more beers. She opened them and put them between us.

"She wasn't supposed to be driving. Josh was. He wasn't wearing a seat belt, and he always did. There were no skid marks. No signs of avoiding the loss. And the notes from her brother you found?"

Rita was frozen in my thoughts in front of me.

"He was her twin and he killed himself when they were sixteen."

"Oh my God." She reached up and covered her gaping mouth with her hand. "She was a crazy bitch."

"It was more than that. I think there was something very wrong with Claire."

"Gabe—"

"Still not done." A look of horror settled on Rita's face. "After she died, I began to notice and remember things. The way she clung to Anna. Little comments she'd made about her. Questions about the way I felt about her." Rita wasn't keeping up. "Do you remember the pictures on our refrigerator?"

She nodded.

"I think they were some grotesque storyboard demonstrating how I felt about Anna."

"Gabe—"

"And the fact that she knew. Claire was proving that she was aware the *whole* time how I felt about Anna. I don't know how, but she knew."

Rita didn't say anything. She was the first person I'd told everything to. I'd stifled any words of encouragement she might be able to produce. The cop had been better, but he hadn't known Claire or how I felt about Anna.

"I feel like the accident was as much my fault as it was Claire's." Saying the words aloud made this fantastically grotesque scenario real. This was my life. Somehow, I had no idea what was going on for most of it. I never really knew my wife.

Rita shook her head. "No. You're talking about a woman you think drove a car into a tree and killed her and your best friend . . . on purpose. You didn't have anything to do with that." She was dismissive, but she was also my sister. "What does Anna say about all this?"

"I haven't told her."

Rita's eyebrows rose. "That's why you feel guilty."

"She won't let me. She wants to leave all of it in the past. Anna loved Claire . . . she won't listen to a bad word about her, not even from me."

"You sure that's all of it?"

"What do you mean?"

"Are you sure you haven't figured out how to tell her yet because you're scared you're going to lose her?"

I stared into the opening of my bottle of beer. I couldn't lose Anna or the baby. "I don't know. I tried to talk to her about it even before I knew about the baby. I told her how I felt about her before they died. She just doesn't know everything about Claire." I faced my sister. The only person who'd ever seen through all of my bullshit. "You think I should tell her?"

"I think I'd want to know." The beer sloshed in my stomach. "But it wouldn't change how I felt about you." I hung on to those words and the hope they carried. "It's not going to change anything for Anna either."

I looked at the clock on the oven behind Rita. It was after midnight. Rita yawned, and I remembered that I was intruding on her already full life. Her two little minions would be awake and getting ready for school in a few hours.

"Thanks," I said and put my empty beer in the sink. "I've got to go call her."

"What time is it there?"

"Six in the morning. It's already tomorrow in Italy."

"Lucky them."

"I guess." I kissed Rita on the cheek and went to the basement where her guest room was located. I threw my bag on the bed, collapsed next to it, and I dialed Anna, who picked up on the first ring.

"I didn't wake you, did I?" I asked. She sounded sleepy but content.

"I miss you." I could hear her roll over and imagined myself in her bed. "I couldn't fall asleep without you last night."

"I still haven't been to sleep."

"Oh, Gabe. I'm sorry."

"It's okay. I'm lying down now." I kicked off my shoes and pulled the comforter on top of me.

"Come back," she said.

"I love you, Anna."

"I know. I'll talk to you tomorrow."

"I'll see you soon."

My eyes were heavy. I was having trouble staying awake. I hit end and fell asleep.

When I woke up six hours later, my phone was beneath me. Anna's contact was still up. Her picture was one I'd taken on the terrace at her apartment in Rome. She was bundled in a sweater and you couldn't tell she was pregnant unless you looked at her eyes. She was radiant. She'd left all the bad stuff behind. Except for me.

I booked my flight back to Philadelphia for the next day. Since I'd done what I'd come to Tampa to do, it was time to get started on everything else. Rita was already moving around upstairs—vacuuming. I took a deep breath and headed up the stairs to talk to my obviously impatient sister.

"Morning," I said when I reached the top step.

"Oh, you up already?"

I pointed to the vacuum. "Sure am."

Rita only smiled, admitting she was ready for me to be awake. "I couldn't sleep. I kept thinking of Claire and what you must have been going through all these months. No wonder you were such a wreck."

"Thanks."

"Seriously, Gabe. Maybe you should talk to someone."

"The person who should have talked to someone is dead."

"Every word Claire ever said ran through my mind last night."

"I must have handed this over to you, because I slept great. I think I needed to tell you."

"There's someone else you need to tell."

I knew. Before I'd even told Rita, I'd known. I shouldn't have left Italy without telling Anna everything, but she didn't want to hear it, and the baby . . .

"What are you going to do?" she asked.

"I'm going to tell Anna everything, and I'm going to ask her to marry me."

"Did you get her a ring?"

"Not yet."

"I was thinking about it," she said and opened the cabinet above her desk.

"You *were* up all night."

"If you want, you can give her this." She opened an old ring box that held our grandmother's opal ring. It was a large oval and surrounded by tiny diamonds, but it appeared soft and gentle. "It was Grandmom's. I got it when she died."

Grandmom had been dead since we were teenagers. "Why didn't you offer it to me when I proposed to Claire?" I raised my eyebrows at my sister. "You never liked her."

Rita took the ring back and studied it. "Claire told me once that she liked my ring because the diamond was big. She'd said an engagement ring, 'Screams to the world that he loves you.'"

"So?"

"So this ring doesn't yell a thing. It whispers just to the person you give it to."

I looked down at the ring again. Anna would love it.

38

Anna

GABE HAD SAID HE NEEDED two weeks at home to get everything in order. After the sixteenth day, my internal dialogue was fucking with my head. He didn't want to have a baby. He'd just been nice when I'd told him. He wasn't even really in love with me.

Nothing he said to me on the phone quelled my horrible thoughts. The only thing that would satisfy me was seeing him walk off an airplane, but on day eighteen, he still wasn't here. I got up the courage to ask him if he was having second thoughts about me and the baby—when he called this morning, I'd be ready. I set my alarm to make sure I was awake before he called, but I didn't need it. My eyes opened and I flipped the switch to off twenty minutes early.

I brushed my teeth. After all, there was no greater evidence of awakeness than brushed teeth. Since a shower was another marker, I turned on the water and stepped in. If he didn't want us, we'd be okay. We had money. I was starting to make friends in Italy. This little girl and I could make a life for ourselves without Gabe Hawkins. I braced myself against the shower wall and cried at the thought of him never coming back.

I remembered his call and rushed out of the shower. I opened the door while I dried off so I wouldn't miss the phone ringing. I still had fifteen minutes before he usually called. This was going to be a long, horrible day if Gabe said he wasn't coming back to Italy. I considered my options and whether I could return to the States to be with him. If he'd even want me to. There were so many things he could reject about this situation.

I'd deal with them as they came.

"Anna." His voice was followed by a knock on my apartment door. "Anna, wake up before I wake everyone in the building."

My phone began to ring. I ran to the door and yanked it open without any clothes on. I jumped into Gabe's arms, fully aware that my days would never continue if he'd told me he wasn't coming back for us.

Gabe dropped his bag inside the door and held me as he crossed the threshold. "Hey," he said. His words were gentle and brushed across my neck. "Are you crying?"

At the mention of it, I couldn't hold back. Every fear I'd had since he'd left came flooding to my eyes. I buried my face in his neck and sobbed. He couldn't ever leave me again. I couldn't lose him, too.

"Anna, what's wrong?" He closed the door to my apartment and carried me to my bed. "Talk to me."

I held him tight against me. "I thought you weren't coming back."

"I'm sorry." He held me close, but I wiggled until I was straddling his lap and kissing him. I was so desperate for him.

"Anna, wait." He pulled back, and the sinking feeling returned. He lifted me off him and placed me on the edge of the bed. Gabe stared at his bag on the floor by the door and ran his hand through his hair. He was torturing himself or he was afraid. Either way, I was trapped in my own hell sitting on my bed, naked, without him.

"Gabe?" It didn't sound like my voice.

He sighed and shifted until he faced me with his hands hanging at his sides. "Anna, you and this baby mean everything to me. I thought all of this was going to turn out so differently, but here we are." He looked down at my belly. I'd grown since he'd left. "All of us."

I reached up and covered the baby with my arm. I was protecting myself more than her. Keeping her with me always.

"I feel alive." He took a step closer to me. "Because of you." He kneeled down on the floor in front of my bed. "Anna." Gabe paused and swallowed hard, as if my name was difficult to get out. "Will you marry me?"

I searched his face for information. Gabe stayed still, and I finally breathed. He'd asked me to marry him. Right now. In front of me. "I don't have any clothes on," I said, and Gabe laughed.

"I said it was unplanned." He lowered his head, refusing to meet my eyes. He'd just proposed to me in my apartment, and I have no clothes on, and it seemed to me that it was absolutely perfect.

"Yes," I said. I reached down and tilted his face toward mine. "Yes. I'll marry you." Everything I'd been thinking for weeks vanished. He was here. We were together. I didn't ask him if he was sure. He was Gabe. Nobody else. I could count on him. He was left here with me for that reason.

Gabe made love to me twice that morning and then he fell asleep in my bed. He woke when the oven timer went off. I'd made us a pizza for lunch. To celebrate him being home. *Home.*

"What is that smell?"

"It's pizza."

"You cook now?"

"Sometimes. Sophia downstairs is teaching me everything she knows." I removed the oven mitts and inhaled the aromas of the tomatoes and anchovies. "She said it shouldn't take but a few days to learn it all."

"We can just eat out for the rest of our lives."

I glanced over my shoulder at him. He was standing by the bed and pulling a shirt over his chest. The muscles in my groin contracted. I wanted him again. "Or order takeout."

Gabe smiled, knowing exactly what I'd meant. "Do you feel well enough to go out today?"

"Of course. I'm only six months." It was the middle of April in Rome. Gabe was back. For good. I shut off the oven and turned to face him. "You're really here?"

"I'm with you forever, and this is where you are."

"I love you."

★

We ate the pizza and made love again. I'd never tire of his body. The contour of his chest. The muscles in his arms. The weight of him—at least what he would allow—on top of me as he came.

When we finally ventured outside, the sun was already dipping in the sky. We bought gelato and walked south to the Pantheon and then cut across to the Trevi Fountain.

"What are they doing?" Gabe asked as some tourists threw coins over their shoulders in into the water.

"Legend has it if you toss a coin into the fountain, you'll return to Rome one day."

"Oh." Gabe searched through his pockets. "Why don't we throw one?"

"Because we're not leaving."

He pointed to me. "Right. I'm still getting used to the idea."

I took his hand and led him away from the fountain. We settled onto the Spanish Steps near the bottom, which was quickly becoming "our spot". I threaded my fingers in his and leaned onto his shoulder without a word.

"I have some things I need to talk to you about," he said and kissed the top of my head.

The monster was returning. Our past needed to be beaten

back again.

I kissed him to forget what he was talking about.

"Anna." He kissed me lightly on the lips and stood up. "I'm sorry about the way I asked you to marry me." The memory of it put a smile on my face. It was exactly how he should have done it. Right before making love to me. "It was unplanned and poorly executed."

"I thought you were magnificent." Gabe blushed a little, which pleased me.

"I'd been missing a key step." He stepped down and kneeled on the stair below me. "Anna, keeper of my life, mother of my son." There was a glint in his eye. "Will you please do me the honor of marrying me?" His voice was silky smooth. There wasn't a hint of hesitation. Gabe reached into his pocket and pulled out an antique ring box. He opened it, and an opal surrounded by diamonds captivated me. The entire ring was set in rose gold. It was unusual and unexpected and too beautiful to be true. I could only stare at it. "Anna?" Gabe said and smiled when I looked up at him. "People are watching."

All around us was silence as couples and families waited for me to say something to the striking man on his knee in front of me. He was mine. All of him. I was overcome with gratitude for more of a life than I'd imagined, but with Gabe anything was possible. Maybe even forever.

"Yes."

After a short discussion while lying in our bed, we settled on a civil ceremony in Rome, officiated by the mayor. I wore the pink maternity dress with the ruffles and a flower in my hair. Gabe wore a suit. The same one he'd worn to Laura's wedding. Sophia and her boyfriend served as our witnesses, and I was Gabe's translator. We ate alone afterward on the rooftop of the

Hotel Minerva. The domes and building tops were lit up below the full moon in the sky.

When Gabe went to the bathroom, I stared out at the city. It was my savior as much as Gabe was. I'd left my remains in Delaware and reclaimed my life in Rome. Gabe came up behind me and wrapped his arms around me.

"Rome is known as the eternal city," I said. He kissed my cheek. His lips dragged up to my ear, where his warm breath told me the night was ending. "Are you ready to go?"

"I am, Mrs. Hawkins." I was thankful Claire had never taken Gabe's name. I'd never replace her. I'd just taken my rightful place by the father of my baby. I hoped she'd be happy with how things had turned out. Claire would have wanted them this way.

39

Gabe

"HUNDREDS OF BABIES ARE BORN around the world every minute," Anna said as if the child lying across her chest was anything short of a miracle.

"Who says?" I asked.

"The books I have about babies."

I nodded and moved even closer to her. I ran my fingertips up the side of her arm just to be near her. "I'm glad you've gotten some new books." *New everything,* I thought. "You were right."

"I know." She smiled down at the baby and then up at me. "I don't know exactly what you're talking about, but I'm sure I was right."

"That she's a girl."

The baby moved her lips in a tiny sucking motion and sighed. Her eyes didn't open. She'd barely stirred, and Anna and I were mesmerized. She had dark hair and blue-gray eyes, but all I could see was Anna. Her nose and lips. They were her mother's. They were perfect, like her.

She'd been here only forty minutes, but I couldn't imagine a life without her. Claire had been with me for years—

"What about Amanda for a name?" I said to silence my thoughts.

"Didn't you already suggest that? Are you trying to back

door Amanda in?"

"I would never. Gabriella?"

"No." Anna had already said no to anything like either of our names a hundred times. She wanted this baby to grow up with none of the baggage of our histories. "I was thinking Louisa."

"And we'll call her Louie?" Overweight, cigar-smoking, short men came to mind.

"Or we could call her Louisa."

I felt my lips pinch just a tiny bit at the name. I didn't like it, but for some reason I found it hard to say no to anything Anna asked.

I stood up and kissed my daughter and then kissed my wife. "I want to take you home."

"Just a few days here," she said as she shifted the baby's weight so she could sit up more.

"No." I leaned down until our eyes met. "I want to take you both back home with me."

Anna's mouth opened a little as she realized I wasn't talking about the apartment in Rome. She needed air. Her eyes opened wider. It was more fear than excitement. I should have waited to bring it up, but there was so much I needed to tell her. The first thing was that I wanted to move her and our baby back to the States.

She swallowed, looked down at the baby, and then her eyes came back to mine. She was more relaxed. The shock had worn off. "You don't like it here?"

"I love it here. It's the place she was born. The country I first learned she existed. I proposed, and you said yes . . ."

"Then why do you want to leave?"

"Because even with all that, it feels like we're running. We don't have to hide from the past."

Anna moved the baby and raised her knees. She rested her

there, facing us both with her eyes still closed. "How about we call her Eva? It's Italian meaning 'life.'"

I couldn't say another word. Anna and the baby took my breath away. I was going to live wherever she wanted to be. Nothing else mattered but the two of them.

"And we'll move home," she said.

"Not just for me?"

"I would do it just for you . . ." She leaned up and kissed me on the lips. "But you're right. She should know the United States as her home." Anna took a deep breath and settled into the decision. "Plus, my mother will love you for bringing us back."

"She doesn't love me already?"

"Kind of." Her voice was full of concern. "Things have moved a little fast for her. She'll be fine. I promise."

The day after the next, I took my *wife* and my *baby* home to our apartment. I'd undergone a rebirth of my own. While Anna had been in the hospital, I'd tossed and turned in her bed, trying to let go of Claire and Josh and everything that had come before Eva. Nothing would ever come before her again.

Anna was exhausted, but grateful to be out of the hospital. I was happy to have her home. Yet, when she left me with Eva while she showered, I panicked. I'd been to Afghanistan and Iraq, and sitting in a room alone with my three-day-old daughter was the most terrifying thing I'd ever been through.

I stared at her until she woke up, and then I chastised myself for possibly contributing to her waking. Eva Larue Hawkins yawned, looked at me, and proceeded to scream her head off.

"Shh, shh, stop screaming." I picked her up out of the bassinet she'd been so peaceful in, but apparently woke up wanting to set on fire. Women would be the death of me. I held her head the way the nurse had taught me and bent at the knees. Deep lunges until the muscles in my thighs burned and my ears throbbed from her screeching.

The door to the bathroom was closed. I bounced some more and told myself Anna wouldn't mind. She loved us. I dragged my feet, feeling incapable, but was relieved as I knocked on the door and Anna told me to come in.

I yelled over Eva, "She keeps screaming at me."

"I can hear." She peeked out from the behind the shower curtain. "What did you do to her?"

"Nothing," I yelled over the baby.

"I'm kidding." Anna shut off the water and stepped out. She took the towel off the bar on the wall and wrapped it around her body. She couldn't move quickly enough to satisfy me. As soon as Eva was in Anna's arms, the two of us calmed. The tension exhaled with my breath.

"I love you, but you're never showering again."

Eva's face was blotchy from the fit she'd thrown and her tiny fist kept rubbing back and forth against her lips.

"She's already calmed down." She looked at me with some expectation I couldn't meet. "Take her back."

"What?" I shook my head. Violently.

"Talk to her. She knows you."

"What should I say? 'I'm the guy whose enormous cock kept hitting you in the head?'"

Anna shut her eyes halfway and shook her head. "Maybe try something appropriate." She was so much better at this than I was. She was a mom. "Tell her what you're afraid of. You two can bond." She reached over and transferred the baby back to me. Eva began to stir. The muscles in the back of my neck tensed. "Talk," Anna said.

"Hi, Eva." It was a strange version of baby talk and guy-speak. It was only missing a "Yo." Anna kept encouraging me with her eyes. God help her, she still loved me. "I love you," I said to Eva, and she appeared to stop and listen. "I love your little lips and your loud screams and your ability to assert yourself." Anna laughed next to me as she stepped out of the bathroom and got dressed. "You're going to make an excellent person who screams someday. Perhaps a cheerleader or the person who sits on the end of a boat and yells at rowers to pull."

I stopped pacing and bouncing so I could watch Anna for a second. Then Eva made some pissed-off sounds, and I started back up again.

"She's cold since we left the bathroom. Keep her covered up."

"How do you know that?"

"Because I'm cold since we left the bathroom."

"Oh. Right. If we're going to use common sense to raise her, I'm not going to be much help."

"You're wonderful." Anna stood on her tiptoes and kissed me.

"Eva, I'm afraid you're going to turn out more like me than your mother. She's perfect."

Anna sighed. I hoped she wasn't thinking the same thing.

40

Anna

GABE WAS STRONGER THAN ANY human being I'd ever met. He got up in the middle of the night and brought Eva to me when she cried. He navigated Rome without speaking Italian as he bought diapers and wipes and everything else we've needed. Not once in the six weeks since she'd arrived had I sought space from him. Gabe created a cocoon Eva and I would be happy to never leave.

All of this he did while searching for a house and a new job in the States. It amazed me what he could accomplish. Josh had always described Gabe as a gifted leader, but to watch him in action with the realtors, head hunters, U.S. Embassy in Rome, and everyone else who would be involved in our relocation, was impressive.

He juggled the details of our future as if they were min-iscule in comparison to what time Eva's last feeding was. We were the center of his universe. I couldn't have chosen a better father for Eva if I'd been given the chance.

Sometimes, when Gabe was out of the apartment and couldn't hear me, I'd tell Eva about Claire. "She was a little wild and sometimes loud. She'd have sung to you and taught you all the bad words, I'm sure of it."

Eva listened. She always smiled when I spoke to her. Whenever it was about Claire, she'd reach up to touch my lips.

In my head, I'd say thank you to Claire for the love and the kindness, for leaving Gabe here for me, and for telling me I'd be a great mom.

I wanted her to know Eva, but more than anything, I wanted her to be here now . . . with me.

"Anna," Gabe said as he dropped the mail on the table.

I was lost in thoughts of Claire with my eyes closed and Eva in my arms.

If Claire were here, Gabe wouldn't be mine.

"Babe?"

I looked up at my husband. "Sorry. I was just thinking."

He walked over and kissed me. Gabe stared into my eyes and asked, "About what?"

With my free hand, I pulled him down and kissed him again. "How lucky I am."

"You are." He kissed Eva on the forehead. "It's beautiful out. Let's take Eva for a walk."

The sun was shining onto the terrace that had become my and Eva's playground. We'd spend the mornings out there while the gray birds sang.

"She's not going to remember how beautiful it is here."

Gabe was putting on the baby backpack thing that strapped Eva to his chest, which he'd gotten much better at fastening over the last few weeks. "We'll bring her back. I promise." I trusted him.

With Eva strapped to his chest, we walked to the Trevi Fountain, and Gabe tossed a coin over his shoulder.

"That one's for Eva," he said and kissed me. I almost cried. My emotions were still so close to the surface of every waking moment, but Gabe got me every time. He overwhelmed me with his love. He pulled me close to him and said, "You're a mess."

"I'm a mom." With that, the tears streamed down my face.

Gabe wiped them away and kissed me over Eva's head. He took my hand, and the three of us walked home. I was a mother. It'd barely been a year since I'd been told I couldn't have any of this.

"What do you think about moving to Maryland?" He squeezed my hand knowing he was breaking through some serious thoughts in my head.

"Maryland?"

"I have an interview for a job there." He stopped walking and faced me. "And it's not Delaware and it's not Pennsylvania . . ."

"And it's close to our parents."

He nodded. "And it's where Eva was conceived. It's the one place that's ours."

He left off, *and not theirs*, but I heard it anyway. Since Eva had arrived, their names were rarely spoken between us. Eva occupied that space.

"Maryland sounds perfect," I said.

We walked home and made love. Our baby slept in the bassinet next to our bed. She had no idea of where she was or how she got here. All she knew was love.

Gabe was drinking a glass of wine as he scrolled through screens on his computer. He'd been quiet the entire evening. "I need to talk to you about something." Gabe was stern, which was a disposition I hadn't seen since Eva was born.

"Sounds serious." I sat down at the table next to him, even though all I wanted was to go back to bed with him. I never had this feeling when we were making love. "Did you find a house you like in Maryland?" I asked, knowing it wasn't the subject he wanted to address.

He shook his head. "No." I poured myself a glass of wine from the bottle on the table and then leaned a bit to top his glass off. "This is all going to sound crazy, but I need you to know. I needed you to know months ago when I found out. Before I proposed. Before we were married. Before my life all started to make sense again."

I sat back in my chair and braced myself. "What is it, Gabe?"

"When you told me you were pregnant. The first time I came to Italy . . . I was going to tell you that I thought Claire caused the accident on purpose." Her name hurt me. The rest of his words didn't. Gabe looked over at Eva and back at me with the same expression I'd seen before whenever he wanted to talk about Josh and Claire. I'd let him have this one time so it would be the last. I never wanted to see this guilt on his face again. He couldn't change anything that had happened, and, as I glanced to our daughter, I knew that I didn't want him to.

"She wasn't drunk. There were no skid marks. Even the cops think Claire hit that tree on purpose."

"Why does any of this matter now, Gabe?"

"That's the thing. It doesn't matter. But it's here . . . between us. It's this giant thing that is hovering over my head, simply because I know and you don't. I need to tell you these things so that I don't feel like I'm hiding them from you."

There was no guilt in his eyes, not hate or self-loathing. Just honesty. So, I nodded my acceptance and let him continue.

"You know how I told you that I had feelings for you before they died?"

I nodded again.

"That's why she did it. Claire realized how I felt about you and she killed herself because of it." Gabe's gaze lowered to his hands on his glass in front of him as if he couldn't face me. *Me.* The idea that he should be ashamed was the most insane part of the four of us.

"So, you're confessing some responsibility for their deaths because of the way you felt about me?"

"Anna—"

"It doesn't matter. None of it matters. Claire did this. Their time was up. That's how this works."

"Are you hearing me? Claire murdered Josh."

My fists clenched together. He shouldn't say murder. It wasn't like that. Claire was good. "Stop! That's enough. I heard every word you said."

Gabe shook his head and studied me. "How can you not hate her?"

"Gabe—"

"It's like you still love her. She killed your husband."

"It wasn't like that."

Gabe's voice was quiet when he asked, "What was it like then?"

I was on the verge of tears, but for Claire, I wouldn't cry. She wouldn't want that. "I understood her," I said, and Gabe's expression twisted from guilt and anger to absolute repulsion. "And I've never been happier than I am with you. I can't keep going back to them."

He peered at me through his confusion and said, "Anna—"

"It's our time now." I stared at him, willing him to believe me. To let them and the accident go. I had given him the chance to talk, to rid himself of whatever guilt he had about keeping what he'd discovered away from me. When his silence moved me, I stood, walked over to him, and pulled his head against my stomach. I leaned down and kissed the top of it.

We stayed that way for what felt like forever, but then Eva cried out, and Gabe slipped from my arms to go pick her up. He rested her on his chest. He was her father. Her safety. His words were replaced by the peace that came with our baby. Nothing bad could happen to us because she was here to make everything right. Gabe softened with Eva in his arms. He believed it, too.

"I just needed to tell you," he said as I walked into the bathroom.

I looked at myself in the mirror and whispered, "I already knew."

EPILOGUE

Anna

I WASN'T A SOCIOPATH. ALTHOUGH I did look up the definition to be sure.

Two weeks after Josh told me the clinic had called, the clinic called *again*. Only this time, they called me. They wanted to make sure that I understood the other options available to us. That Josh's sperm should be retested, because although, "There were deficiencies found, they could represent a brief abnormality. That even without his sperm, there were many, many options available to us."

I was only confused for a second. Other wives would have assumed the mistake was on the clinic's part, but I knew. Looking back, I sensed from the way Josh had told me—so cold and detached—that he'd been lying. He was ready to get right back to work as if nothing had happened. We were fine because he was fine.

When Josh had gotten off the phone that day, I was speechless. There were so many emotions to work through. I had to deal with the loss of hope, and then I had to work through my husband's insistence on us moving on and abandoning the idea of children all together. Josh had moved so fast that he left me behind. In my efforts to catch up to his acceptance, I didn't question his sincerity.

He'd set all this into motion. My loving, strategic husband

may not have planned the accident, but his part in its occurrence couldn't be overlooked. "The tests on me all came back fine," he'd said. I kept still. I was at my computer at the kitchen table. I knew Josh was sitting at his desk at work with his office door shut. "It's you there's an issue with." He thought I'd let the whole thing go. He was a liar and a thief. He stole my future from me, or at least he tried to.

I didn't exactly lie to Gabe. Josh *had* told me there was something wrong with me. That I couldn't have children. For two weeks, I'd trusted my husband's words. If the truth had been that Josh's body was the problem, I wouldn't have thought less of him for a second, but in believing it was me, I was left empty and filled with anger.

A woman's body was created to bear children. My marriage, our house, the four-door car I drove no longer made sense. What was I even doing on this earth if I couldn't have a baby? It was crazy, of course. I loved my life before Josh brought up a baby. Our marriage could have been full and rich and wonderful if I could somehow just have gone back in time and remembered not wanting to be a mother. Instead, I spiraled into the notion my life had no meaning and there I stayed for two weeks. Until the clinic called *again* . . . and what I thought was forever meant nothing to me anymore.

On the night of the accident, I was planning to tell Josh I wanted a divorce. I'd worn the red dress in honor of the event. I wanted him to remember exactly the way I looked when I said the words aloud. I wanted him to remember for the *rest* of his *life*.

I didn't know what Claire was going to do. She was so brilliantly spontaneous. Without ever having considered it, though, I knew Claire would die for me. Not only because she loved me, but because Claire was the type of person who wasn't afraid to die.

I knew the moment the police officer was standing on the other side of Gabe and Claire's threshold that she'd done the unthinkable, which, to her, was probably the only reasonable solution to the problem.

There were many times Josh had underestimated me. He'd completely dismissed Claire, but I found her to be very simple to understand. She had to know you'd always be there—consistency was paramount to her security. She was easy if you listened, but Josh wasn't a very good listener. I often wondered what she said to him and how she got his seatbelt unbuckled.

Claire had a different plan than my divorce. Hers was better. She hand-selected Gabe for me. She loved me more than she loved herself and now, I'd never be able to thank her. I liked to think I was as good of a friend, but I could never have done what Claire did. She was the bravest woman I'd ever known.

Gabe's feelings for me were between him and his wife. I never sensed a thing but friendship until the night Eva was conceived. I'd wanted him then, and I'd wanted him when we were all in the bar the night Josh and Claire died. I wanted him still.

He was wrong about one thing, though. Claire didn't kill herself because she knew Gabe loved me. She killed Josh because *Claire* loved me. Gabe would never understand all of that the way Claire did, and that was why he'd never know.

Given one more chance to talk to her, I wouldn't ask any questions. I'd let her tend to the details the same way she always did and just tell her that I loved her.

Claire understood. She always did.

ALSO BY

ELIZA FREED

The Devil's Playground
(Book One in the Faraway Series)

Former U.S. Attorney, Meredith Walsh, took some time off to raise her children. But the time took away everything she once trusted about herself. She's lost within the mundane confines of her children's schedules of lacrosse, soccer, Cub Scouts, and math facts. Desperate for a sliver of her former passion, and isolated in the small town her corporate husband relocated her to, she counsels herself on risking her family for the rush of a fling.

But Vincent Pratt, the local chief of police, weakens Meredith's abhorrence of affairs and her dedication to her family. With him, she finds a new version of herself, one capable of contributing in her new world, and thriving in her lonely home. In spite of the fact, she's not the kind of woman who has an affair.

Please turn the page for an excerpt from *The Devil's Playground*.

There were times when I felt completely alone.
Even when he was standing right next to me.
He would tell me that's ridiculous.
He would convince me I never felt it.

one

I SCANNED THE BALLROOM OF the Downtown Club in Philadelphia. Brad was standing near the bar, laughing with his high school friends, the ones he rarely saw anymore. He towered over most of them. His six-foot-three body an anomaly among his childhood friends. His height matched his power. He could stare you down with his jet-black eyes, or melt you with them, and he always knew which way to proceed. Most people were at his mercy. I was at his side.

I barely smiled, but Brad caught it and winked at me. He kept watching me as he half listened to his friends talking. There was little Brad didn't notice.

"Meredith, I want to introduce you to my father," the bride said, pulling me away from Brad's stare. I stood even straighter. The introduction was the reason I'd been excited about the wedding. It was why I'd spent weeks finding a dress. And it was why I'd barely drank a sip of alcohol the entire day. The bride's father was Judge Warren of the U.S. Court of Appeals. He was an Army veteran and Harvard Law grad who'd made his way to Philadelphia and an appointment to the Third Circuit. One didn't fall into that position.

I followed the bride across the dance floor. My Norwegian cream skin, the same as my mother's, was perfectly highlighted in the light-green dress I'd saved three months to buy. I'd been told before that I was angelic. Looking, at least. My skin and light eyes—not quite green, not quite blue—had garnered comments from passersby even as a child.

"She's beautiful. Why she looks like an angel."

My mother would take me aside each time and tell me *they* say that to everyone. "You're no prettier than anyone else, which is fine, because beauty will get you nowhere."

Beautiful or not, I'd capitalized on others' views of my appearance since they'd first noticed me. I knew what colors looked best, what cuts of clothing to wear to accentuate my lean figure. I wasn't voluptuous or petite. I was statuesque. At least that was the word my mother's boyfriend chose when he'd inappropriately blocked the doorway to my bedroom to discuss my future plans.

I'd been high at the time, like the rest of my senior year. I'd skipped school as much as I could and had driven the three and a half hours east to the shore. I wasn't challenged by my coursework, not inspired by my teachers, and easily ranked in the top of my class. If it wouldn't have killed my father, I'd have dropped out and surfed every day.

I was sitting on the floor of my room, leaning against my bed, and he was standing at the foot of it. I hadn't noticed the thirty extra pounds he carried around his waist or the bald front of his head until that day. He was a drycleaner. My mother had brought him home for dinner after having a pair of pants tailored at his store.

He picked up my bra from the hamper and held it to his nose. He closed his eyes and tilted his head toward the ceiling as he inhaled deeply. He ran his fat fingertips over the lace at the edge of the cups and pressed the silk against his cheek. My stomach churned with disgust. No one—man or woman—had ever made me feel that afraid.

His grotesque leer had made me want to change something. Something bigger than anything I'd ever imagined while swimming in the ocean, or lying on the sand. I stopped getting high and started making a plan. It started with locking my bedroom door every night until I moved in with my father.

"Dad, this is my friend, Meredith." Judge Warren turned and paused at the sight of me. The candles' soft light highlighted the chiffon crossed at my chest and tied behind my neck. "She's an attorney with the Justice Department."

His eyes widened, and he took one step to my side, blatantly appraising me in front of his daughter. She smiled to put me at ease, but I wasn't uncomfortable, I was prepared.

Game on.

The judge and I spoke of his path to the bench. We went all the way back to his military service, and I memorized every word he said. Judge Warren was the human equivalent of a tufted leather chair in a warm, ornate library. He was broad and upright, commanding attention, but reserved. He was a powerful man, whose generous smile relaxed you immediately. And to me, he was fascinating.

I was intelligent and interested and, above all, innocent in my intentions. I would not sleep with this judge to get ahead. But I would learn from him in whatever limited time I was allotted.

When he asked for my business card, I presented him with the one I brought with me. It'd been placed in the side pocket of my purse, all by itself, waiting for the judge to request it. I promised to have lunch with him the following week. He wanted to discuss my future, the one he knew would be bright. The judge had found me "remarkable." My work here was done.

I walked back to our friends, still high from my introduction. Two pregnant wives anchored the table; waters with lemon rested between their swollen fingers. One was due that month, the other the next. Both were uncomfortable, tired, and annoyed by the shots their husbands poured down their throats and chased with beers, and I couldn't bring myself to sit with them and listen to their complaining. My life was too short.

"Do you want to dance?"

My body relaxed at the sound of his voice. It would forever be recognizable. I turned to find Brad standing just inches behind me. His smile was collusive. He was saving me from this table of lost joy, and it reminded me of the first night we met. He had rescued me from a guy hitting on me in a bar. He'd walked up and asked me if I was ready to leave. And without even knowing his name, I'd left with him.

"Yes," I said, and he took my hand in his and led me to the dance floor. The orchestra slipped into a slow cadence, and Brad held me the way he had a thousand times before. I'd been dancing with him for four years. Through weddings and promotions and thirtieth birthday parties and drunken holidays together. We'd been to the mountains, the islands, and to Europe, and we hadn't found a reason to stop dancing. But this would be the last dance for a while. The babies were beginning to come; the parties were beginning to end.

Brad leaned in as he whispered in my ear, "Frank and Tom were just telling me how lucky I am you haven't begged me for a baby yet."

"Is that how it works? We women beg you for your DNA to make the perfect baby?"

"According to them." He laughed and pulled me closer. "You smell amazing." He wanted me again. He'd had me when we woke up that morning, and again in the shower before the ceremony.

Brad's needs were simple. He wanted me, and power, and money. Not always in that order. Brad didn't care about changing the world. He cared about running it. But somehow we worked. Our goals were completely different, but the road we traveled to reach them was perfectly balanced between us. I forgot what we were talking about and let Brad lead me.

"I saw you wrap His Honor around your finger. I almost felt bad for the man." The smile on my face hid my disappointment. Lately, I'd sensed tiny moments of jealousy from Brad. Not jealousy of other men, but of me. As if he feared I might eclipse him. It reminded me of my mother. "Do you want to have a baby?"

I leaned back to see if Brad was kidding. "You want to talk about babies now?"

"Yes. You're twenty-nine. I'm thirty-one." Brad kissed me again. His eyes lit up with the same excitement of the days we'd set our wedding date and settled on the condo in the city. Brad liked when things were decided.

"I have so much left to do."

"None of our friends died when they had their babies," Brad said, pointing out the obvious, of which I was still not convinced.

"I don't want to have a baby just because everyone else is having one."

"You won't. You've never given a fuck what everyone else is doing. It's part of your charm." Brad admired me with the strangest expression. He was right next to me, and yet felt so far away. As if suddenly he didn't know me at all. "You're beautiful," he said, but *they* say that to everyone.

The song ended and took the discussion of babies with it. Brad and I walked over to the windows overlooking Independence Mall. The Liberty Bell was lit up, proclaiming our independence on this hot summer night. Brad handed me a glass of champagne. He put his arm around me and stared out the window as well. I leaned into him, feeling him solid beside me and forgot the last few minutes. No, it was not time for babies. We were on the verge of something brilliant.

two

NINE YEARS LATER

"MOMMY, CAN BRIAN HAVE A snack?"

I'd started locking the bathroom door, but I was too nervous to lock it while I showered. What if one of them fell and hit their head and bled to death while I was shaving my legs? What if I couldn't hear their screams, or their banging on the door? No matter how old they got, I never felt sure they'd be okay.

"Brian who?" I told Liv never to open the door for anyone. No one was allowed in the house. *Do. Not. Open. The. Door. Do you understand me?* I said it every time I got into the shower.

"This Brian." Through the fogged shower glass I could see Liv and the four-year-old boy from across the street staring at me in the shower. Brian was not fazed by my nudity.

I opened the shower door and stuck my head out. "Brian, can you wait in the hall for a minute?"

He shrugged and walked out of the bathroom, probably wondering what was taking so long with the snack.

"I thought I told you not to open the door?" My teeth were clenched. She would be the death of me.

"I didn't. I unlocked it, and then *he* opened it."

"It's not funny, Liv!"

"He's hungry. And that's not funny, either. You fed that dog the other day. The one that was lost."

"Brian's not a lost dog. He has a kitchen across the street."

"Does that mean no snack?" She had the sweetest face, that of an angel. And even though I knew that she knew exactly what she was doing, it was impossible to be mad at her.

"I'll be down in a minute."

As I walked into the kitchen, James told Brian hot dogs were the gross part of pigs. "Like all the stuff you'd never want to eat on a pig." Brian insisted he didn't want to eat any part of a pig, and Liv told him he had to eat a pig to have bacon, and everybody loved bacon. It seemed every conversation was some equally mind-numbing variation on the gross parts of a pig. I tried not to listen. *How much can one woman take?*

"You know a hamburger is made from a cow," James said.

"Milk, too," Liv added.

"Nobody likes milk."

"Lots of people like milk. Mommy, don't lots of people like milk?"

I nodded my head and grabbed three bowls from the cabinet. I poured goldfish into the bowls and took a handful for myself. My hair still had soap in it. I was in my robe. I wanted to be standing under a hot shower, not feeding these tiny people fish.

"Without milk, there'd be no ice cream."

"That's not true."

"Yes, it is."

Brad walked through the door. His eyes were glassy. He had that goofy I'm-kind-of-drunk smile on his stupid face. "Hey, Brian! What are you doing over here?"

"He's scavenging for food," I said.

Brad's smile disappeared. He looked like he wanted to disappear. My nasty tone was ruining the afterglow of his golf outing. I couldn't even pretend as if I cared. At least not until I rinsed the soap from my hair.

I carried a glass of water to my plant dying in the foyer and watered it. It continued to die. It couldn't stand hearing about the gross parts of the pig either. "Why can't you live?" I asked the plant, and heard Liv walking around, searching for me.

"Mommy, can you make ice cream without milk?"

My eyes bulged at Brad as I walked back into the kitchen, and then I closed them tightly, attempting to shut all of them out of my mind.

"Man, you're an angry woman," he said without an ounce of sympathy.

"It's because I can't be clean. Even inmates are allowed a shower. Not me, though."

"Go shower now. I got this." He opened a beer and sat down at the island. "Do you want me to shower with you?" He winked.

God, I hate you.

❧

I DID SHOWER. I SHOWERED for forty minutes. I was in no rush to be anywhere else. We were always late whenever we left the house, but that was because I never wanted to be where we were going. I had 77,000 miles on my car. Three hundred and ninety-eight were to places I wanted to be. But who was counting?

After the shower, I put the kids to bed. I sat on the couch and listened to Brad's day. Who he golfed with. What business was conducted. How it affected him. He didn't ask a word about my day. He'd stopped a long time ago. He'd stopped after the thousandth time he'd returned home to find me unhappy.

His arrival was usually timed perfectly after I'd cooked dinner, listened to the kids' riveting conversation while we ate, cleaned everything up, and completed elementary school homework. I packed their lunches and signed their assignment books. Tomorrow's outfits were picked out, and notes were written. Permission slips were signed and money was paid. And then Brad would walk through the door and wonder why I was miserable. *Don't you want to hear about my day? I cleaned two fish tanks and plunged the toilet.*

I wanted to *need* to take a short shower. I missed having someplace to be. Having something to talk about that was about my life and not Liv's and James'. I let my mind drift to when the next interesting thing in my life might occur. Five years . . . ten years . . .

Maybe I'll cut my hair.

The Devil's Playground
Available Now

Please see the next page for an excerpt of the stunning first installment of The Lost Souls Series.

Forgive Me

one

"My soul is forgotten, veiled by a boring complication"

MY FOOT WILL BLEED SOON. Judging by the familiar curve in the road, I'm still at least two miles from home. Of course I end up walking home the night I'm wearing great shoes. The pain shoots through my heel as the clouds flash with lightning in the dark sky.

Maybe I'm bleeding already. I mentally review the last few hours. Anything to distract me from the agony of each step. The texts, the endless stream of drunken texts, run through my mind.

We're soul mates. I roll my eyes. Brian deserves a nicer girl-friend; someone sweet like him. Someone who doesn't roll their eyes at this statement.

We belong together. Bleh.

What does it say about my relationship when the only thing I ever tell people about my boyfriend is, "He's a really nice guy"? And how, after two years of being apart, did I ever take him back? The last three weeks have felt like years, years I was asleep.

We're perfect together. My mother thought we were perfect. Hell, this whole town thought it.

No one is ever going to know you the way I do. He was watching me as I read this one and I had to work hard to keep a straight face. At the time I wasn't sure why, but here on this deserted road, in the middle of a thunderstorm Brian would never walk through, I know it's because he never knew me at all. Or my soul. It's not his fault. I'd nearly forgotten it myself.

I stop to adjust the strap on my sandals and two sets of eyes peer out from the ditch next to the road. They're low to the ground, watching me. I've always hated nocturnal animals.

"Anyone else come out to play in the storm?" I say to the other hidden night life. I move to the edge of the shoulder, facing the nonexistent traffic, and give my new friends some room. I wince as I step forward, and watch as a set of headlights shines on the road in front of me and the scene around me turns mystical. The steam rises off the pavement at least five feet high before disappearing into the blue tinted night. The rain only lasted twenty spectacular minutes, not long enough to cool the scorched earth.

I'm lost in it as the truck pulls up beside me, now driving on the wrong side of the road, and Jason Leer rolls down his window. I glance at him and turn to stare straight ahead, trying not to let the excruciating torture of each step show on my face.

"Hi, Annie," he says, and immediately pisses me off. I might look sweet in my new rose-colored shorts romper, but these wedges have me ready to commit murder.

"My name is Charlotte," I say without looking at him, and keep walking. The strap is an ax cutting my heel from my foot. *Why won't he call me Charlotte?* Of course the cowboy would show up. What this night needs is a steer wrestler to confound me further. The same two desires he always evokes in me surface now. Wanting to punch him, and wanting to climb on top of him.

"What the hell are you doing out here? Alone—" A guttural moan of thunder interrupts him, and I tilt my head to determine the origin, but it surrounds us. The clouds circle, blanketing us with darkness, but when the moon is visible it's bright enough to see in this blue-gray night. We're in the eye of the storm and there will never be a night like this again. *God I love a storm.* The crackling of the truck's tires on the road reminds me of my cohort.

"I'm not alone. You're here, irritating me as usual." I will not look at him. I can feel his smartass grin without even seeing him, the same way I can feel a chill slip across my skin. It's hot as hell out and Jason Leer is giving me the chills.

Lightning strikes, reaching the ground in the field just to our left, and I stop walking to watch it. Every minute of today brought me here. The mind-numbing dinner date with Brian Matlin, the conversation on the way to Michelle's party about how we should see other people, the repeated and *annoying* texts declaring his love, and the eleven beers and four shots I watched Brian pour down his throat, all brought me here.

"If you're trying to kill yourself by being struck by lightning, I could just hit you with my truck. It'll be faster," he says, stealing my eyes from the field. His arm rests out his truck window and it's enormous. He tilts his body toward the door and the width of his chest holds my gaze for a moment too long.

"Annie!"

I shake my head, freeing myself from him. "What? What do you want? I'm not afraid of a storm." I am, however, exhausted by this conversation.

I finally allow myself to look him in the eyes. They are dark tonight, like the slick, steamy road before me, and I shouldn't have looked.

"I want you." His voice is tranquil, as if he's talking the suicide jumper off the bridge. "I want you to get in the truck and I'll drive you home." Thunder growls in the distance and the lightning strikes to the left and right of the road at the same time. The storm surrounds us, but the rain was gone too soon. Leaving us with the suffocating heat that set the road on fire.

I close my eyes as my sandal cuts deeper into my foot, and Jason finally pulls away. My grandmother always said the heat brings out the crazy in people. It was ninety-seven degrees at 7 p.m. The humidity was unbearable. Too hot to eat. Too hot to laugh. The only thing you could do was talk about how miserably hot it was outside. By the time Brian and I arrived, most of the party had already been in the lake at some point. Even that didn't look refreshing. The sky unleashed, and Michelle kicked everyone out rather than let them destroy her house.

I stop walking, and shift my foot in the shoe. The strap is now sticking; I've probably already shed blood. Jason drives onto the right side of the road and stops the truck on the tiny shoulder. He turns on his hazard lights and gets out of the truck. *He's a hazard.* I plaster a smile on my face and begin walking again. As soon as he leaves I'm taking off these shoes and throwing them in the pepper field next to me.

Before I endure two steps, he's in front of me. He's as fast as I remember. Like lightning: always picked first for kickball in elementary school. His hair is the same thick, jet black as back then, too. The moonlight shines off it and I wonder where his cowboy hat is. He's too beautiful to piss me off as much as he does. He blocks my path, a concrete wall, and I stop just inches from him.

"I'm going to ask you one more time to get in the truck." A lightning strike hits the road near his truck and without flinching he looks back at me, waiting for my answer.

"Or what?" I challenge him with my words and my "I dare you" look on my face. He hoists me over his shoulder and walks back to the truck as if I'm a sweatshirt he grabbed as an afterthought before walking out the door.

"Put me down! I'm not some steer you can toss around,"

I yell, as I fist my hands and pound on his back. He's laughing and pissing me off even more. I pull his shirt up and start to reach for his underwear and Jason runs the last few steps to the truck.

"Do you ever behave?" he asks, and swings the truck door open. He drops me on the seat and leans in the truck between my legs. I push my hair out of my face, my chest still heaving with anger. "Why the hell are you walking alone on a country road, in a goddamned storm, this late at night?"

My stomach knots at his closeness and this angers me, too. Why can't Jason Leer bore me the way Brian Matlin does? Jason raises his eyebrows and tilts his head at the perfect angle to send a chill down my spine.

"Brian and I broke up tonight."

"And he made you walk home?" Shock is written all over his face. Brian would never make me walk home. He is the nicest of guys. Not great at holding his liquor, but nice.

"No." I roll my eyes, calling him an idiot, and he somehow leans in closer, making my stomach flip. "He proceeded to get drunk at Michelle Farrell's party and I drove him home so he didn't die." I think back to all the parties of the last six years, since Jason and I entered high school. Besides graduation, we were rarely in the same place. I've barely hung out with Jason Leer since eighth grade. At the start of high school everyone broke into groups, and this cowboy wasn't in mine.

"Why didn't you call someone for a ride?" He breaks my revelry.

"Because apparently when Brian gets drunk he texts a lot. My battery died after the fiftieth message professing his love for me."

"Poor guy."

"Poor guy? What about me? I'm the one who had to delete them, and drive him home. I thought he'd never pass out." I'm still mourning the time I lost with Brian's drunken mess.

"Why didn't you just take his car?"

"Because I left him passed out in it in his parents' driveway. I got him home safe, but I'm not going to carry him to bed."

At this Jason lowers his head and laughs. My irritation with him twists into annoyance at myself for telling him anything. For telling him everything. I want to punch him in his laughing mouth. His lips are perfect, though.

"It's not easy to love you, Annie."

"Yeah, well I've got fifty texts that claim otherwise. Judging from the fact you can't even get my name right, everything's probably hard for you." Jason leans on the dash and his jeans scrape against my maimed foot, causing my face to twist in pain. Before I can regain my composure, his eyes are on me. He moves back and holds my foot up near his face. He slips the strap off my heel and runs his thumb across the now broken and purple blister. I close my eyes, the sight of the wound amplifying the pain.

"My God, you are stubborn," he says, his eyes still on my foot. Thunder groans behind us and he straightens my leg, examining it in the glimmer of moonlight. I'm not angry anymore. One urge has silenced another, and awakened me in the process. He pulls my foot to him and kisses the inside of my ankle, and a chill runs from my leg to both breasts and settles in the back of my throat, stealing my breath.

I swallow hard. "Are all your first kisses on the inside of the ankle?" I ask. His hands grip my ankle harshly, but he's careful with my heel.

His eyes find mine as he drags his lips up my calf and kisses the inside of my knee. I shut up and shudder from a chill. There are no words. Only the beginning of a thought. *What if,* arises in my mind against the sound of the clicking of the hazard lights.

The lightning strikes again and unveils the darkness in his eyes. He lowers my leg and backs up, but I'm not ready to let him go. I grab his belt buckle and pull him toward me. Jason doesn't budge. He is an ox. His eyes bore into me and for a moment I think he hates me. He's holding a raging river behind a dam, and I'm recklessly breeching it.

With a hand gripping each shoulder he forces me back to the seat and hovers over me. Even in the darkness I can see the emptiness in his eyes and I can't leave it alone. He kisses me. He kisses me as if he's done it a hundred times before, and when his lips touch mine some animalistic need growls inside of me. He's like nothing I've ever known, and my body craves a hundred things all at once, every one of them him. With his tongue in my mouth, I tighten my arms around his thick neck and pull him closer, wanting to climb inside of him.

Jason pulls away, devastating me, until I realize there are flashing lights behind us. His eyes fixed on mine, he takes my hands from behind his head and pulls me upright before the state trooper steps out of his car and walks to our side of the truck.

"CHARLOTTE, HONEY, ARE YOU GOING to get up? I heard you come in late last night."

I roll over and put my head under the pillow. I don't want to get up. I don't want to tell my mom that I broke up with Brian . . . again.

"Is everything okay?" She's worried. I take a deep breath and sit up in bed. The sheet rubs against my heel and the pain reminds me of Jason Leer.

"I broke up with Brian last night."

"Oh no. I have to see his mother at Book Club on Wednesday."

"I can't marry him because you can't face his mother at Book Club."

"I'm not suggesting you marry him, just that you stop dating him if you're going to keep breaking his heart." My mom leaves my room. Her face is plagued with frustration mixed with disappointment. I climb out of bed and lumber to the bathroom. My green eyes sparkle in the mirror, hinting at our indelicate secret from last night. I wink at myself as if something exciting is about to happen. My long blond hair barely looks slept on. I think breaking up with Brian was good for me.

"JACK, SHE BROKE UP WITH Brian again." I catch, as I enter the kitchen.

"Through with him, huh?" My father never seems to have an opinion on who I date as long as they treat me well. Brian certainly did that.

"Dad, he just didn't do it for me." Jason's eyes pierce my thoughts again, haunting me. The trooper sent us home and I left him in his truck without a word. There wasn't one to say.

"Do what? What did you expect him to do for you?" my mother spouts. She's not taking the news well.

"When he looks at me a certain way, I want to get chills," I start, surprised by how easily my needs are verbalized. "When he leans into me, I want my stomach to flip, and when he walks away I want to care if he comes back." My parents both watch me silently as if I'm reciting a poem at the second-grade music program. They are pondering me.

"What? Don't your stomachs flip when you're together? Ever?"

"Does your stomach flip when you look at me, Jack?" she asks.

"Only if I eat chili the same day," my dad says, and they both start laughing.

"Charlotte, I remember what it was like to be young. And your father did make my stomach flip, but I think you're too hard on Brian. He's a nice boy."

"Yeah yeah. He's nice." I butter my toast and move to sit next to my father at the table. *He is nice.* For some reason Brian's kindness frustrates me. He's a boring complication. "I ran into Jason Leer last night." *And he kissed the inside of my leg.* I smile ruefully.

My mother's eyebrows raise and I fear I've divulged too much. My father never looks up from the newspaper.

"Butch and Joanie's son?"

"That's the one." I try to sound nonchalant as a tiny chill runs down my neck.

"I haven't seen him since Joanie's funeral. Poor boy. She was lovely. Do you remember her?"

I nod my head and take a bite of the toast. "From Sunday school."

"Jack, do you remember Joanie Leer? Died of cancer about a year ago."

"I remember," my dad says, and appears to be ignoring us, but I know he's not. He always hears everything.

"If you don't want to be with Brian, that's fine, but please not a rodeo cowboy," my mother pleads, not missing a thing.

"I only said I saw him. What's wrong with a rodeo cowboy?"

"Nothing. For someone else's daughter. I really want you to marry someone with a job. Someone that can take care of you."

"Can't a cowboy do that?" *From what I've seen, he can take very good care of me.*

"Charlotte, please tell me you're not serious. They're always on the road. Their income's not steady. It's a very difficult life." My mother's stern warning is delivered while she fills the dishwasher, as if we're discussing a fairytale, a situation so absurd it barely warrants a discussion. She's still beautiful, even when she's lecturing me. "I know safe choices aren't attractive to the young, but believe me you do not belong in that world and he'd wither up and die in yours. Do not underestimate the power of safety in this crazy life."

"How do you know so much about rodeo cowboys?" I ask.

"Yeah, how do you know so much?" My dad asks. He stares at her over the newspaper.

"Is your stomach flipping?" She asks, and gives him her beautiful smile she's flashed to quell him my entire life.

"Yes," he says, and winks at her.

Forgive Me
Available Now

ELIZA FREED

ELIZA FREED GRADUATED FROM RUTGERS University and returned to her hometown in rural South Jersey. Her mother encouraged her to take some time and find herself. After three months of searching, she began to bounce checks, her neighbors began to talk, and her mother told her to find a job.

She settled into corporate America, learning systems and practices and the bureaucracy that slows them. Eliza quickly discovered her creativity and gift for story telling as a corporate trainer and spent years perfecting her presentation skills and studying diversity. It was during this time she became an avid observer of the characters she met and the heartaches they endured. Her years of study taught her that laughter, even the completely inappropriate kind, was the key to survival.

She currently lives in New Jersey with her family and a misbehaving beagle named Odin. As an avid swimmer, if Eliza is not with her family and friends, she'd rather be underwater. While she enjoys many genres, she is, and always has been, a sucker for a love story . . . the more screwed up the better.

www.elizafreed.com

Made in the USA
Middletown, DE
15 November 2016